CW00862731

Roulette - Text copyright © Emmy Ellis 2023
Cover Art by Emmy Ellis @ studioenp.com © 2023

All Rights Reserved

ROULETTE

Emmy Ellis

Chapter One

Goldie stared at his two moles, Karen Jacobs and Teddy Marshall, who sat across the table in the back room of his tanning shop, Golden Glow. He liked gold. He ran The Golden Eye Estate and didn't give a single fuck that people laughed behind his back about his obsession with the shiny stuff and naming most things he owned to reflect that. They'd be laughing on the other side of their faces when he came up trumps from robbing The Brothers' casino, Jackpot Palace (he'd have called it Golden Goose). Gold would be coming out of his ears in the form of all that lovely money, whereas those sneering people would still be penny-pinching arseholes without a pot to piss in.

Jealousy was a nasty trait.

He inspected his plate of full English one of the tanning women had collected for him from the café down the street. It came in a polystyrene tray, but he'd die rather than eat it out of that. You had to have standards, didn't you, and his days of being seen as 'less than' were far in his rearview mirror. His dinner service from Pinkhouse Mustique had cost him over three grand. If *that* wasn't standards, he didn't know what was.

He picked up his gold-plated knife and fork and cut a sausage in half. Fat shot out and stained the front of his Paul Smith shirt. Fuck it. He dabbed at it with a napkin and told himself to buy a replacement online later.

He smiled at his employees. "Giss an update, then."

Teddy stared at Goldie's food like he hadn't eaten for weeks.

"I'm sorry, did you want breakfast?" Goldie asked, genuinely pissed off at himself for assuming they'd have already eaten.

Teddy, with an air about him of suave sophistication (it might have something to do with his sculptured quiff, his light-grey, drainpipe-trouser suit, and white grandad shirt), leant back, his elbow on the arm of a red velvet carver chair, a finger beneath his nose. "Err, it's all right, boss, we can nip to the café after."

"Fucking nonsense," Goldie said, then shouted, "Babs? Babs! Get in here!"

Tanning Tart Babs poked her head round the door, her bottle-blonde hair fleshed out with extensions, her body nice and brown from the free tans he allowed his employees to have. She blinked, her eyes haloed with thick, false lashes.

"Yeah, oh Golden One?" She winked, chewed gum, and blew a pink bubble.

"Get breakfasts for these two, please, love." Goldie nodded at his moles. "Dish it up on plates from the safe." Mad, some would think, to keep dinnerware and his cutlery in a safe, but there were people brazen, and desperate enough, to nick it if it was stored in a lowly cupboard. Some of the customers and residents hereabout were the light-fingered variety, and he didn't want to put temptation their way.

Babs closed the door.

Goldie smiled. "Now that's sorted, like I said, giss an update."

Teddy took a notebook out of his suit jacket pocket. So he'd said, his great-grandmother had taught him shorthand, which was just as well, because if he wrote snippets just *anyone* could read, Goldie wouldn't be happy.

"The takings have gone up this week." Teddy grinned. "They're pulling in shedloads. We're talking a million plus sitting in the safe on a Friday night."

A million plus? Fuck me…

Goldie swallowed a mouthful of sausage. "Gamblers, they just don't know when to stop, do they. Imagine how many people out there are now having to sell their houses because they've fucked up at the tables. Tragic." He continued eating, a mocking voice in his head telling him that if he didn't get out of London sooner rather than later, he'd lose *his* house an' all. He'd lose *everything*, including his freedom.

He couldn't afford to get caught for the shit he'd been involved in.

Teddy tapped a finger on his notebook. "As you know, George and Greg make an appearance once a week on a Saturday night, but this week, they came on the Friday, too."

Goldie frowned. For the few months Teddy and Karen had been working at the casino, the twins had stuck to a rigid routine, which was unlike them and, in Goldie's opinion, fucking stupid to let people know where you'd be at a certain time on the weekly. "Why the change in pattern?"

"Jacques Bernard was in town."

"Ah, that French ponce who sings all that rap rubbish. What, are The Brothers fans of his or summat?"

"No, they're not usually bothered by famous people attending, they're not the arse-licking type, but Jacques brought an entourage with him, and the press were out the front, waiting to pounce. The twins wanted to oversee the night in case something kicked off."

"Don't they trust Ichabod and Two-Time to handle it?"

"Well, yeah, but with Jacques being in the news after his split with Queenie, and her being rumoured to also be going to the casino that night—with her new fella, one of her dancers—you can see why the twins wanted to be there. Journalists will do anything to cause a scene, and The Brothers didn't want any of them getting inside the casino and wreaking havoc."

"*She* sings crap an' all," Goldie said, stabbing a mushroom as if it were Queenie's head. The woman thought she was Madonna and got on his man tits for no other reason than her impersonating one of his idols. "It's all fucking noise to me. No idea why anyone would want to listen to it. Now Madonna, on the other hand…give me 'Vogue' any day."

Tanning Tart Babs shouted, "Can someone open the door? I've got me 'ands full."

Karen jumped up to do the honours. Goldie liked her. She was an eager beaver, although she wasn't into Madonna, which was a shame. Despite the latter, she was a good employee. Some people you just gelled with from the off, and she was one of them.

Karen took the plates from Babs, Goldie cringing internally in case she dropped them, broke them. She placed them down carefully, and he heaved a sigh of relief. Babs tottered across in her high heels and deposited the cutlery, a couple of paper napkins with the café logo in the corner, then left.

With Karen and Teddy tucking in, Goldie let them fill their bellies while he finished filling his. He mulled things over. The Brothers going to the casino on a Friday night had naffed him off—that was the night he planned to rob the place at some point in the future. It would be busy, customers and staff too rushed off their feet to take any notice of what was going on in the money-counting room (his best men frightening the head cashier with shotguns aimed at her face). According to his moles, *all* evenings were busy bar Mondays, but Friday was the bee's knees—and it was the night the most money was on the premises.

Breakfast over, he stacked the plates and poured them all a coffee from the carafe on the worktop in the kitchenette behind the table. He carried his Pinkhouse cups and saucers on a tray and put it on the table, admiring the Palms and Coconuts print, white china with blue trees. It reminded him of the end goal—moving to a place where palm trees were the norm and the sky was always blue, a hot sun beating down on him, giving him a natural tan. A dream, one he'd had since a nipper. Running The Golden Eye Estate was all well and good, but he didn't want to do it forever. A man had to put his gangster life behind him at some point, didn't he, and retirement at forty wasn't something to be sniffed at. Unfortunately, the money he'd made from a certain enterprise had dried up, his plans to use it to jet him off to a home in the sun thwarted until he'd come up with the heist idea. With the proceeds of the casino in his pocket, plus all the cash he'd funnelled into offshore accounts from his dealings as a leader and his part in the enterprise, he'd be golden.

He laughed to himself at that, golden, and sat to continue the chat with his employees. "So, I'm thinking I'll have to add a contingency plan in case the twins are at the casino on the Friday night I've earmarked for the robbery."

"When *is* that?" Teddy asked.

Goldie wasn't about to tell him. "The less you know the better. You've been told how to react and behave on the evening of the heist, and that's all the info you need."

"So you don't trust us to know beforehand?" Karen asked.

He took in the sight of her. Brown-black hair, a Spanish or Mexican look about her, and these pale-blue eyes that had him thinking things he shouldn't. She was sexy as fuck but twenty years his junior. To others, it'd be too close to robbing the cradle if he asked her out on a date—being seen out in public with someone so young would get people thinking he was a paedo. Behind closed doors, however…

He had a rep to maintain, and being a known pervert wasn't on his agenda. But if he'd met her when he was her age, he'd have gone for it.

"It's not that," he said. "If you don't know exactly which Friday it's going to happen, you can't let it slip if, say, the twins get wind and interrogate you. Also, the element of surprise, even though you know it's going to happen, will appear more genuine to anyone watching. And you can bet the camera footage will be gone over and over by The Brothers so they can see if any employees are acting dodgy on the night. Remember, you've got to work there for at least a year after the event so they don't suspect you. No obvious spending of your portion of the heist either. I can't stress that enough. They'll be watching for people to splash the cash."

"Right." She let out a long sigh. "I'll be honest and say I didn't realise how much this would play on my nerves. Don't get me wrong, I'm confident I appear like any other Cardigan employee, but a small part of me worries, well, you know how it is."

Goldie wasn't bothered by her little wobble. "I do, and it's natural to feel that way because you're constantly under pressure to seem innocent. You've been fine for months so far, and you'll be fine in the future. You two look like you're just a pair of employees who enjoy their jobs."

"How do you know?" she asked.

"You don't think I'd let you go there without being monitored from time to time, do you?"

"Ah, I get you. Undercover customers who can also scope the place out."

"Exactly." Goldie eyed her critically, pleased with the reports on her so far. "You'll do fine, I have every faith in you. Like I said to you before, you *have* to be fine. If you don't pull this off, you're dead." He watched his words sink in for the umpteenth time—he liked to repeat himself so no one could accuse him of withholding information later down the line. "I don't get sentimental with my staff in case I have to off one of them. While this may sound harsh, and I don't much give a fuck if it does to be fair, I won't let anyone or anything derail my ambitions. If you mess up, tarra, know what I mean?"

Karen nodded. "I won't mess up. I haven't so far, have I?"

Goldie shook his head. "Nah. As long as it stays that way, all's well that ends well. Now then, what about this Two-Time fella. What's he been up to, Teddy?"

Teddy had been tasked with getting close to Two-Time, some bloke with double scars down his face from where he'd been slashed with a blade. He was one of the twins' more recent recruits, and Goldie was surprised they trusted him with heading security for their precious Jackpot Palace. He'd have thought they'd have chosen a more long-standing member of their firm, maybe that Will character, but maybe they had something on Two-Time, some insurance. Sensible. The same went for Ichabod. He hadn't been in their top-trusted group for long, but as Goldie knew, sometimes people proved their worth behind the scenes, so the wiry Irishman was clearly someone they held in high regard if he was the face of the casino.

"He calls himself T-T now. We went out for a pint yesterday lunchtime," Teddy said.

"Where?" Goldie already knew, but he liked to ask questions to see if he got the correct answer.

"The Angel."

"Right. And how did that go?"

"We chatted about football, stuff like that, nothing to do with the casino. I thought it was best to act like a mate rather than a colleague. If I ask too many questions too soon, he'll clock me as suspicious."

"Good boy. So what's your impression of him?"

"He doesn't suffer fools gladly, put it that way."

"So he's definitely one to watch." Goldie made a note of that in code in his little navy-blue, leather-bound book. He stabbed a full stop at the end of the sentence: T-T MIGHT BE A PAIN IN MY ARSE. "Anything else to report?"

Teddy nodded, his quiff bobbing. "You know we thought Ichabod would be easy to take down?"

"Yeah."

"Turns out he's a martial arts expert."

"Fuck me sideways. That changes things." Goldie fanned through the aspects of his plan in his mind and put an asterisk beside Ichabod's name to remind him he needed more consideration. He'd have to go down a route he didn't want to. Ichabod might have to be shot to incapacitate him more than a punch to the head would—which he'd likely deflect, seeing as he was into all that ninja shit. "Not to worry, I'll iron out the kinks."

"I wish I'd found out sooner," Teddy said, "but he plays things close to his chest. He mentioned it in passing when news came in that Jacques would be arriving. Said he wasn't bothered about the press because he's a black belt and could knock the lot of them out inside two minutes."

"Let's just be glad you found out when you did—*before* the robbery. Afterwards would have naffed me off. Anything else?"

Neither of them supplied any info.

"What about the other women, Karen?" he pressed. "Any of them likely to cause me any grief?"

"The only one concerning me is some bint who calls herself Cinnamon Bun."

"You fucking what? Who calls themselves after a cake?"

"She does. Says the customers like it because it's cute. I've had to play my part as a loyal Brother employee by grassing on her."

"What's she done?"

"She picked a gambling chip up off the floor—worth a hundred quid—and put it in her pocket. I watched her for a bit to see what she'd do, but she carried on working on the roulette table. I excused myself from blackjack, didn't I, Teddy, and went to tell Ichabod. He took us both into the office and made me repeat what I'd seen. If looks could kill, I'd have been dead on the spot. Anyway, she reckons she was going to hand it in to the cashier after the game had ended, then she took it out of her pocket and passed it over. She's a good actress, I'll give her that, because for a minute there I was convinced she'd told the truth. Ichabod seemed to believe her, too, and he must have, because she's still working there."

"Unless the twins have told him to keep her on purposely, so they can observe her." Goldie would have done the same. Bided his time. Waited for her to nick again, then killed her.

Karen shrugged. "But she isn't likely to repeat her theft attempt because she knows they'll be watching her."

Goldie chuckled. "People like her can't keep their sticky mitts to themselves for long. She'll be at it again, you mark my words. Do you know enough about her to understand why she'd need to steal?"

"I'd like to say she's got kids to feed, but no, she's always guffing on about expensive shoes, being single and whatever."

"Right, so she's just greedy. Well, good luck to her, because the twins will sort her in the end. Stupid cow. You'll need to be careful. She might be watching *you* now, waiting for a time she can grass you up. I don't need to tell you having eyes on you like that isn't welcome."

"No, but at the same time, because I act squeaky clean, it'll only make The Brothers and Ichabod think I'm on the level even more."

"True." Goldie liked the way Karen thought. She was always one or two steps ahead. He might give her a bonus out of the spoils if she kept this attitude up. "So why do you think she'd give me hassle?"

"There's just something about her," Karen said. "I can imagine her running round like a headless chicken when the guns come out, putting a spanner in the works. You said you didn't want anyone killed, just the money."

"I did."

"I agree with Karen's assessment," Teddy said. *Then Miss Bun needs taking care of.* "What's her real name?"

"Even worse than Cinnamon Bun," Teddy said. "Rainbow Archer. Wish I was joking."

"Stone me. Right, if that's everything, get yourselves a tan before you go. Tell Tanning Tart Babs to fit you in."

Karen frowned. "Won't it look a bit weird if we *both* rock up to work tonight all brown?"

"Nope. As far as everyone at the casino is concerned, you two are shacked up together, planning to get married, so it's feasible that as a couple you decided to get it done. Whatever. If you don't want a tan, don't get one, it was just a kind offer."

Karen studied him, probably to see if his 'kind offer' was actually an order. "Okay, fine by me. I

16

could do with one. I'm looking pasty. Thanks, Goldie."

"You're welcome. Now sod off out of here. I've got a tan of my own to get done." He admired his already golden skin that went perfectly with his golden hair. He was a walking bullion bar.

His moles left the room, and he checked his notes, gritting his teeth about Ichabod being a black belt. Would the Irishman risk doing hand chops and daft leg swings when faced with the business end of a gun? Goldie didn't want to take the chance. Better to knock him unconscious if he discovered Goldie's men in the money-counting room.

He stood, took off his clothes, and put on a robe and flip-flops. On his way to the tanning booths where he'd be sprayed to within an inch of his life, he pondered on his interaction with that scummy slimeball last night in Swindler's Ship, his favourite boozer. The gobby twat had muttered that he looked like Donald Trump, his tan orange. No, it was fucking *golden*, just like him. Goldie had followed him down the street later, whipped his gun out, and shot the fucker in the back of the head.

Some people really didn't know when to keep their opinions to themselves.

Orange, my arse.

Chapter Two

Cinnamon Bun fast-walked to work in her comfy flat shoes. She'd change into her heels once she arrived, touch up her makeup, and fluff her hair. Her job at the casino paid well, but not enough to pay all her bills and keep the fridge and cupboards stocked to the max. Her colleagues thought she was some dumb blonde bitch who loved Gucci and Prada, that she was single and only out for a good time, the impression she'd fed them to keep her real life private. The reality was, she had two girls under five and rent arrears that would have Mum and Dad spinning in their joint grave.

Life was hard, but it hadn't always been that way. It was having kids that had done it, their father fucking off with some tart to live on The Golden Eye Estate. He didn't pay her any money, didn't visit the girls; it was as if the trio who had once been his world—supposedly—no longer existed. She'd plodded on, ashamed she'd been reduced to being a single mother, but determined to prove she could do this by herself despite London prices. Every day she wished Mum was still here to help her out. Not necessarily with money but advice—Mum's had been sage and had got Cinnamon out of a spot of trouble on more than one occasion. To not be able to pick up the phone and ask for guidance was the biggest sting of all.

She weaved through the dark East End, contemplating how she'd almost got into trouble over that gambling chip. Well, she *had* been caught, Karen had grassed her up to Ichabod, but

Cinnamon's quick thinking had saved the day — and her skin. Ichabod had accepted her explanation, and she still had a job, although she sensed she was being watched more than she'd been previously.

Mind you, Cinnamon was doing a bit of watching of her own. She hadn't liked the way Karen hadn't confronted her about the theft first, instead going behind her back like a goody-goody, sucking up to Ichabod. Cinnamon had picked up on a couple of interesting things between Karen and Teddy, especially the fact they didn't go home to the same gaff, yet they'd told everyone they lived together as a couple and were getting married next summer. That was fishy, and after thinking about it for days now, Cinnamon had made the decision to inform Ichabod tonight so he could pass that snippet to George and Greg. If they were lying about their living arrangements, what else were they lying about?

She'd intended to give the money from the chip to her one and only friend, the woman who lived in the flat next door, the one who babysat her kids every night. Anna could have cashed it in for her a few days later and no one would have been any the wiser. Cinnamon had needed the money for the leccy meter — that thing swallowed cash like no one's business, and with it being the arse end of winter and still cold, she couldn't turn the heating off any more than she already did.

The mould was becoming a problem. With the flat nippy, no windows being opened to keep in the meagre heat they did have from a short burst of the rads being on, peach stuff had been making itself at home on her bathroom tiles, and black spots lurked in a couple of corners in her bedroom. The council weren't interested, said it was her fault, so she relied on Astonish Mould and Mildew Blaster, although it felt like she constantly sprayed the stuff.

She worried what it was doing to her daughters' lungs.

Turning the corner, she headed up the last residential street before she'd enter the road leading to Jackpot Palace and hoped she'd get lots of tips tonight. Unlikely, because it was Monday and people didn't tend to get as drunk or free with their cash then, but she could hope.

Hope was her best friend.

A shadow ahead between the splashes of streetlights caught her eye, and she squinted at it, trying to make out what it was. It morphed into the shape of a person, and she supposed they'd either come out of their house to go somewhere or were on their way indoors. Whoever it was must have clicked a key fob; a *blip-blip* echoed, indicator lights flashed, and the person opened the back door of a dark SUV.

She kept walking. They'd be gone by the time she got there.

Except they weren't.

Uneasy now—because *why* hadn't they got in the bloody car?—she shifted across the pavement so she was closer to the houses. The shadow bent its head inside the back of the vehicle, so she took the opportunity to scoot past and walk faster once the SUV was behind her. Just a few metres to the end of the street now. Three houses to pass. At the midpoint between two lampposts, she quickened her pace.

"Rainbow?" someone said behind her.

She spun round, confused as to why anyone around here would know her name.

"Rainbow Archer?" the shadow asked. Male.

"Um, yes? How do you—?"

A burning sensation speared her thigh immediately before the sound of a *pfft* filled her

23

ears. She stared at the shadow—they had a balaclava on—and the gun in their gloved hand didn't shake, so whoever it was, they weren't afraid of using the weapon. All this information inside a split second. She automatically slapped a hand to her thigh, her palm sticky with blood, and the enormity of what had happened hit her harder than the bullet.

Had The Brothers sent someone to kill her because of the gambling chip?

"Oh God, oh fuck…"

She turned to run, but another burn in her backside, another *pfft*, and she went down to the pavement on her hands and knees. Agony scooting through her, she moved to get up, staring at the bloodied handprint she'd left on the pale doorstep of a house with a white door, a number two on it.

"Help me," she shouted. "Help…"

She staggered to her feet, the burning in both sites ramping up, and hobbled to the end of the street, waiting for another shot, worrying it would be in the back of her head. The sound of an engine rumbling relieved her at first, but then dark thoughts came. What if the shooter was coming after her? What if they weren't going to let her get away?

She veered around the corner, her option to knock on someone's door gone now — all that was ahead of her was a long road that led to Entertainment Plaza. She spotted a garden gate in the side fence of number two and stopped to open it, but it must be padlocked from the other side. She hammered on the gate, shouting for help, staring up at a bedroom window. Someone looked down at her, shaking their head, shrugging, the light from the room casting them as a silhouette, and she'd swear they were trying to tell he they couldn't help her, they'd been warned not to. Of *course* they'd do that if the twins had ordered this. They'd have had a visit beforehand.

Desperation filled her — the whole fucking *street* would have been warned, so going back there wasn't an option. She had no choice but to attempt to escape to the casino, or the bowling alley, the cinema, the restaurants, anywhere. The road ahead with scrubland either side presented as a tunnel, where the light at the end of it was too far for her to reach. The pain in her backside and thigh hampered her progress, and she panicked she'd bleed to death before she got to safety.

She thought of her daughters. Who'd look after them? Her ex wouldn't want to, so would he opt for them to be put into care? Would Anna step forward and take the girls in? For the first time, Cinnamon had been forced into thinking about her mortality, how her absence would affect the little people in her life. She should have put measures in place, secured her daughters' futures, but she'd thought herself too young for all that. Instead, she'd believed she was invincible and she'd see them grow into adults.

Tears stung, and she staggered on, the engine growing louder. A car door slammed, and she glanced over her shoulder. The shadow got out. He stood behind the shield of his open driver's door, gun up and aimed at her.

"Oh, Jesus Christ. Don't let my babies grow up without me," she whimpered and carried on lurching up the street, waiting for another bullet to sink into her.

"Oi, what the *fuck* do you think you're doing?" a man shouted.

It wasn't the shadow's voice. She recognised it. *Shit.*

Despite the danger the newcomer represented, instinct told her to stop. She turned. Shadow Man stood facing two blokes who'd parked behind the SUV and held guns of their own. She'd never been so frightened to see other people in her life. She should be pleased, but…

Shadow lowered his gun and spun to face them. Then he quickly raised it and fired. Neither of the other men shouted in pain, they just stood there, staring. Shadow seemed to work out what his best option was since he'd missed either target. He darted inside the SUV, speeding away towards the plaza, one of the men firing at the vehicle. The rear tyre popped, the SUV skewing across the road, but it kept going regardless.

"Follow that prick," one barked. "I'll deal with her."

Fear pummelled her as Greg dived into their BMW and George stalked towards her. Had they come to ensure Shadow killed her? Had one of them asked what he was doing, in effect enquiring why she wasn't dead yet? If so, why shoot Shadow's tyre if he was one of their henchmen? Had that been done because he'd failed to carry out their orders?

"I'm…I'm so sorry," she said. "I was going to hand the chip in, I swear."

"Chip?" George asked. "What fucking chip?"

Oh God, he didn't *know*? Or was he testing her? You could never tell with the twins whether they were playing with your mind or telling the truth.

"I thought…" She swallowed, wincing at a fresh wave of pain. "I thought he was here to kill me because of the chip."

"Look, love, I don't know what you're on about. I'm more concerned with the blood coming out of your arse and leg. He shot you, yes?"

She nodded.

"Hang on while I get help." He sent a message then lifted her, his arm brushing her backside accidentally as he scooped her into a cradle hold.

Agony speared, and she cried out, biting her lip.

"Sorry," he said. "What the fuck have you done to get yourself in this mess?" He walked towards Entertainment Plaza, still too far in the distance, face set in a grim mask, every step he took jolting her.

She snatched in a breath at the extra pain it brought. "There was a misunderstanding with a chip at work," she said. "I found it on the floor by the table I was working so put it in my pocket to hand in to the cashier later. Karen told Ichabod I'd nicked it. I didn't, I swear."

"That's news to me. Ich must have believed you else he'd have informed us. So, like I said, what have you done to get yourself in this mess?"

"I can't think of anyone who'd want to…want to s-shoot me."

"Pissed anyone off lately?"

"Not lately, no."

"When, then?"

"A couple of years ago, when my ex left me, I burnt all his stuff and sent him a text message telling him. That's all I can think of. I haven't seen him since, so why would he send someone after all this time?" If the bullet wounds hurt her even more, she'd pass out. It was reaching unbearable levels.

"Well, *someone's* miffed with you. Don't worry, Greg will sort him out."

"There's something…something I need to tell you."

"What's that? Ah, here's Ich."

She stared at headlights coming their way. "Will he take me to hospital? They'll ask questions because I've been shot and—"

"No, you'll be going to the clinic we use. Private. Confidential."

A swath of discomfort cut into her body, and she sucked in a sharp breath. Everything went fuzzy at the edges, and she closed her eyes. "My daughters are with my friend. A neighbour. Anna. Can you…will you tell…?"

Her eyes drifted closed, and the shock of it all caught up with her, sending her into the darkness of sleep, and she let it carry her along.

Chapter Three

*S*tanding in the living room, five-year-old stubborn, proud, defiant little George stared up at the face looming over him. He'd had his trousers pulled down, so he knew what was coming, but he'd take it. He'd do it every time if it meant Greg didn't get a wallop. Slaps waited in the near future. He didn't like his father, he was mean and smacked him a lot, even when he hadn't *done anything. A pinch when Mummy wasn't looking. A cuff round the back of the head when Daddy walked past. A sly foot sticking out to trip him. The hits, so sore and sharp, itched afterwards, leaving red handprint shapes. The punches were worse, and for days after a beating, George had great big bruises on his tummy, legs, and the tops of his arms, all places the teachers and neighbours couldn't see when he had clothes on. Mummy saw them at bath time, and she cried, saying sorry over and over again. George didn't understand. If she was so sorry, why didn't she take them from here and run away? She had bruises, too. Did hers hurt as much as his when he poked them at their blackest?*

George wished Daddy wasn't his daddy. Greg did, too. When they couldn't sleep at night, worrying he would come in from drinking too much at the pub and hitting them for no reason, they whispered into the darkness and made up a world where Daddy wasn't it in. It was just them and Mummy, and they lived a long way from London where green fields backed onto their imaginary cottage. They played in the long grass, had picnics with jam sandwiches, and for afterwards, they'd have sweets in the small, blue-and-white-striped paper bags like old Mr Bum Head used at the corner shop.

32

George didn't like Mr Bum Head either, a name he'd made up because the man had a deep line down the middle of his forehead, but he loved having sweets. They didn't get many, and if they did, when Mummy had extra in her purse, and Daddy saw the bags, he snatched them away, saying they didn't deserve treats, they were nothing but the devil's spawn.

If they all escaped to the dream cottage, they wouldn't miss Daddy, nor Mr Bum Head, who always shouted at them and told people, "Watch it, The Brothers are about. They might nick your handbags." That had only happened once, the handbag thing, and George hadn't nicked it as such, he'd just taken a fiver out of the purse inside so Mummy could have it for buying food.

Loads of people called them The Brothers instead of their proper names. Greg didn't mind, he reckoned it was the same as being called 'the twins', but sometimes, George wished he could be known for being Just George, a boy all to himself instead of being lumped in with Greg all the time, as if they were one person.

The slap to the back of his thigh brought him out of the place he forced himself to go whenever it was obvious Daddy was going to hurt him. Mummy was down at the bingo—Daddy had sent her there to win some money—and Greg was upstairs in their room playing with his red car, the one Mummy's best friend, Francine, had given him. George had one, too, except his was blue.

"Where's your mother?" Daddy slurred, his breath all smelly from the beer.

"B-bingo," George said, his tummy bunching and hurting.

"Fucking wasting money on the bingo? That bloody bitch..."

George hated it when Daddy did that, saying one thing when he'd said another before. "You t-told her to g-go."

Daddy slapped George's leg again. "Are you calling me a liar? Are you saying I don't know what I said and what I didn't?"

The third slap was expected, and George had been ready for it. A horrible feeling swirled in his belly, hot, and he felt sick. He knew he'd likely get a beating for what he said next, but he couldn't stop the word from tumbling out. "Yeah."

Mummy said his defiance would get him really hurt one day, and if George could just be a good boy, everything would be okay. But how could he be a good boy when something inside told him to egg Daddy on, *to push his luck? It was like another part of himself came alive, and George had more courage then.*

Daddy's eyes darkened, like they always did when he was in a state. His fist rose to beside his head, arm bent, then it came rushing towards George's stomach. It landed, whooshing the air out of him, the agony deep and boiling, and no matter that he wished he was a man, or at least a bigger boy so he could cope with it better, the pain still barrelled through him. Wishes didn't bring you anything. It didn't stop him stuttering in front of Daddy. All wishing did was upset you because, like dreaming of the cottage where they'd all be safe, George had to come back to his real life.

To this.

Mummy said that wasn't true. If wishing didn't get you what you wanted, then you had to do something about it, make it happen. Why hadn't she tried, then? What was keeping her here? Why couldn't she run away with her sons?

The things George wanted most in the world were Daddy dead, Mummy happy, and to always shield Greg from being hurt. When George was a big boy, he'd get it all, he'd make it happen.

Daddy picked George up by his hair and dangled him high. His scalp screamed for George so he didn't have to; George kept his mouth shut, teeth gritted, and thought of all the other times Daddy had done this to him. A little kid he may be, but his insides clenched with hate.

"The day you two were born was the worst of my bleedin' life. Fucking little bastards, the pair of you. If I could turn back the clock, I wouldn't have looked twice at your slag of a mother."

George didn't like it when Daddy called her names, and that horrible feeling came back, his anger so great it took away the pain in his head from Daddy clutching his hair. Even though George knew he shouldn't, the other part of himself piped up, and he kicked him in the willy. Daddy dropped him. On the floor, his hip banging with a nasty ache, George looked up at him and wanted to laugh—that part of him found this funny, that they'd got their own back on him.

Daddy had bent double, and he glanced at George, his eyes watering. "You'll pay for that when I get my breath back. Spiteful little cunt."

The front door slammed. It could be because of the wind and Daddy hadn't shut it when he'd come in from The Eagle, but Mummy's heels clicked on the tiled hallway floor. George loved that sound when she was coming home, but not when she was going out without them. He wanted to be with her all the time so he could protect her if Daddy raised his fist, get punched himself instead like he did for Greg. But there was school, and the times Mummy told them to go out to play so she could mop the floors, and then there was Daddy, when he gripped George's and Greg's ears and marched them to the front door, putting them on the step and kicking their backsides, shouting, "Don't come back until the streetlights turn on. Can't stand the sight of you."

Mummy appeared in the living room doorway and, as usual, she didn't ask Daddy what had been going on. If she did, he'd hit her, tell her to mind her own business. Once, she'd got the devil in her and said it was her business because they were her children.

Daddy had muttered, "Don't I know it, you filthy whore."

George still didn't know what that meant, the first bit, not the whore bit. He knew what one of those was because Ron Cardigan had said it outside The Eagle once, and he had explained to them, when he'd caught them staring, that whores were women who let men put their willies inside them for money.

Did Mummy do that?

"Everything okay?" Mummy asked, smiling at Daddy then giving the trousers around George's ankles a quick glance.

"No, it fucking isn't. That son of yours just kicked me in the nuts." Daddy stood upright and glared at her. "Did you win?"

"Forty quid."

"Give it here."

Mummy got it out of her purse and held it towards him.

Daddy snatched it. "Sort him out. Teach him some manners. I'm going back to the pub."

The monster in their lives stormed out, and Mummy came to crouch on the floor in front of George.

"Why did you kick him, love? You know how he gets."

"He slapped my legs and punched me in the tummy. I hate him."

"I do, too," she whispered. "He needs to be six feet under."

He blinked back tears—ones he tried not to let out because it would make her feel bad. "What?"

"Nothing," she said and helped him to stand. She checked him over, crying and saying sorry. Kissed the slap marks and the red fist shape on his belly in the middle of two older bruises. Sorted his trousers, then held his hand. "Where's your brother?"

"Upstairs."

"Did he get sent up there?"

38

"Nah, he was playing with his car."

"Guess what?" Mummy's eyes sparkled.

Hope lit up his heart, because when she looked like that after bingo, it meant she hadn't given all the winnings to Daddy. "What?"

"We can get some treats." She tugged him from the room. "Shoes and coat on." Then, calling, "Greg! Come on, we're going up the shop."

Greg's footsteps scrambled, and he came to the top of the stairs, peering down at them. "On our own?"

Mummy coughed, like George did when he stopped himself from crying.

"Yes, on our own. He's gone to the pub."

Greg all but tumbled downstairs and grabbed George in a hug, whispering, "Did he hurt you, cos I heard him shouting. I stayed away like you said."

"Yeah," George whispered back. "But it's okay because it means you didn't get hit."

They held hands with Mummy all the way, one on each side, and she stopped from time to time to speak to neighbours and other people she knew, saying she was fine and smiling, which she always did, even if she wasn't fine. Inside Mr Bum Head's shop, she picked up a basket and sent them off to find some sweets, and they chose what they wanted then found her at the fresh food section. Mr Bum Head's wife, Margaret, was a baker, and she manned the till when he was having a break.

George spied his favourite bread. Mummy said it came from a place called the Netherlands and the name was from the stripes of a tiger, and he reckoned if he ate enough of it, he'd be as strong as those big cats and could hit Daddy back really hard.

She had chicken and mushroom Pot Noodles and a block of Anchor butter in her basket already, a proper treat, and when she reached out and grabbed a loaf of tiger bread, George nudged Greg.

"Cor, look what we're having for dinner."

Back at home, their noodle pots steaming, thick slices of bread and butter on a plate in the middle, they all tucked in, George pretending Daddy wasn't alive and their kitchen wasn't in London but at the dream cottage. For the first time in a long time, he felt safe, and afterwards, they shared their Revels with Mummy, who never ever bought much for herself.

"But I want you to have them," she said.

George smiled. "And we want you to share. When we're bigger, we're going to look after you and buy you loads of flowers and chocolates and dresses and Daddy will be dead."

Mummy glanced at the door, the fearful look back. "You mustn't say things like that, son."

40

"Why not? He's a fucking little bastard."

Greg wet himself laughing, his mouth open, chocolate stuck to his teeth.

Mummy stared in shock. "George! Where did you hear that?"

"Him."

Mummy tried to be angry but held back a smile. "Please don't say that in front of him, for God's sake."

"But I can say it in my head. Cos he is one, like that other thing he said."

"What was it?" Greg kicked his legs back and forth so they brushed against George's.

Mummy sighed, pursing her lips in that way she did before she always warned, "Boys..."

George laughed and whispered to his twin, "A spiteful little cunt."

Greg laughed so hard he peed himself.

Chapter Four

The cubicle in the women's loos at Friday's restaurant in Entertainment Plaza smelled strongly of cleaning products. Goldie cursed himself for going after the Rainbow Cinnamon bitch. He should have delegated, kept well off Cardigan turf, but no, he'd wanted to do it himself. What a dick. And when would he learn?

He was so close to early retirement now, yet it seemed his brain wanted him to take little detours. Yes, Miss Bun could be a potential problem, but would it have really mattered if she'd run around like a headless chicken as Karen thought she would? A smack to the head during the heist would have solved that, yet here he was, hiding from one of the twins in a fucking *toilet*.

He'd already stuffed his balaclava in the sanitary products bin beside the porcelain throne, turned his interchangeable jacket inside out to reveal a light-blue side instead of the black, and his gun nestled safely in the inside pocket, his gloves in there with it.

He ran his hand through his hair to tidy it; God knew what state it was in. Phone out, he put the camera app on and took a gander at himself. His barnet wasn't as bad as he'd feared, so he smoothed out a couple of iffy spots and shoved his mobile away.

A creak sounded, and he jumped. He recognised it as the one the main door had bleated out when he'd entered. He cringed at footsteps echoing, then sagged with relief. They clip-clopped rather than thudded like Greg's would, and they were accompanied by another set that dragged. The door of the cubicle next door banged, and he glanced down. Shadows of someone in there pasted the floor tiles.

Of all the gin joints in all the towns in all the world, she walks into mine.

"On you get," a woman said.

"I don't want to poo here, Mummy. I want to go home."

"Better here than in your pants, puddin'."

Lovely. Not only was he standing in a restaurant bog, he had the imminent smell of a kid's shit to contend with. While they were busy, he took a chance and opened his door.

He left, thankful no one stood in the corridor to spot a man coming out of the ladies', then went into the restaurant and spoke to the greeter at the door. Asked to be seated. He hadn't had dinner yet, so it was the ideal time to take a pew and wait it out.

Taken to a table by a server, near the window—his request—he settled in to look at the menu once the fella had noted his drink order and rushed off to get it. The lad didn't appear to know who Goldie was, and while that would ordinarily piss him off, he was grateful for it tonight. The less people who knew he'd been on Cardigan the better. He opted for The Deluxe Wagyu Burger and informed the kid of what he wanted when he returned with his Tanqueray No Ten, a citrus gin, then pondered how the hell tonight had gone so wrong.

He'd got cocky, that's what it was. Thought he had all the time in the world, that he had the situation sussed. He should have shot her in the head after he'd confirmed her name, but something in him had wanted to only wound her so he could take her back to Golden Eye and finish the job there. Do a bit of torture to remind him of the old days, when he'd been younger and so eager to prove to his residents and fellow leaders he was someone to be feared. It had been heady back then, him desperate to make a name for himself, to become a face no one forgot. In recent years he'd stepped back from doing the dirty work himself, so tonight's detour would be considered abnormal. He wasn't even going to be present at the Jackpot heist, instead creating an alibi where numerous people could vouch for him.

He'd spotted the infamous BMW barrelling down the road after him and had sped up, the busted rear tyre creating problems with going too fast. As soon as he'd entered Entertainment Plaza's vast car park, he'd hopped out, legged it into Bowling Bonanza's side door, marked STAFF ONLY, and hoofed it out the back way, much to the chagrin of employees who'd shouted at him, although some had appeared alarmed at a masked man barging through. He'd given them the finger and ran through the yard, along the way a bit, and entered Friday's delivery area where he'd hidden behind a line of large wheelie bins. Someone had come along, their footsteps and heavy breathing had given them away, and Goldie had worried Greg had found him. If it *was* him, why hadn't he checked behind the bins? What kind of leader was he to forget to do a thing like that?

Goldie had held his gun, ready to shoot Greg if necessary, but he'd ended up waiting half an hour after whoever it was had gone, then took the balaclava off and stuffed it in his pocket. A worker had come out for a cigarette, and while they'd wandered to the wooden gate to make a phone call, he'd slipped into the building. Fate had been on his side. The corridor led to another, where the loos were.

The SUV wouldn't be a problem. It had been stolen earlier from Moon's estate — a calculated move — had fake plates, and he'd worn gloves. The twins would undoubtedly look into it, go in the wrong direction, and Goldie would be well in the clear. Even if he was spotted in here now by Greg, which he sensed he would be, there was no law against him eating on another estate.

A woman and her son came and sat at the table beside him, joining a man and a teenage girl who scowled a lot; she clearly didn't want to be here with what he assumed was her family.

"Feel better now, puddin'?" the man asked

Great, Poo Boy. Goldie listened to their conversation for a while, sipping his gin, and checked in on his to-do list in life. No, he still didn't want kids. Didn't even want a wife, who had the potential to clean him out. But someone like Karen...he could handle a permanent relationship with a woman of her calibre, providing she didn't tell him what to do or how to spend his money. Going by experience, all the women he'd picked in the past had only wanted him for the pound signs, which was why he'd gone into the enterprise and shagged people who didn't know how much he was worth.

48

Thinking about that reminded him he had something to attend to before he got on a jumbo jet and fucked off out of here.

His food arrived, and he mourned the lack of his Pinkhouse plate. Still, he got over it and concentrated on eating and keeping an eye out of the window. Entertainment Plaza, built in a U shape, had a massive courtyard, a large, lit-up fountain in the centre. At night, a lightshow played out like in Vegas, the water droplets sparkling with colour, people seated at the edge of the fountain on the circular bench that surrounded it. Friday's, on one side of an upwards part of the U, stood opposite Jackpot Palace on the other. The casino spanned what amounted to three units, its name on a sign in capital letters, flashing bulbs around it, reminding him of those fancy mirrors some women used to put on their makeup. Said sign drew you in, enticed you to enter the confines, to discover the promise, the anticipation of winning big, to change your life. He'd give it to them, the twins had done their homework, and the place looked top-notch.

Beside Jackpot, Bella Italia, then, totally out of whack in the somewhat posh area, a well-known burger place that seemed to be everywhere these days. Next to that, a Brazilian restaurant, amongst others on the base of the U. The whole plaza glittered beneath a black sky, a place to come and forget your worries for a while, although it'd no doubt lessen your bank balance.

Then Goldie spotted him. Greg stood outside Jackpot, arms bowed, T-T beside him—Two-Time had shortened his name so it wasn't the same as when he'd worked for Sienna's sister behind the twins' backs, saying this job was a clean slate. They talked, Greg scanning the area, then he nodded, and the pair parted ways, T-T going into Bella, Greg storming across the shiny-tiled plaza towards the bowling alley next door. The bloke was lax. Surely the bowling alley was the first place he should have gone—he *must* have seen Goldie legging it in there, and it had to have been him investigating Friday's yard. Had he been so riled up he hadn't checked properly? Maybe he'd returned to the bowling alley to question people again.

Goldie chuckled quietly, looking forward to their confrontation.

It came ten minutes later, Greg entering Friday's on a mission, chatting to the greeter by the door. Greg gave the place the once-over, his gaze finally landing on Goldie, then it shifted to Poo Boy and his lot. His expression clouded over.

Good, he knows he can't make a scene with kids nearby.

Greg made his way over, a few people knowing who he was, smiling at him or averting their gazes. He commanded respect, and people feared him, which was only right, considering he was a leader. Goldie enjoyed the same on his estate, although he wasn't as built as The Brothers and didn't think he was viewed with quite the same awe. A bummer, that.

Greg pulled a chair out opposite and sat. "What are you doing here?"

Goldie indicated his food. "Err, eating? Like people generally do in a restaurant?"

"You know what I mean."

"What, are you asking why I'm on your estate? Why not? It's a free country."

"How did you get here?"

"Someone dropped me off."

"When?"

"About fifteen minutes ago. What is this, the Spanish Inquisition?"

Greg scowled. "Apart from sampling a burger, what else are you here for?"

"Bowling."

"On your own? Don't make me laugh."

Goldie sniffed. "Can't see what's funny about a bloke throwing balls down a lane myself, but whatever hits your funny bone is your business."

"Talking of business. Are you doing, or have you done any, tonight?"

"Now why would I do that without informing you first?"

Greg stared at him.

Intimidated a little but not showing it—Greg's eyes seemed to want to seek out his secrets—Goldie waved a hand over the remains of his meal. "If that's all... My food's getting cold."

"You've only got a couple of chips left."

"So?"

Greg glanced at the Poo Boy family then back to Goldie. "You'd better not be lying to me."

"What, about my chips being cold?" Goldie held in laughter. He enjoyed winding this bloke up.

"*Don't* fuck me about."

Goldie supposed he'd better rein it in. "What have I got to lie about?"

"There's been a shooting."

"And? That's your problem. Your estate, not mine. What do you want, my help? I don't think so. I don't do collaborations, you know that."

Greg stood. "Go bowling, then fuck off home."

Goldie raised his eyebrows. "Swearing in front of kids. My, my…"

Greg planted his hands on the table and leant close. "I'll swear near who I fucking like, mate."

Goldie glared into his eyes. "Mate? Didn't think you had any. I *could* bring this up at the next leader meeting. You know, you harassing me."

"Bring up whatever you like, I couldn't give a fiddler's. I'm within my rights to question you when there's been an *incident* on my turf. Like I said, bowl, then *fuck off.*"

He strode away, the brick shithouse, and left, swaggering past the window, not bothering to glance inside to give another warning stare. He didn't need to, and he knew it. Greg was confident enough in himself that he didn't have to overegg the pudding. Had Goldie been a mere resident, he'd have crapped himself, but as it was, he laughed at the thought of Greg's face once they found out their casino had been robbed.

He resigned himself to going bowling alone. He couldn't *not* do it—Greg would likely get someone in Bowling Bonanza to keep an eye out for him.

Fuck's sake.

Goldie hadn't bowled for years, was too ham-fisted to get any strikes, the ball inevitably destined for the gutter. God, the things he had to do in order to get what he wanted…

He sipped his gin. Thought about Miss Bun and how George would be helping her now. They'd protect her, probably squirrel her away somewhere until her shooter was caught, so there was no way Goldie could get his hands on her to finish the job.

Unless Karen or Teddy could get information on where she was. Karen could pretend she was concerned.

Goldie swirled a scheme around in his head and nodded. His men could take out any babysitters easily, snatch Miss Bun, and Goldie could do away with her. Or maybe he wouldn't have to bother. She'd be out of commission for a while, what with those bullet wounds, so she wouldn't be at the casino to do the chicken act.

Nah, on second thoughts, he wouldn't trouble himself with her. She was inconsequential now.

He drained the rest of his gin, paid the bill, and went outside. He walked casually to Bowling Bonanza and made a show of checking the price list in the window so any of Greg's minions could see him. Then he took a deep breath and entered, dreading having to play a game he detested.

Roll on retirement.

Chapter Five

Karen, unnerved by what she'd seen earlier, glanced at Teddy who dealt cards on the blackjack table. She stood in her usual spot, where she watched the customers for card tampering and the like, wondering why a red-faced Greg had come stomping in, jerking his head at T-T, both of them going out the front into the plaza.

What had happened? Why was Greg here on a Monday night? And where was George? They were never here on their own, always in a pair. She'd already been worried because Ichabod had disappeared sharpish after receiving a message on his phone.

Had Goldie sent someone to spy and they'd been caught? Shit. She couldn't be doing with everything going wrong. She *needed* the promised money from the heist, couldn't see a way out of her issue otherwise. Her sister, Robyn, needed surgery, had been on the NHS waiting list for a year already, and Karen had sworn she'd find the cash so she could pay to go private. The specialists clearly didn't think she needed a procedure called laparoscopic ovarian drilling anytime soon, which would hopefully help Robyn with her fertility issues. The pain Robyn experienced from polycystic ovary syndrome wasn't good either, and all Karen wanted to do was take the discomfort away and give her sister a ray of hope that she might one day be able to have a child.

Failing that, Karen would be a surrogate.

The refusal of a medical loan had been the last straw in the search for funding, so Karen had suggested going down the self-pay route, where she'd save enough to fund the op outright. Seeing Robyn so depressed all the time meant Karen became more and more frantic to help as the months wore on. When Goldie had approached her about the heist at her job in Golden Glow, she'd been over the moon, but at the point he'd told her she had to work at Jackpot for a few months prior, she'd sagged, her balloon popped. She now only got wages from the twins, so her savings pot hadn't increased that much. London prices sucked up most of her earnings.

Robyn had said it didn't matter, she'd waited for ages already, so what was another six or so months? Fair enough, but Robyn's mental state had deteriorated, and her behaviour had affected her marriage. Karen loved her brother-in-law, Cal, like a sibling, and she had the burning urge to fix everything for them as soon as possible. To see them smile again. Be happy.

She owed it to Robyn who'd protected her throughout their tumultuous childhood from a manipulative father who'd taken his anger out on Karen.

With Greg turning up and Ichabod doing a vanishing act… What if they *had* rumbled Goldie and the heist didn't go ahead? What would she do then? She didn't have a mortgage, and neither did Robyn and Cal. All of them had been refused unsecured loans, including medical insurance, because their credit ratings were up the swanny. As she lived on Cardigan as part of her cover, she could be cheeky and ask the twins to lend her the money, but she doubted they'd do that. They'd probably send her to Sienna, the woman who bore a creepy resemblance to Alice from *Luther*. Sienna had set up a loan business with the help of the twins not too long ago. But what were the chances she would lend Karen that amount of money? Maybe if Karen, Robyn, and Cal approached her, with their combined wages, she might consider them.

"Concentrate," Teddy whispered.

She pulled her mind from her problems and planted herself firmly back in work. As well as looking pretty and flirting with the male customers to encourage them to drop more cash, she glanced every so often at the rest of the casino, stopping short when she couldn't see Cinnamon at her usual table. Maybe she was ill, although Karen swore she'd seen her walk down her street earlier.

Shrugging, she attended to a man's hand that had found its way to her backside, firmly removing it and smiling at him in a way that told him not to touch her again, *ever*. He winked, played with his stack of chips, and she resisted rolling her eyes. He was letting her know he had the money to pay her for sex, and she'd lost count of the many times blokes had made the same move, the same assumption. Some mistakenly thought she was for sale, but Ichabod always put them straight: if they wanted women, they were welcome to go to Debbie's Corner and select one—providing they were prepared to hand over their name and address and go through a police check to prove they were safe.

Greg barged back into Jackpot, creating a stir. People swivelled to glance his way, but he paid them no mind, intent on marching forward. T-T entered then, heading straight for the staff area, the same as Greg. Something was definitely going on, and Karen's stomach cramped.

Please don't let it be about the robbery, please…

T-T went through the staff door after his boss, and she jolted in shock at Jimmy Riddle coming out seconds later. He prowled the floor in his tartan suit. Jimmy acted as manager for two nights a week so Ichabod could have time off, but Monday wasn't his night, Tuesdays and Wednesdays were, and even then, Ichabod sometimes came in because he said he enjoyed the atmosphere so much and it saved him being bored on his own at home.

Why was Jimmy here?

Maybe someone's been seen on camera, nicking, and that's why T-T walked out earlier to go and find them.

It was driving her batty not being able to find out, but if this wasn't anything to do with the heist and she deviated from her usual pattern, it would be noticed.

Jimmy Riddle went round and spoke to each member of staff at every card table. Karen held her breath, desperate to know what he was saying, but she'd soon find out: he came her way. She smiled at the punter beside her (everyone secretly called him Handsy), then directed her attention to the others at the table, acting diligent in case Jimmy got suspicious.

He greeted the customers, then said, "Please excuse us for a moment."

He took Karen a metre or so away, his hand on her elbow. She all but shit herself, panicking. Why was he moving her away when he hadn't with the others? He'd leant close to speak to them, so how come he wasn't doing the same now? Did he know she was one of Goldie's moles?

He let her arm go. "Keep your reaction to a minimum. We don't want customers knowing."

"Knowing what?" she asked, breathless with fear.

"Cinnamon was shot on her way to work — you all need to know in case everyone who works here is a target. The reason I pulled you over here is because of that bloke there." He pointed to Handsy. "He's got a thing about her, and we don't want to alarm him or give him an excuse to leave if he knows she won't be in for a while. He spends too much for us to not have him in attendance each night."

"Shot?" Karen whispered. "What the *hell*? Why?"

"Pass it on to Teddy once this game's over, but for fuck's sake, do it quietly. Off you go." He walked on to another table.

Karen returned to hers, butterflies and all sorts rioting in her chest. Had Goldie done it? She'd told him earlier about Cinnamon potentially being a problem, so had he sorted it so she wouldn't be at work on the heist night? Did that mean the robbery was going ahead *this* Friday?

Relief at it possibly being this week, but concerned that Goldie might pick off any other employees in the meantime, creating unrest in the twins, which may then have a domino effect and fuck up the heist plans, she pasted on a smile and waited for the game to end. Once it had, and several people had got up to chance their arm at other tables, she tugged Teddy's sleeve to get his attention and gripped his shoulder to draw his face down to hers.

In his ear, she whispered what Jimmy had told her, then eased back to look up into his newly tanned face. "What do you think?"

"I won't answer that, not here." He shifted his attention to Handsy, one of two men who'd remained. "But it's got me worried, I'll tell you that much." He raised a hand to his cheek and dragged his palm down it. "Listen, the table's filling again. Let's just get to work and talk about it once we're out of here."

"Come to mine after we've finished?"

"Yep."

Teddy's place was closer, but they couldn't go there and discuss anything as his boyfriend would be at home and he didn't want to get involved in Goldie's business more than knowing what they were up to. She took a deep breath and launched herself into her role. She'd phone Goldie on her break and tell him about Cinnamon—in case he'd had nothing to do with it. He'd expect that of her, especially as she'd have to let him know which croupier had taken Cinnamon's place so he knew who'd be in attendance on heist night.

She swore to God, if it wasn't for Robyn, she wouldn't even have contemplated being involved in a robbery. Goldie being her leader and boss at Golden Glow or not, she'd have told him she wasn't the right fit for the job.

The idea of visiting Sienna with her sister and brother-in-law floated through her mind again, but even if she got the cash that way, she was still stuck in this mess. If she walked away once she'd secured the funds and didn't stay at Jackpot for the required year, Goldie would come after her. He wouldn't trust her to keep her mouth shut.

Unless she found herself incapacitated, unable to go to Jackpot at all. Surely he couldn't blame her if she was so ill she couldn't work. No, he'd make her. Too much time had been spent on this with her part cemented in stone. If she was absent, it would mean cocking up the whole scheme. She had an important role to play.

But maybe there was another way to get herself out of this.

Either way, though, she might find herself dead.

Chapter Six

George, seven now, cowered at Dad's feet. He could push back at him as much as he liked, but it still didn't mean he wasn't scared of him. Adults could be frightening, and Dad was the worst. George had just been kicked in the back, and it hurt, his eyes stinging where he held off tears. He wouldn't cry in front of

Dad, not when the man seemed to like it, but a sob built, asking to come out.

"Tell me where that cricket stump is, Greg."

Greg stood in the corner where George had pushed him before the attack so he was safe.

Dad put on his other voice, the one he used to try to get them to do what he wanted. "If you tell me, I'll buy you some sweets."

Neither of them believed that. He'd promised sweets before and not come through.

"I d-don't know," Greg said, just like George had told him to.

Dad went back to his usual voice. Snarling. Loud. "So then you must know, George, because your useless mother wouldn't need a cricket stump."

Greg had stolen it so George could keep it under his mattress for the times when Dad came into their room to hurt them. George dreamed of stabbing their father with it, sticking it in the side of his neck, then pulling it out so all the blood spurted like it had on that film Lonnie James told them about at school. The idea had sprouted in George's head ever since, growing wings, so not only did he stab the neck, he stabbed him all over.

"I don't know nuffin' about no cricket stump," George said.

"It's missing from my bag, and seeing as I haven't been in the cupboard under the stairs lately, and your mother says she didn't take it, then it's one of you two. Are you protecting your brother, George, is that what you're doing?"

"No. He hasn't got it and neither have I."

"Well, someone has." Dad moved back, took aim, and kicked again.

The agony in George's side hurt more than anything Dad had done to him before. Mum had a sore side last week, and she said one of her ribs had cracked when she'd slipped over on black ice. Had the same happened to George? Would he move like an old man now, the same as she had?

"Tell me," Dad said, "or I swear — "

"It was me," Greg blurted.

"No, it was me," George said and gave his brother the stare: Don't.

"So we're back to playing games, are we?" Dad paced. "What have I said about doing that? Other people might not be able to tell you apart, but I can, and I know this is something you would do, George."

George stared up at him. He wanted to cry because he hated this man, hated him so much. He was cruel and nasty, always shouting or being cross, apart from the times Mum read notes from him that he'd propped *on the mantelpiece. For a couple of days after they appeared, Dad left them alone. For as far back as George could remember, they'd all been afraid of him, worried in case he blew up, Mum asking them to be quiet and good if Dad was home, to not provoke him. Greg had stolen the cricket stump last week when Mum and Dad had been at work, so they'd stuck to their promise and had only been naughty while they were out.*

"Father Christmas won't be bringing you any presents, then," Dad sniped.

George didn't believe in stupid Father Christmas anyway, he'd caught Mum wrapping the presents last week. She'd said she had to help wrap them because the elves were too busy, but Lonnie had told him the man in the red suit didn't exist anymore, he was just some bloke from years ago who'd helped poor people, and he was dead now, so how could he get in a sleigh that flew and travel around the world?

"I don't want any," George said.

"You ungrateful shit." Dad kicked him again.

George rolled away from him, gritting his teeth so he didn't cry. He didn't dare touch his ribs, but they ached, and something seemed to be poking into his insides. Had he cracked one of them?

"I've never wanted to buy you any presents. I wouldn't spend a penny on you if I could help it."

"Is that why you don't hardly give her no money, then?" George snapped back. "You're horrible, you are. A pig."

Dad dropped to the floor and pummelled George with his fists. George curled into a ball, vaguely picking up the sound of Greg shouting for their father to stop. The faint tap of Mum's shoes, a gasp, and then Dad was gone, away from him, where Mum had dragged him back.

"You can hit me, but don't you dare hit my sons."

Mum usually got in the way before Richard could hit either of them if she was home, George doing the same for Greg—he'd learnt from the best. But Dad had taken to hitting them while she wasn't there, dishing out the threat that if they told her what he'd done, he'd kill her while she slept.

"Go to Mrs Deal next door," Mum said. "Both of you."

George stood, his whole body screaming. Greg came over and slipped his hand in his, squeezing tight.

"No," George said. "Greg, you go, but I'm staying here."

"Do as you're told." Mum stared at him, her eyes saying: Please.

"He'll hit you if we go, and I don't want him to."

"No he won't," Mum cajoled. "Will you, Richard?"

"I won't touch her, kid. Now get out of my sight."

Greg tugged him out of the room and down the hallway. He opened the door and, outside, stuck his arm around George's shoulder. "What if he hurts her."

The chilly winter air hit George's hot cheeks. "I'm going to tell Mrs Deal. Then she can get help."

"Mum said we weren't allowed to tell anyone."

"I don't care."

George knocked on Mrs Deal's door, and she opened it, staring down at them with what George had come to know was pity. She was one of the only people around here who didn't call them little bastards, instead being kind to them. Her grey hair in curlers gave him comfort, like the Pot Noodles and tiger bread.

"He's been at it again, hasn't he." She sighed and adjusted her glasses. "Come on. I'll make you a hot chocolate, and I've got some of those Penguins you like."

They followed her into the kitchen, with its smell of recently baked cakes which sat on the worktop on a wire rack, the tops all iced white, like the frosty pavement, sprinkles on top. They wouldn't beat

72

Mum's rock cakes, but George could already taste them, nonetheless.

She wafted a hand at the cakes. "I've no doubt you'll want one or two of them an' all. Help yourselves."

They sat at the table, side by side, Greg's thigh against George's. He always needed to touch George after Richard had gone off on one or when he was feeling weird inside. That was how he put it. Weird inside. Was it the same weird George felt? That madness that told him to chat back at Richard?

Mrs Deal plonked a plate of cakes in front of them. "Just leave three for my Sid for when he gets home from the pub, all right?" She bustled off to the fridge to get the milk out.

George and Greg took a cake each, staring at each other, and Greg nodded, giving George permission to confide in their neighbour. He had that look about him that said he was as tired of this as George and they needed someone to step in, regardless of Mum telling them it had to stay between all of them.

"He hits us all the time," George said.

Mrs Deal blew out a puffy breath. "I know, son."

"Why don't you tell the police for us, then?"

"Because your mother asked me not to." She poured milk into a saucepan.

"But they need to arrest him."

"They do, but sometimes, it isn't as easy as that. Involving the police... Look, your mummy doesn't tell me much, but from what I've gathered, she can't go to the police, okay? Just be good, and he won't hit you."

"But he does it even when we're good!"

"I know, love, I know."

George ate his cake. It didn't make sense, what she'd said. The teachers at school said if anything horrible was happening at home, they could get it stopped. George thought about what Mum had said when he'd told her Miss Flag might be able to help them run away: "No, George, no! We mustn't tell anyone."

"She'll be ashamed, I'll wager," Mrs Deal said. "A lot of women are." Then she muttered, "Although if someone like him battered my kids, I'd take a ruddy knife to him."

Adults did a lot of that, muttering to themselves, like they thought George couldn't hear what they'd said. He picked a lot up that way. From what he'd gleaned, it was too dangerous for Mum to go to the police. Was it because of Dad or something else?

Someone else?

Stirring the milk, the old woman said, "I know it doesn't help you now because you're so little, but one day, you can get your own back, you'll see."

"I'm going to kill him," George said proudly, then bit into a second cake.

"I do believe you will," Mrs Deal said, then another of those mutters: "Just don't get caught."

She shouldn't be saying stuff like that to a small boy, George knew that, but so many grown-ups around here said things they shouldn't.

It confused him, and he finished his cake, reaching for another one. Their hot chocolate would be ready in a minute, and he concentrated on that rather than what might be going on at home. There was no shouting coming through the wall, no thuds, so maybe they weren't arguing. He didn't want to think of what else could be happening instead.

Later, after their front door slamming had shook Mrs Deal's house and they'd scoffed two Penguins each, she waited on the doorstep to see them home as it was dark now, the stars bright. Mum opened the door, smiling as if nothing was wrong, although she hobbled down the hallway.

The twins went inside, George thinking about the cricket stump and all the holes he could make with it.

Chapter Seven

George sat in a private room at the clinic on Moon's estate while Cinnamon had surgery. Moon, Alien, and Brickhouse had arrived, as George had received info from Greg that the SUV the shooter had used had been stolen from The Moon Estate.

"What the fuck's all this about then, then?" Moon stood by the window and peered into the darkened garden where patients sat or walked during their recuperation in the daytime.

He pulled the blind down and sat on an armchair in the corner.

"You want me to repeat myself?" George asked. "Have you suddenly gone Mutt and Jeff?"

Moon gritted his teeth. "I'm not that old, son. Yet." He pondered the news George had given him. "A stolen car? Someone shooting at one of your residents? Fucking bastard."

"Greg and T-T visited every place in the plaza in search of the wanker, but the only person who stood out as iffy was Goldie."

Moon took a silver hip flask out of his pocket and swigged, probably because he wasn't allowed to smoke his cigars in here and he needed something to calm his nerves. "Why would he want to kill Belgian Bun?"

"Cinnamon Bun," George said. "No clue. She passed out and didn't come round again even when I brought her here. She went straight into surgery. I'll ask her when she's back and wakes up, see if she knows him or has had any dealings."

Brickhouse huffed. "Fucking rude that Goldie didn't ask for permission if he's shooting people on your estate."

"Cheeky fuck," George muttered.

"My thoughts exactly," Moon agreed. "All right, me, you, and Greg don't ask for permission to mess about on each other's estates anymore because we've come to an agreement we don't have to, but Goldie? He's a dickhead and needs a talking-to. At the very least it should be brought up at the leader meeting. The others need to know if he's poncing about without asking. What if he gads off to one of theirs and pulls a stunt like this? Tick-Tock won't stand for it, and neither will the rest."

Alien, a big Canadian, paced. "There's always the chance he wasn't the shooter. Did Greg speak to him or just spot him hanging around and assumed?"

George recalled what Greg had said on the phone. "He was eating in Friday's and said he was going bowling—alone."

"Fuck right off, was he." Moon scowled. "That's a load of old bollocks. Like *he'd* do that by himself. He's usually got two of his thugs with him these days as bodyguards."

Brickhouse held a hand up. "What if he was the shooter and he didn't tell any of his men he was doing a job? That would explain why he was by himself."

George had already considered that. "Greg said the bloke in the SUV had black clothing on, plus a balaclava. Goldie's jacket was light-blue. Before you say anything, yep, I know he could have changed it, but the reason I brought it up is, what if he'd left a spare jacket somewhere in Bowling Bonanza or Friday's so he could switch them afterwards? I'm also concerned that if it *was* him who shot Cinnamon, not only do I want to know why, but I want answers as to what gave him the right to nick a car from *your* estate, Moon. To deliberately send us in the wrong direction? Or do you two have a beef and he's after putting a wedge between us because we'd think someone from your area had come and shot one of our residents, so we'd take it up with you?"

"Whatever it was, the fact he ate and bowled on his tod..." Moon sipped from his flask then tucked it away. "Sounds fishy to me. So what are we going to do about it?"

"Greg's already got someone watching him. Ichabod's the best we've got when it comes to tailing a subject covertly, so Jimmy's taking over the casino in his absence. At the minute, Goldie's at home. Alone as far as Ich can see."

"We could pay him a visit now," Moon said.

George shook his head. "Nah, we'll leave it, see what pans out. And also see what Cinnamon has to say about her involvement with him, if any."

"Fucking weird name," Moon grumbled.

"Her real one is Rainbow Archer."

Moon furrowed his eyebrows. "Don't play me for a fool, son."

"I'm not!"

"Have hippy parents, did she?" Moon rolled his eyes.

"No idea. But she checked out fine when we looked into her after her initial interview to work at Jackpot—obviously, otherwise we wouldn't have taken her on."

Moon grunted. "People *are* clever enough to dupe you, you know."

"I'm aware of that. So what are you suggesting?"

Moon took a deep breath. "Let's throw this scenario out there. Cinnamon works for him. She's at Jackpot to see how you run it—maybe

Goldie's after opening his own money-spinner and wants pointers. Maybe he asked her to do something dodgy. I dunno, like nick gambling chips, enough that you'd suspect another employee. It'd cause uproar, because we all know you'd go fucking mental at the thought of someone stealing from you, that it'd rock the boat. Goldie might just be playing a game where he creates enough angst that you two take your eye off the ball and Jackpot fails. He's the jealous sort. He won't like you coining it in more than him."

"A few chips going missing wouldn't piss us off *that* much," George said, "although what you've said has disturbed me because before she passed out, Cinnamon mentioned a chip she'd put in her pocket. Reckons she was going to hand it in, but Karen told Ich about it before she could. Ich hasn't mentioned it to me, so I assume he bought her story, but I'll be having a word with him about it."

"There you go, then. It's like I said. She's probably told you about it so it gets her out of the shit when you find out what's *really* going on. She'll do what everyone else does and say it wasn't her fault, she was forced to work for

Goldie, blah-de-fucking-blah—God, that excuse really bugs the crap out of me."

"What if she *was* forced, though? She's been a Cardigan resident all her life. We owe it to her to help if Goldie's making her do shit."

"She should have come and told you straight off the bat."

Ordinarily, George would have said the same, but he'd finally learnt that not everything was so black and white. "What if she was too afraid?"

"Are you having one of your soft moments, George? You know how they get you into trouble."

Bog off, mate. "I don't want to jump in feet-first without all the info to hand. I won't accuse her of anything without proof to back it up—all right, I usually torture stuff out of people, but in this case, I want to gather all the info I can. Hence why I've got our PI, Mason, on it, plus Ich's watching Goldie. If anything dodgy is going on, they'll find it."

Moon nodded. "In the meantime, we'll have a root around on my estate to see if we can discover who nicked the car. How did Greg find out it was from my estate so quickly?"

"He checked the VIN and got hold of our copper. The car had been nicked earlier in the day. Some poor cow had parked it at the supermarket and came out with screaming, bored kids in tow, realising it'd been nicked."

"Got a name for her?"

George racked his brain. "Daisy...Daisy..."

"Give me your answer, do," Moon sang.

George laughed. "Pack it in, I'm trying to think. Ah, Daisy Barlow. Lives in College Road. I asked for her address so we could offer her a car to drive while we get hers repaired. Greg shot the tyre, so we feel obliged."

Moon waved that idea away. "I'll sort that. You get on with finding out info from Cinnamon when she finally makes it back in here."

"It's been three hours, so she should be arriving soon."

The clatter of a bed being pushed along announced her arrival, then a knock at the door.

"What did I tell you," George said.

Moon opened up. "All right, Bill?" he asked the porter.

"Yes, thanks. You?"

"It's all fucking gravy with me, son." Moon moved out of the way so the bed could be wheeled in.

Cinnamon, half awake, woke up even more once she spotted the men in her room.

"Calm your tits, love," Moon said. "We don't bite."

Alien chuckled.

Bed in position, Bill looked at George. "Do you want me to get the doctor so you can have a chat?"

George shook his head and stood. "No. Someone already came and gave me the gist. The bullets had to be removed, all that jazz. I'll settle the bill on my way out."

Bill nodded to everyone, left, and closed the door.

Cinnamon tried to sit, but her arms failed in helping to push her upright. Obviously exhausted from the anaesthetic, she flopped back down. "If it's about the chip, I can explain."

"You already did," George said.

"No, explain properly. I lied. Christ, I'm so sorry. I *was* going to steal it. Fuck…" She blinked. Tears seeped down her temples and into her ears. "I'm not who I let people think I am."

"Here we go," Moon muttered.

"Who *are* you, then?" George asked. "If you're talking about having nippers, we know that. We didn't mention it to anyone else because it's your business if you want to go round telling people you're fancy free. What I'm interested in was why you felt it was okay to nick a chip. How much was it worth?"

"A hundred quid."

"That's rude," Moon said. "What did you need it for, drugs?" He stared at her in disgust.

"No! The leccy." She closed her eyes, clearly ashamed.

This wasn't the first person who'd needed leccy money lately, and it really got George's goat that because of the rise in energy costs, his people were suffering. *Other* people were suffering all over the country, maybe even the world. He'd slipped people money to top up their meters during the winter, unable to stand the thought of them freezing their tits off. And now, here was another one.

"Why didn't you just come to me or Greg if you needed leccy money?" he asked gently. Aware of Moon mentioning his soft side, he kept a hardened part of himself on standby, just in case.

"It's embarrassing. I can't afford all the bills on my wages. I get a Universal Credit top-up, but I'm still on the breadline. Below it, if I'm honest. The rent's sky-high. The flat's got mould because of the condensation. The council won't do jack shit about it. I have to pay a babysitter so I can work."

"Is that why you make out you're well-off and have a thing about name brands? To hide the fact you're skint? Are you that bothered about what people think of you?" Fuck, George's eyes stung. Tears were annoying bastards, and they'd paid him a visit a lot this week because of memories gate-crashing his mind. She must have underlying issues from childhood or something for her to pretend like that. Someone had made her feel lower than a tart's knickers, and she wanted to prove them wrong. "I've seen you in Gucci at work. How did you afford that sort of clobber?"

"I went to your shop, got lucky in finding a few nice dresses and whatever for cheap."

Vintage Finds, their little emporium, had grown in popularity since two Ukrainian refugees had taken over running it. The sisters, now with new identities, had settled into London life well after their ordeal. They'd been lured here just before the war had broken out, with the promise of jobs and housing. What they'd stumbled into was a room full of mattresses, a boarded-up window, and the position of sex worker to rich people who'd used them as if they were dolls to pose and do with as they pleased. Zoe, their little Miss Marple, had been keeping a close on eye on them and had declared they weren't still in with The Network who'd arranged for them to come to the UK. All had ended well with that saga, although not all Network members had been apprehended.

He couldn't let Cinnamon's plight steer him into Mr Mushy until he'd established the real story here. The one she'd told might well be it, but further digging was needed before he'd be satisfied.

"What do you know about Goldie?"

She frowned. "The music producer or the leader?"

"The leader."

"Not a lot. Why?" She sounded too tired to continue.

George didn't care. "Is that the truth or bollocks?"

"The truth," she slurred. "Bloody hell, sorry, I can't keep my eyes open."

Moon stepped up to the bed. "I'll help you with that." He used the pointer finger and thumb of each hand and prised the lids apart.

George would have laughed normally, but in the current circumstances, Moon's methods could be detrimental. "Leave off, will you?"

Moon grinned and stepped away.

Cinnamon blinked, likely to get moisture back in her eyes. "I don't know him except that he's one of you. What's going on?"

"So you don't work for him, then?"

"*No.*"

George visually checked in with the other three to get their take on it. The men shook their heads: *the state she's in, she'd confess; she just wants to sleep.* George nodded his thanks and addressed her again.

"While you were having your op, I got hold of your neighbour, Anna. You told me about her before you passed out, remember? She's happy to have the kids for however long you need. They're all at a safe house we own. Will's with them. We didn't want to put them at risk in case the shooter goes after them next."

She became instantly alert.

The love of a mother.

She shrieked, "Oh my God, I have to go to them."

"It's fine. They're in the best place they can be. Listen, this is important—and serious. We think Goldie shot you. Now why would he do that?"

"*What*? Can you prop me up? I might not fall asleep if I'm sitting."

George and Moon took an arm each and hauled her into a better position.

"I don't understand," she said. "I was just walking to work. He was at the end of the street at his car. I went past, and he called me by my real name—and shot me in the leg. I went to run, and he shot my arse. I fell over but managed to get round the corner. Then you and Greg came. I don't know anything, I swear." She frowned. "But this might help. There was someone in number two, they were looking down at me from a back bedroom. They shook their head as if they *couldn't* help."

So they'd been warned. Fuck-up number one, Goldie, issuing orders to our people.

He recalled their earlier conversation. "You told me you had something to tell me, before you conked out."

She slowly raised one hand and rubbed an eye. "Karen and Teddy. They don't live together like they say they do. I go home the same way as them, and he went into a house on Moorgate Street. She said she'd see him tomorrow, then went into a block of flats down Diamond Road."

"Didn't they see you following?"

"I was a fair way back but close enough to hear. I just find it weird that they're supposedly living together and getting married next year — that's what they've been telling people — yet they *don't* live together. Why lie?"

Why indeed. "Thanks for telling me. How long have you known this?"

"Two days. I wasn't sure whether to say anything or not, that's why I never got hold of you or Ichabod."

"Right, you'll be staying here, guarded, until you're allowed to leave. Then you'll go to the safe house. You're not going home until we get to the bottom of this. Anna's already dealing with phoning the school in the morning so the kids' absence is accounted for — stomach bug. In the meantime, rest up. When you're better, we'll discuss upping your wages or finding you another position that caters to school hours, then you won't have to pay a babysitter every night. Have you got your leccy payment card in your bag?"

She nodded. "It's in my purse."

"Then I'll go and top it up. We'll deal with you paying us back another time." He silenced whatever protest she planned to make by raising his hand. "Be quiet. Sleep. Our man will stay outside in the corridor." George had already phoned for one of their heavies to stand guard. "And we'll say no more about that chip, other than if you do it again, there'll be trouble."

She closed her eyes, more tears falling.

"Do you want to lie back down?" he asked.

"Can you put me on my side so I haven't got pressure on my bum?"

They did that. Her chest rose and fell slowly; she was already sinking into oblivion. He gestured for Moon et al to follow him out, then closed the door, telling the guard Cinnamon wasn't allowed any visitors other than clinic staff, George or Greg, or Moon, Alien, and Brickhouse, unless he said otherwise.

They marched down the corridor, Moon and his men continuing out of the main doors, George going to the reception desk to settle the bill, his mind ticking over. If Goldie *hadn't* shot Cinnamon, he was still up to no good just by breaking his usual pattern by eating and bowling alone.

Something was up, and George wouldn't rest until he'd discovered exactly what it was.

Chapter Eight

Goldie paced his living room, eyeing the steel shutters on the outside of the floor-to-ceiling windows that looked nice and decorative but were for his safety and to keep anyone from nosing in. A man like him who didn't have them was a fool, and he wasn't one. Well, he *had* been tonight, muffing up his mission, but he wouldn't dwell on it. By now, Greg would be gunning for whoever had nicked the SUV from Moon's estate, and George was likely grilling Miss Bun—she must have had an op by now, he couldn't see George not getting her some medical help. If she had any sense in her head, she'd keep her mouth shut through fear Goldie would investigate her life and find one of her family members to shoot next. She must know the way of the leaders because she was employed by two of them. *All* residents of London were aware of how it worked, so if she told them exactly what had happened, she was thick as pig shit if she thought he'd take it lying down.

Maybe he *would* poke into her anyway, see what nuggets he dug up.

Karen had phoned while on her break. She'd informed him of the goings-on at Jackpot while he'd been suffering at Bowling Bonanza—the Poo Boy family had come in, taking the lane beside him. Poo's screeching had done Goldie's head in, and it had been a close call as to whether he beat him around the head with the heaviest ball or pretended he couldn't hear it. Kids were like vermin, they got everywhere. To top it off, he hadn't liked having to bowl when he didn't usually do *anything* he did want to.

Karen's news had been welcome—he'd trained her well to get hold of him immediately if she thought it meant the heist would be compromised. Once again, he wished she was older so he could whisk her away to the palm trees with him, see her in a bikini.

On one hand, it pleased him that Greg had been red in the face and fit to burst with anger, but on the other, knowing Ichabod wasn't there in his usual capacity, prowling the casino trying to appear tough, well, that was a worry. Jimmy Riddle had taken his place, so what had the Irishman been sent to do?

The fluttering of panic in his chest gave him concern. It wasn't unheard of that people his age had heart attacks from stress, but would fate be so unkind as to make him have one when he was so close to his goal? Taking a few deeps breaths and letting out some *ohms*, he deemed himself calm enough to think properly.

Right, mind made up, he went upstairs to spy through one of the lenses he'd installed in the shutters. No point in using the one downstairs. High bushes surrounded his property, and he wouldn't see fuck all from the living room or kitchen unless someone stood in the front or rear gardens. Any cars with people inside, observing, would be out of sight.

He entered his large bedroom and headed straight for the front window, activating the camera installed in the lens by using a keypad on the wall beside a display monitor. He manoeuvred it from side to side, counting the parked cars on the screen and checking for anyone watching from the driver's seats.

No one.

He relaxed, telling himself he wasn't being paranoid but diligent. After his interaction with Greg earlier, Goldie being as belligerent as ever, he couldn't take any chances. His attitude could have pissed Greg off, and the man might have sent someone to follow him.

He swept the camera slowly this time, inspecting everything more closely. The spaces between the iron fencing struts. The gaps between cars. No, there definitely wasn't anyone out there. All of the houses opposite appeared the same as normal, a couple with lights on, the glow peeping from the sides and tops of curtains, the cul-de-sac of superior homes either gated, fenced, or standing proudly behind hedges. *His* hedge had barbed wire and glass embedded inside it, so if anyone thought of clambering over, they'd get a nasty surprise, hopefully a vicious stab to the nuts. Was it legal? He didn't give a fuck. His safety meant more to him than a smack on the wrist by a copper.

Next, he went to one of the back bedrooms and did the same sweep, then once again checked the front. He wished he could take some time to spy on the blonde woman in the house opposite. Marleigh. She liked to get undressed with her lights on and the curtains open, probably thinking no one could see her, but he had things to think about, and indulging in voyeurism sadly wasn't on the cards tonight.

Satisfied he could have a proper good drink now he'd shrugged off the distasteful experience of bowling alone, having to get into a taxi instead of Bronson driving him — *Jesus fucking wept* — and checking he hadn't been tailed, he returned downstairs, going straight to his notebook on the kitchen island to amend a few things. With Cinnamon out of action in time for Friday's heist, all he had to do was write down whoever was taking her place, plus whether Ichabod or Jimmy would be the manager that evening. Ichabod may have been sent on a mission that was nothing to do with Goldie.

That brought another mad idea to mind. With the Irish ninja possibly out of the equation, it would go much better if Jimmy was in attendance.

Hmm. Maybe Ichabod needed a little visit to ensure he didn't come back…

An hour after he'd jotted down some bits and bobs, he went to the third storey and slid the key in the lock of the door that led to the loft. He secured it behind him and put the key in his pocket, then climbed the stairs.

He walked into the room at the top and glanced over into the corner. Smiled. Felt a bit sad, to be honest. There had been some good times in this private space, where he'd convinced himself things weren't how they actually were. It was easy to do with your eyes closed, to pretend, to lie to yourself.

"Such a shame I can't take you with me," he said. "But there wasn't enough time to train you to keep your pretty little mouth shut. Mind you, I want it well and truly open now." He undid his trouser zip and approached. "Get your gob around that."

Chapter Nine

*M*argate was the best place George had ever been to. They'd travelled on a coach for the weekend. Dad and Francine's husband, Jeff, had stayed at home. Francine had persuaded Dad to let them go—how, George didn't know, and he didn't care. They were here, on a sandy beach making sandcastles, and that was all that mattered. Francine's kids were there, too, and George was glad—he loved Gail.

Last night, they'd been to a fair, going on all the rides, George worrying about where the money had come from to pay for it. They'd had so much fun, not to mention candy floss, his fingers sticky with it all the way back to the hotel. Despite Mum saying they should take the double bed, George and Greg shared a single, top to tail, so she could have the big one all to herself. There was a bathroom, much nicer than their one at home, with fluffy white towels and free soap that smelled like talcum powder.

Mum had said she was in her element, whatever that was, and if that meant she was happy, then he wished she was in it all the time. Toes in the sand, she smiled a lot, drank from her bottle of pop, and stared out at the sea as if she wished she could sail away. George wished they could, too. Or stay here forever under the hot sun, building the castles and listening to people chatting, kids shrieking.

Greg flicked sand at George using his spade, and George flicked back. Greg did it again, and some shot up into Mum's eye. She blinked, her eye watering, and playfully clipped them round the earholes.

"Pack it in," she said and stood. "Who wants an ice cream?"

George's heart lightened—he'd been upset that messing about had hurt Mum's eye—then he fretted, because ice creams cost money, and Dad had told her she wasn't to spend much. Francine and Jeff had paid *for the hotel, and they all had breakfast free there every morning, dinner at night, so that was all right, but...*

Mum bent down to stroke his head. "Don't worry. I did extra cleaning."

He knew what that meant. She'd saved some, hadn't handed it all over to Dad. She must have been doing it for a while, because she took her purse out of her bag and showed him all the notes.

"We're here to enjoy ourselves for once, okay?"

"Can I come with you?"

She nodded.

Greg dropped his spade and tugged George up, holding his hand. He didn't like not being with George, and anyway, George had assumed going with Mum meant Greg would, too.

They walked up the beach holding her hands, leaving Francine, her two little boys, and Gail behind with promises that they'd bring them an ice cream back. The sand hot on his feet, George had never felt so free. How brilliant it was not to have Dad around to be afraid of. No fear that he'd come storming up to them and give them a clout. This was what it would feel like if he was dead, and George prayed really hard that when they got home, he wouldn't be there. He'd be gone. Someone would have killed him, chopped him up and put him in the river so the fishes could eat him.

They walked past some donkeys who trotted along with children on their backs. George wanted to ask for a go, but even though Mum had money in her purse, he kept his mouth shut. They never asked for anything, except to leave Dad, and he wouldn't start now.

"I don't want to go home," Greg said.

"Me neither." George wanted to stay here forever.

"Nor me," Mum said, "but we have to."

They'd arrived last night, and today was Saturday. Tomorrow afternoon, they'd have to get back on the coach.

George didn't want to think about it.

They reached the little striped shack which sold ice creams, sweets, drinks, crisps, sandwiches, loads of things. Sticks of rock poked out of a tall tube on the counter, boxes of fudge stacked beside it. George's mouth watered, and he thought about nicking a box but stopped himself. They weren't at home now, they weren't hungry, so he didn't need to steal, but he reckoned Mum would love some fudge because she looked at it for ages while she waited to be served.

Mum handed them their ice cream cones then carried the others back, all wedged together in both hands. The sun was so hot the ice cream had dribbled onto the cornets a bit by the time they got to their area. Mum handed the cones out, and they sat on their towels, George watching the kids playing while he ate his. None of them had bruises like he did. Mum had said for him to keep a T-shirt on so the ones on his belly and the tops of his arms didn't show. Dad hadn't kicked him for a while, so his legs were all right, sticking out of his red shorts. Mum had long sleeves on even though it was hot, and her skirt reached her ankles.

They spent the afternoon paddling in the frothy waves, playing with a ball, and making more castles. A picnic lunch, bought by Francine at the hotel, had beef paste sandwiches, crisps, and a piece of fruit cake each with thick icing on top. Gail shared a big bag of sweets Francine had pulled out of her handbag, and they each had a Panda Pop.

Life couldn't get any better.

They waited to cross the road from the promenade to the hotel opposite. A fancy car drew up, a BMW, and George stared at it in awe. It was so posh and shiny, and he promised himself that one day he'd have one. A man got out of the driver's side, a black peaked cap on, his suit jacket buttons done up, even though it was still hot at four in the afternoon. He opened the back door, and another man appeared. Big, wide, a grey suit and red tie, his dark hair slicked back.

"Shit, can you believe it." Francine nudged Mum. "Of all the places he could have come…"

Mum stared across the street.

"You'd think he'd have picked a posher hotel," Francine said. "Not a cheap and cheerful one like ours."

"Maybe he's doing business there." Mum held George's hand tighter.

"Who is it?" Gail asked.

"That's a leader," Francine said. "He's called Sultan."

"Sultan?" Greg said. "That's a weird name."

"It's what he calls himself," Mum said. "He thinks he's a king."

"What's a leader?" Gail asked.

"You know, like Ron Cardigan," Francine told her.

"Oh. So he's scary?"

Mum and Francine looked at each other.

"Not if you do as you're told, love," Francine said.

They crossed the street, reaching the other side just as Sultan put his foot on the bottom of the steps that led to the double doors of the hotel. He paused, as if sensing their interest, and turned, his almost-black eyes finding George.

"I like your motor, mate," George said.

Sultan nodded to the mums then returned his attention to George. "You do, do you?"

"Yeah. I want one of them when I grow up."

"If you're savvy, you'll get one."

George didn't know what savvy meant, but he'd be that and everything else if he could drive around in one of those cars. "Are you rich? It looks like you have to be rich to buy one."

"I do all right for myself." He glanced at Mum. "London?"

"Yes. East End."

"Ah, Cardigan's lot."

"Unfortunately." Mum smiled.

"Hmm, he's…in a league of his own, shall we say." Sultan put a hand in his pocket and brought out a wallet. He opened it, then looked at Mum again. "Do you mind?"

"No, it's fine."

He handed each child a five-pound note, and George clutched his with wonder filling him up. A whole fiver to himself? That didn't seem right. As one, George and Greg held the money up to their mother, and she stared down at them, tears in her eyes.

"No, you keep it this time," she said.

"It's like that, is it?" Sultan said, his voice low and rumbly.

"You could say that." Mum smiled again.

"Father not providing for them?"

"Um, no."

"Who is he? Sounds like he needs a kick up the arse."

Greg giggled at 'arse', and George nudged his brother's shoe. Something told him this wasn't funny, what the adults were talking about.

"It's okay," Mum said. "I work."

Sultan handed her a card. "If you ever need help…"

George's heart leapt. Help? This big man was going to help them? Should he keep his mouth shut? Or open it and take the hand this man like a king offered? "We need loads of help, cos our dad, he—"

"George!"

He snapped his mouth shut, upset he'd let out a part of their secret. Angry with himself. He knew better, but this Sultan, he seemed kind, like he cared what happened to them. The sort of leader they needed, unlike Ron who was always grumpy and went round killing people, and Mum and Francine got all funny whenever someone talked about him.

"Sorry," George whispered.

Sultan watched him, eyebrows going down, then cocked his head. "Work hard, son. Get yourself that car."

Then he was gone, indoors, his driver sitting behind the wheel reading a newspaper.

In the hotel, George caught sight of Sultan entering the lift. The big man caught George gawping and nodded. A feeling of being safe wrapped around George, and he waved as the doors closed. If things got too bad at home, he could find that card Sultan had given Mum, then ask him to tell Dad to leave them alone. He could save them all, and Mum would always be in her element, then.

"Don't even think about it, George," Mum said.

His shoulders slumped, and they waited for the other lift to come. All the way up to their room on the fourth floor, he thought about Sultan's clothes, that car, all that money in his wallet and how he'd dished it out like it was nothing.

One day, when he was a man, George would be like that.

Work hard, son…

He promised himself he would.

The next day, before they went home, he bought his mother a box of fudge with that fiver.

Chapter Ten

Karen and Teddy had finished their shift and walked down the long road that led away from Entertainment Plaza towards the nearby housing estate. Other employees were far enough behind that she reckoned they wouldn't hear their conversation, but Teddy had put paid to talking about anything to do with the heist by telling her to keep her mouth shut until they were farther ahead. Instead, they chatted about their bucket lists, and she was surprised to hear he wanted to work on a farm next summer, mucking out pigs and whatever. He didn't strike her as the type to get dirty, what with his tidy quiff, posh suit, and the way he grimaced if he had to shake anyone's hand.

"My boyfriend comes from a farming family," he said quietly, likely so any eavesdroppers didn't pick up on it, considering he was supposedly marrying Karen. "His stories about growing up got me wondering what it'd be like to get out of my comfort zone. I'm the type to shower twice a day, always look in the mirror any chance I get, and I need to loosen up, not be so bothered about my appearance."

It was nice to talk to him like this, about something not related to the heist or Goldie or The Brothers. "How come you're like that, d'you know?"

"My mother. You have to be perfect around her, otherwise, what *would* her friends think?" He grunted. "God, I was so suppressed growing up."

"What does she think of you being gay?"

"She doesn't know."

She felt bad for poking into what must be a sore subject. "Sorry to hear that."

He shrugged. "Some parents can't hack their child being what they consider 'imperfect'. She is how she is, and I'm used to it."

"Do you see her much?"

"Not if I can help it."

"What are your plans for after…you know?" She'd nearly said *heist* but had stopped herself in time.

"I'm going into the farm business with Oakley. You know, putting a big deposit down on a mortgage, seeing what it's like to get dirty without worrying about whether I have water nearby to wash it off. I want to be *different*, know what I mean? I don't want to be like this anymore, the way my mother made me behave. It limits how I live."

"Is it a compulsion or something, being clean?"

"My therapist thinks so."

That was another surprise, him seeing one of those. Karen ought to really, and there was one on offer if she wanted to take the twins up on it. Therapy was free if you worked for The Brothers. They'd been given a business card for a bloke called Vic Collins who ran his practice from an old pub/cottage in a street behind The Angel. Karen had been sorely tempted, just to talk about Robyn and Cal's problems and how she could deal with them better without letting it all get on top of her. She didn't know if she could ever open up about her childhood with anyone except Robyn, though.

"Do you see Vic Collins, then?" she asked.

"No, someone on Golden Eye."

"Ah, right." She felt she'd probed enough.

He shoved his hands in his pockets. "What would you do if you had a lot of money?"

She admired the way he'd said that. Anyone listening would think they were just dreaming. "That's easy. I'd give some to my sister."

"How come?"

"She needs it."

"Is she in shitloads of debt or something?"

Should she confide in him? It wasn't her story to tell, but because she was so involved, surely it'd be all right to relieve her burden, wouldn't it? "No, she needs an operation."

"Oh. Shit. Sorry."

"It's all right. You weren't to know."

"Only because we're not meant to be talking to each other about stuff like this. I don't know why

116

Goldie said we should keep it to just business. No harm in being friends, is there."

She gently bumped into his side. "No. It's been nice to natter. I've got no one other than my sister and her husband, and they've got their own problems and don't need me going round there because I'm lonely."

"You should come round to mine for dinner sometimes. Oakley won't mind. Go round the back way so nobody sees you if you're worried about being spotted."

"All right, thanks."

They turned into Moorgate Street.

She glanced at Teddy's house as they passed it. "Oakley's still up, then."

"Hmm. He knows I won't be back until later. I messaged him."

"You've said before he knows what we're doing."

"Um, yeah."

"My sister does, too."

"Then we're both in the shit if You Know Who finds out we blabbed. The thing is, how could I *not* tell Oakley? I mean, I had to give a proper reason why I'd decided to work at a casino all of a sudden when I'm usually up to my neck in it doing other stuff for *him*. Plus we had to move to Cardigan. I couldn't expect him to up sticks without an explanation. Anyway, he wouldn't tell anyone, he's just worried about us getting caught."

She whispered, "How *will* we get caught, though? Our roles mean when the other You Know Whos look into finding whoever did it, we appear innocent."

"True. Shh now. Sandra and Craig are still behind us."

They entered Diamond Road, and she got her keys out. They went inside her building, the two from work continuing past, Karen watching them through the glass in the communal door. Neither of them glanced back.

Karen led the way to her flat and, once inside, stuck the kettle on and whacked the heating up from low to high. She'd only keep it on long enough to take the chill off. "Bleedin' cold in here." She rubbed her arms on the way to the cupboard to get the mugs out.

Teddy sat at the little table. "You didn't bring much stuff with you, then."

"No point," she said. "Goldie's paying the rent on my flat on Golden Eye while I'm here instead of the wages I used to get at Golden Glow. The perks of working for a leader, eh? I bought some cheap basics for this place. I call it the minimalist look."

"We didn't bother keeping the old place on, even though he offered me the same deal, so I've got all my gear around mine. Come on, no point putting it off. We need to chat about your call to Goldie."

She sorted coffee granules, sugar, and milk in the mugs and leant her backside against a cupboard, arms folded. "He said he wasn't anything to do with the shooting, but he sounded...I dunno, off."

"In what way?"

"Agitated."

"He's got a lot on his mind."

"Maybe, but he went on to say he'd bumped into Greg in Friday's."

Teddy's eyebrows shot up. "What, at the *plaza*?"

"Hmm."

"What the fuck was he doing *there*? He said he wasn't going to go anywhere near Jackpot so he was never caught on CCTV and couldn't be blamed for scoping the casino out."

The kettle clicked off, and Karen poured boiled water into the mugs. "I know. So if he wasn't anything to do with the shooting like he reckons, what *was* he doing there?"

She glanced at Teddy.

He rubbed his fingertips over his mouth. "Shit. Do you think he lied to you about popping a cap in Cinnamon?"

She nodded and handed him his mug. "What other explanation is there? He said Greg asked him what he was doing on Cardigan, and Goldie told him he was eating and going bowling. On his own. *Everyone* knows he doesn't go anywhere without at least two bodyguards lately. Even when he's at Golden Glow they're stationed at the front and back doors. Something's off, and I'm worried it's going to affect us."

"How?"

"The twins will be on alert now he's been to the plaza. They'll be wondering if he shot Cinnamon and why. There'll be more security for the staff at Jackpot, which will fuck things up for the heist if we're not told in time what measures have been put in place. Goldie needs to know who's in play every Friday night, you know that. I've got a feeling it's going to be this Friday."

"Fuck. What do we do?"

"There's nothing we *can* do but continue as we've been told and tell Goldie if things change so he can amend his plans."

Teddy put his elbows on the table and held his head in his hands. "I just want this over with so I can start a new life. With Goldie retiring soon, I can't stand the thought of working for a new leader, whoever the hell that will be. I want out of his world."

She smiled. "To get pig shit on your new wellies?"

He laughed. "Yeah."

The doorbell rang, and she jumped, slapping her gaze onto Teddy in fear. Her heart rate ramped up uncomfortably, and she swallowed tightly.

"Who the fuck's that?" Teddy hissed.

"I don't know! No one ever comes here but you, not even my sister." She bit her lip, her stomach rolling over. "What do I do?"

"Check through the peephole before you make a decision."

She walked down the hallway, Teddy behind her. With her eye to the lens, she looked out.

"Oh God," she whispered.

"What's the matter?" Teddy whispered back.

"It's George."

"*What?*"

She turned to find Teddy pacing, panic scrunching his features. "Calm down."

The bell rang again, and she felt sick.

"I'm going to have to see what he wants," she said. "Go back in the kitchen. It's weird with you lurking."

Teddy walked off, and once he'd disappeared, she blew out a breath to steady her nerves and opened the front door.

"Oh, hello." She frowned, as anyone would if their boss turned up at their home. "Everything all right? Did I forget to do something at work? Or is it about Cinnamon and that chip?"

"No. I need to come in."

She stepped back. "Fancy a cuppa? The kettle's not long boiled."

"Don't suppose you have a coffee machine, do you?"

"Only instant. We're waiting for the wedding presents and hoping we get a Tassimo." She laughed, hoping it didn't sound forced.

"Instant will have to do, ta."

She walked down the hallway, leaving him to shut the door. She didn't glance across at Teddy, just put the kettle back on and found another mug. In the downwards curve of the hot tap, she caught George's skewed reflection in the stainless steel. He stood in the kitchen doorway, the actual door shielding him from Teddy.

"Talking of weddings," George said. "When's yours exactly?"

"Next year at some point," Teddy said.

George poked his head around the door. "Oh, I didn't expect you to be here." He went to sit opposite Teddy, hands clasped into a double fist on the table.

Is that a threat?

"Eh?" Teddy looked from Karen to George. "Why *wouldn't* I be? I live here!"

"That's what I thought." George smiled, but it was the false kind, where he was tense about something but hiding it. "Interesting."

"What is?" Karen sorted his coffee and handed it over.

"Cheers." George placed it on a coaster. "A little bird told me something else."

"Like what?" Teddy asked.

"That you two *don't* live together."

Karen's titter distracted Teddy from saying anything else. "That's just daft, that is. Want a biscuit?"

George nodded. "Got any with chocolate on them? Failing that, custard creams?"

"Do birds shit on windscreens?" She opened a cupboard and pulled a new packet of Hobnobs out. "Will these do?"

"Yep." George received them with a gleam in his eye and got on with the business of opening them and dunking one in his coffee. He bit into the soggy part and closed his eyes. "Fucking handsome."

Karen sat and drank some of her going-warm drink. "So who said we don't live together, then? A bloody nosy beak, I'll bet."

"An employee. I won't go further than that."

"A bit weird, someone saying that." She nicked a biscuit and bit into it.

"So what were you doing the other night, then, Teddy?"

Teddy reached for a Hobnob. He didn't seem fazed at all now he had his game face on. "What other night?"

"The one where you went into a house on Moorgate Street. The one that's registered to you and someone called Oakley Hartley."

"Err, that's my brother."

"With different surnames?"

Teddy shrugged. "Different mothers. Mine doesn't know he exists. She'd have my dad's knackers if she found out he'd been playing away before she had me."

"How come you're on the electoral roll as living there, then?"

"Because I *was* living there. I didn't move in with Karen until four months ago."

"Yet you both rented that house and this flat at the same time. On the same day. I checked." George's grin turned feral.

Karen dredged up the cover story they'd already worked out for an occasion like this. "That's because we both used to live on Golden Eye and wanted to come to Cardigan. We heard the leaders are nicer here." She smiled. "We both had separate flats on Golden, see. The plan was for Teddy to move in with Oakley for a bit until he'd got settled. Oakley's not good with relocating, he likes things to stay the same. Takes a while for him to adjust. Anyway, him and

125

Teddy had a barney a couple of months after they'd moved in, so Teddy came here, and that was when we told people at work we lived together. I don't get what the issue is."

"I visit him after work sometimes, which I did the other night," Teddy added. "I kip over every now and then. I don't see a problem with that either. Is there one?"

"Yeah." George took another Hobnob and broke it in half. "Not with you, but with Karen." He swung his attention to her.

She held down her need to bolt. Christ, his stare shit her up. "What problem?"

"Why you've still got a flat on Golden."

"Oh, *that*." She smiled, mainly with relief but to also throw him off the fact she trembled with nerves inside. "My sister uses it from time to time."

"And you can afford *two* rents at London prices?"

"Not really, we're all struggling, but I go without so she can use it." There was no way she could tell him Goldie paid the bloody rent on it.

"Why does she use it?"

"A bolthole from her husband."

George's eye narrowed. "Is he hurting her? Does she need help?"

"God, no, he just gets on her pip. She likes her space. She used to come and stay with me often when I lived there and can't be arsed with coming all the way over here."

"The two-rent thing. Weird, because going by this place, it doesn't look like you even have *any* spare money." He gestured to the kitchen. "There's fuck all here."

"Like I said, we're waiting for wedding presents."

He turned to Teddy. "Why's your name still on the Moorgate tenancy agreement if you moved in here?"

"Oakley wouldn't have been given the place if I didn't go in with him. On paper, it looks like he can't afford the rent on his wages, but he does cash-in-hand stuff, so…"

An awful feeling came over Karen. "Just nipping to the loo."

She left and went into the bathroom. Lifted a new toothbrush out of a pack she had in the cupboard under the sink. Popped it in the brush holder beside hers and the tube of toothpaste. From a basket hidden behind the sliding bath panel for just this situation, she took out a few men's toiletries and placed them on the side of the bath, then grabbed a man's shirt and draped it over the hook on the back of the door. She closed the panel, flushed the loo, and loitered for half a minute so it seemed like she'd washed her hands.

Back in the kitchen, she sat and helped herself to another biscuit from the rapidly dwindling packet.

"I could do with a piddle myself," George said.

Once he was gone, Teddy looked at her to silently ask if she'd put the things out like Goldie had specified she should do if anyone from work wanted to come over. She nodded, ate her biscuit, and waited for George's return.

He swaggered in and retook his seat. "All I can say is, you'd better get married sooner rather than later because this place is barer than a newborn's arse."

The tension flowed out of Karen, and she finally relaxed.

It was going to be all right.

Until she spoke to George alone at some point and grassed Goldie up.

Chapter Eleven

George left Diamond Road, satisfied Cinnamon had got the wrong end of the stick. Karen's and Teddy's explanations sat well with him, so he got in the BMW and drove to the shops a few streets away. He entered the twenty-four-hour newsagent's and nodded to an alarmed-looking Yiannis, the Greek owner, who had dark shadows under his eyes indicating years of working when the rest of London slept. His wife, Dimitra, did the day shift.

"I paid Martin on time, Mr Brother," he said and fanned his chubby neck in panic. "I have never missed a payment. I am a good resident. I even pay all of my *taxes*."

George contemplated toying with him but couldn't be arsed. "Fuck me, I'm just here to buy some Tangtastics and put some leccy on for someone. No need to soil those nice corduroys you've got on. It'd be a shame to ruin them."

"Ah, I panicked. Thought you had come in to grab me by the throat and—"

"I'd have Greg with me if I was going to give you a battering." George reached over to the Haribo stand and plucked off his favourite sweets. Fishing out Cinnamon's electric payment card, he handed that and the sweets over. "Oh, hang on. Back in a sec." He went to the grocery aisle, grabbed four tubs of chicken and mushroom Pot Noodle, and dumped them on the counter.

Yiannis rang up the purchases, his hands shaking. "How much on the meter, Mr Brother?"

130

"Three hundred, and seeing as you're such a good bloke, it's George to you."

Yiannis shook his head. "Right, Mr Brother."

George sighed. Yiannis was too respectful for his own good.

Yiannis quickly added the payment to the system. "That won't last long anymore. The electric is crazy."

"It's fucking disgusting, those prices. Bloody daylight robbery."

Yiannis gave the card back.

George got out his debit card, stuck it in the machine, and prodded in his pin. "Everything going all right here, is it?"

Yiannis put George's things in a bag. "I had a thief last night, a woman with a buggy."

"What did she steal?"

"A loaf of bread and some nappies."

Christ. Was she desperate or a chancer? "What did you do about it?"

"Nothing. I let her walk out. If she were my daughter, I'd want her to have those things. She's normally a good woman, usually always pays, so she must be in a terrible state to have stolen from me as we are friends."

"Charge me for it."

Yiannis came from behind the counter, selected bread and nappies from the aisles, and used the scanner on the barcodes. "You're a good man, Mr Brother, no matter what anyone else says."

"People been chatting shit about me, have they?"

"No more than usual."

George chuckled and paid the bill. "What's the thief's name?"

"Oh, you don't have to pay her a visit, do you?"

"Not the sort you mean. If she's genuinely skint, I'll drop an envelope round."

Yiannis relaxed. "It's Becky Sutton down the road here at number twelve."

"Cheers. See you when I see you."

George picked up the bag, put the nappies and bread back, then walked out, pleased with himself for doing the decent thing. Since the Janet saga and him 'seeing' his dead mother when he had relaxation therapy with Vic, he'd wanted to do whatever Mum would expect him to if the opportunity arose. Paying for Becky's stolen items and giving her a few quid was his Good

Samaritan deed for the day, not to mention helping Cinnamon out.

He put the bag in the car, took an envelope containing five hundred out of the glove box, and wrote on the front of it.

FROM THE BROTHERS.
DON'T NICK FROM YIANNIS AGAIN.
IF YOU NEED HELP IN FUTURE, COME TO US.

He strode down to number twelve, popped the gift through the letterbox, and made a mental note to look into Becky when he had more time. If she was just down on her luck, fine, giving her the money was worth it, but if she was a dodgy cow beneath a friendly veneer, losing five hundred wasn't as bad as the grand he *could* have given her.

Back in the car, he swung by Jackpot to collect Greg who looked like he'd had a bellyful and wanted to go home.

"Where are we off to?" Greg stuck his seat belt on. "I'm tired and need my bed, so I don't want to go gadding about for long."

"We're going to see someone, and it'll take as long as it takes." George explained about the

133

person in number two who'd ignored Cinnamon's plea for help. "Have you found anything else out?"

"No. Ichabod said the lights in Goldie's hallway went off half an hour ago."

"Is Jimmy manning Jackpot overnight instead of Rowan?"

"Yeah."

"Fine."

Rowan, Ichabod's cousin, had come over from Ireland to take the position of manager from two a.m. until ten so Ichabod could get some sleep. Ichabod then pulled a massive shift from ten a.m. until two. It worked for Ichabod, he didn't need much sleep, loved the long hours, and it saved George and Greg the headache of finding a fourth man to trust, as Jimmy Riddle did Tuesday's and Wednesday's. There were plenty of potential managers on their books, but all of them were busy elsewhere and not necessarily suited to work in a casino, given that they were used to beating people up and generally throwing their menace around. They'd shifted some brick shithouses to security at Jackpot, T-T being the head of that little band of bruisers. Sienna had wanted him as her heavy for her loan business, but George had vetoed it and given her one of their other men instead.

George swung into the street where they'd seen the masked man aiming a gun at Cinnamon, then turned into the road they needed. He parked outside number two.

"She told me something that ended up being a load of bollocks," he said.

Greg glanced across at him, clearly annoyed by the vagueness. "Who?"

"Cinnamon."

"What did she say?"

"That Karen and Teddy don't live together. She saw him going into another house, then Karen going into a flat a couple of streets away. She got her wires crossed. The house is Teddy's brother's."

"A brother didn't come up in the background checks."

"Nope, because he has a different mother, and Teddy's old dear doesn't know he exists."

"Fucking hell, talk about 'the secrets we keep'."

"I know. Anyway, it's all sorted. I went round to the flat we have on record for them. They were together, and I nosed in the bathroom. Two

135

toothbrushes, his aftershaves and whatnot on the side of the bath, a shirt hanging on the door. He admitted he'd lived with Oakley—that's his brother—for a bit before moving in with Karen."

"Just to double-check, we'll have a look at the employment records, see if he came to us with the house address then changed it to the flat. If both addresses aren't there, then maybe Cinnamon wasn't wrong after all."

George nodded. "Right, let's go and see this plonker."

They got out and stood by the step.

George stared down at it. "A bloody handprint."

Greg stared down. "Cinnamon's, got to be."

George knocked, then rang the bell over and over for good measure. The top front window flew open, and a tousle-haired head poked out.

"What the fuck d'you want? You're not meant to be here until tomorrow," a man whisper-shouted, squinting at them, obviously trying to wake up properly, the light from the lamppost giving him a sepia-photo appearance.

"You might want to think about the way you speak to us," George said. "Get your arse down here and open the fucking door."

The bloke stared. "Why do you need to talk to me? I did what you wanted."

What?

"You'll find out in a minute," Greg said. "Do as my brother said and get down here. You've got one minute."

"But I'm not dressed."

George huffed out a growl. "Then we'll just have to view your meat and two veg, won't we. Fifty seconds…"

The window slammed shut, then came the thunder of feet on stairs, and the door swung open, the thirtysomething fella standing there in the nuddy holding up a pair of light-pink shorts.

"I've just got to put these on." He spun round, showing his pasty backside, and hopped about trying to get one leg into a hole.

"For fuck's sake," George said. "Piss off into the living room and do that. Hairy arse cracks aren't my bag."

The man stalked off through a doorway on the right, and George stepped inside, fuck standing on ceremony. He rolled his eyes at Greg, but his attention went over his twin's shoulder to an old woman in a long white nightdress and royal-blue dressing gown beckoning him over.

"Stay with this pleb, I'll go and see her."

Greg turned to see who George meant. "Right."

George walked across the street and, ushered inside the house that stank of fish by the white-haired, surprisingly sprightly woman, he followed her into a lounge warmed by an old-fashioned three-bar fire that was trendy in the eighties. It was that old it had a black-and-white material flex that he remembered from his mum's fire when he'd been a kid. The nostalgia hit him pretty hard, and his eyes blurred for a moment.

His host waggled her bony, raised-vein hand to an armchair, so he sat. She chose the other, a pile of orange crocheting on the arm.

"You're here about that man," she said. "Are you checking he did the job properly? And where's my money?"

Eh? Are we on the same page here? "What man?"

"The one in the balaclava driving the SUV."

"What's your name, love?"

"Winifred. Which one's yours?"

"George."

"Right. He came here, if that's what you want to know. Knocked on my ruddy door and wouldn't stop until I answered."

"What time was that?"

"It would have been just after five because I was dishing up me dinner."

"Kippers?"

"Yeah, there's a bit of a whiff, I'll give you that. Anyway, there he was, on my doorstep, scaring me shitless with a woolly mask on. He hadn't even said anything at that point, but a bloke in a balaclava's never good news unless he's skiing, is it."

George wanted her to hurry the fuck up but at the same time didn't want to rush her in case she panicked and forgot important information. "Right…"

She hitched up a saggy boob. "So he says to me, he says, 'Keep your mouth shut about what's going to happen round here. The Brothers will bring a payment round for your silence tomorrow.' What do you think about *that* then?" She slapped the arm of her chair, a crochet hook going flying.

What did he think about it? He was fucking fuming, that's what he thought. Goldie—or whoever it was—had used their name to get what he wanted. "We didn't send him here to do anything. He lied to you."

Winifred blinked at him. "Pardon? I've already spent that money in me head. Are you telling me I'm not getting any?"

"You can have some for giving me this information, but as for the silence, no."

She weighed that up then nodded. "All right, so long as it's enough to get me a few of them steaks off that bloke on the market. I can eat it now me dentures have been sorted."

George took his wallet out, thankful he had a couple of hundred quid in notes on him for moments like this. He removed the money and placed it on her teak coffee table. "That should buy a fair few. Was that all he said to you?"

"Yes, then he walked next door. I watched him go to the houses at this end, on my side and the other, four on each, then he sat in his car for ages until that young woman came along. She comes past at the same time every evening. He got out of the car and made out he was farting around with something on the back seat, you know, bending over so his head stuck inside. She walks past, and he bloody shoots her! I thought to myself, I thought: *She must have pissed those twins off if they're going that far*. She turned to run, but he shot her again, then I couldn't see her because she fell and a parked car was in the way. She got up and legged it around the corner, then he climbed in his motor and followed."

"Is that all you know?"

"Yes, son."

He wished his mother had been given the gift to grow as old as her and *she'd* just called him son. He held back his emotions and stood, dropping two business cards beside the cash. "If anyone ever comes here saying they're doing a job for us again, ring me. The other card's for our therapist in case you need it. He's called Vic Collins, nice fella."

"Ah, I know him from way back. Used to drink in the pub with him and his wife, God rest her soul. Thanks for the offer, but I don't need counselling. I've seen my fair share of shit in my life, and this doesn't even come close to the worst of it. One of your children dying before you puts things in perspective."

"Sorry to hear that."

"So was I. Anyway, off you trot. And thanks for the steak money."

He glanced at the fire and thought of the cost. "Can you afford the leccy for that?"

"I'm all right, thank you. My Brian left me well accounted for. Now piss off and find whoever shot that poor girl."

He smiled at how she wasn't afraid of him and treated him as she would a son or family friend. "What are you doing up so late anyway?"

"Insomnia laced with memories from the past. Lethal combination."

"Right. Night, then."

"Night, George."

He walked into the hallway, worried about her. "Lock the door after me. Put the chain on."

"I will, son."

He left the house, vision once again misty, accompanied by a lump in his throat. He hadn't dealt with his mother's passing properly, had immersed himself in his busy life instead, and reckoned Vic might be right in that he should use his sessions as grieving time instead of bottling everything up. George didn't do crying, and if he let the cork out, he'd be blarting all over the shop. Not a good idea.

He visited the other houses Winifred had mentioned on this side, then the ones opposite, explaining the situation to sleepy residents and promising Martin would be round with money tomorrow to pay for them being disturbed. Then he banged on the door of number two. Greg opened it gripping the homeowner's wrist; he obviously didn't trust him not to leg it while he wasn't in the room with him.

George entered and indicated the lounge. In they went, George and Greg opting for chairs, the bloke on the sofa, George pleased their host now had shorts on.

"What's your name?"

"Austin."

"Austin what?"

"Hunt."

"Why didn't you help that woman earlier?"

"I've told *him* all this." Austin jerked a thumb at Greg.

George frowned. "I don't like your tone or attitude. *Him* has a name. Take that boulder-sized chip off your shoulder and answer me again."

Austin sighed. "Look, I know who you are, and I don't want to be rude, but repeating myself isn't going to make this any better, is it?"

"I don't care. Do as you're told or you'll find my fist in your fucking face, my old son." Mad George was knocking to make an appearance, tensing his jaw, his muscles.

143

"Sorry, it's just I've got to be up at four to do an airport run, I'm a cab driver, and this is wasting time."

"What part of 'I don't care' don't you understand?" George gritted his teeth to stave off his need to punch Austin in the nuts. "You're the one wasting time by not telling me what you know."

"Can't Greg just tell you?"

George shot out of his chair and rammed a fist into Austin's gut. He gripped his throat and squeezed. "Never disrespect a Brother, got it?"

Austin's face, going a fetching shade of purple, appeared to swell. He managed a nod of sorts, letting out a gurgle.

George let him go, planting his hands either side of Austin's head on the back of the sofa, bending low to say, "When I say jump, you ask how high, that's how this works."

"Okay, okay, sorry. Sorry. I just…"

George pushed off the sofa and stood to his full height, looking at Greg. "Can you believe this bloke?"

Greg smirked, the bastard. He must have known Austin was one of *those* types and would rile George up. He'd left any admonishing to

George, probably after Austin had fucked him about while George had been at the other houses.

"Why didn't you teach him a lesson?" George asked his twin.

"Because I've already punched someone at Bowling Bonanza tonight and thought it was only right I let you have this one."

George sighed and gave Austin his attention. "You're *this close* to me battering you to a pulp, sunshine, so I suggest you tell me what you told my good brother here."

Austin hugged himself where George had walloped him. "He told me there'd be what he called a *commotion* outside my house and that if anyone knocked for help, I had to turn a blind eye."

"Did he pay you?"

"Yeah, fifty quid to ignore the door, plus he said you two would be round in the morning to give me more."

"What did you see?"

"He shot her twice, then got in his car. I went upstairs to watch out of the back window. She saw me, and I knew she wanted help, but I was fucked if I'd go down there. I shook my head at her."

"Were you still upstairs when we turned up?"

"Yeah."

"What did you think when Greg shot his back tyre?"

Austin rubbed at his reddened neck. "Dunno, maybe that you were fucked off he hadn't killed her yet or summat."

"What's with the attitude? Most people who deal with us don't behave like you have."

"I'm tired. I always get like this when I've been woken up. I can't help it, shit comes out of my mouth before I've had time to think. And I've got stuff going on, lots of worries, so *this*…I don't need it."

"I pity whoever you marry."

"I *was* married, but she left me."

"I can see why." George inhaled deeply, pondering on what to do with this little prick. Ordinarily, he'd have given him a Cheshire or kneecapped him for his cheek, and he glanced at Greg for direction.

Greg shrugged.

George made the decision. "If we ever have to deal with you again, we won't go lightly."

Austin chuffed out a wry laugh. "You call a punch and strangulation going lightly?"

146

George clenched his fists and held one up. "Do you want another one?"

"Sorry. Honestly, I'm sorry. I can't control myself."

"Then you need to learn how to." George took a business card out of his pocket and threw it at him. "Go and see that man. If you don't, we'll know about it. Tell him you need to work on anger management or whatever the fuck else is going on with you."

"I can't afford that shit."

"It's free. If you haven't made an appointment by this time next week, we'll be back, then you'll understand what *real* lack of anger management looks like."

George stormed from the house before he gouged Austin's eyes out with his fingers. The man's disrespect was a cover for something, he was sure of it, and Vic would get to the bottom of it.

In the car, he messaged Martin the addresses and the amount of money he had to give each resident tomorrow, leaving Austin out. He'd already accepted the shooter's payment, so he didn't need more.

Greg parked his arse in the passenger seat and laughed with his head thrown back.

"What's so fucking funny?" George asked.

"You, getting so wound up over a bloke who's so knackered he can't think straight. I bet by tomorrow he'll be worrying about how he behaved when he properly thinks about it."

"I don't see what's amusing about me being wound up."

Greg sobered, wiping his eyes. "You did well in controlling Mad, by the way."

George slipped his seat belt on then drove away. "Yeah, well, I sensed there's more to Austin's stroppiness. He needs help, not me battering him."

"Unusual for you to pick up on something like that."

In truth, George had recognised a bit of himself in Austin. "I'm trying to be a nicer person in some circumstances. Like Mum would."

Greg lost all his mirth. "Yeah, she was a good old bird."

The rest of the journey was eclipsed by the silence of private mourning that had come far too late—for both of them.

Chapter Twelve

*B*eing thirteen was better than being five. One, George wasn't little, and two, the part inside him that got so angry he couldn't see straight, gave him the courage to stand up for people who couldn't do it for themselves. People said George was a bully, but he saw it differently. He only threatened people who picked on others, and that meant he regularly stood outside the head's office at school, waiting to be told off. Mum worried he'd get suspended or expelled one of these days, and Richard would go ballistic.

Richard. He didn't think of him as 'Dad' anymore. That man wasn't a dad. He was a monster.

The Wednesday sun hid behind a fat white cloud. George sat beside Greg on the grass of the school field at the start of their lunch break, picking at the drying blades next to him, the yellow-headed dandelions seeming unaffected by the heat. It had been well warm lately, and the summer holidays couldn't come soon enough. They'd be able to piss about all day instead of being stuck in a classroom. They'd go up the park with Gail and her brothers or follow Ron Cardigan around to see what the bloke was up to. George wanted to be a leader like him, like Sultan, to run an estate, looking after all the people and damaging the ones who caused trouble.

The rumours said Ron killed people. That he cut throats and shot brains out. George had been giving his own future method of sorting arseholes a lot of thought. He wanted to be known for specific things, for people to do as they were told because they were too scared not to. To give them pain not just at the time of torture but for a long while afterwards. He'd been asking questions about Sultan and would do what he

150

did. Kneecapping had to hurt, and they'd be hobbling around for ages. And what about slicing their faces, a blade between the lips, pressed back and up, creating a permanent smile? It would be George's trademark.

His mind was mixed up. How could he be good like Mum asked him to but at the same time want to be bad, to do those nasty things? He blamed that part of himself, the one who got mad. Did Richard have one of those? Did Greg? Was it normal to have a bad side?

"There's something wrong with you," Greg said, as if reading his mind.

They'd always been like that, knowing what the other was thinking. George was used to it, and he relied on their telepathy a lot when Richard was home, sensing when the bastard was going to blow and warning Greg with a shift of his eyes to get the hell out of the room. Many a time he'd been tempted to contact Sultan, but Mum's warning that it would bring them a load of trouble stopped him.

"What d'you mean?"

"I think you broke Rick's nose."

George laughed. "Good. Serves him right for nicking Emma's sandwiches. I mean, who does that and gets caught? He didn't even wait for everyone to get out of the cloakroom before he went in her bag. Dickhead."

Greg snatched up a handful of pale grass stalks, the lack of water bleaching the green out of them. "Mum said they're poorer than us now. He might have been hungry, bruv."

Laughing didn't seem such a good idea anymore. George's nice side kicked into action, and he imagined Rick so desperate for food he'd had to steal it. George had done the same in various shops. Once, he'd even grabbed a leg of lamb off a market stall, Greg cursing behind him as they'd run home, wetting themselves laughing from the adrenaline rush. George had given it to Mum, and it was as if he'd handed her a diamond necklace, although she'd been worried about him being caught.

The current conversation came back to him. Rick being skint. "How come they're down on their uppers, then?"

"His dad's been sacked, and his mum's poorly. She's got cancer."

Ah, bollocks. "Well, I didn't fucking know, did I."

"Do what Mum said and think before you do stuff. Or ask me. I listen to shit going on around us and think about it, you don't anymore. You just go mental."

Mum had said something about a hair-trigger temper, that George 'flew off the handle' too often and it was becoming a worry—a him-being-arrested worry. More and more, people mentioned The Brothers as if they were deviants, naughty boys who should be in Borstal, not roaming free in the East End, but that wasn't fair. George was the one who should be there, not Greg, who wasn't half as bad. George reckoned if he didn't set such a shit example, Greg wouldn't follow him wherever he went. Wouldn't copy him. Wouldn't want to do these things so they both got the blame, because he said he owed George for all the times he'd taken the flak from Richard.

"I can't help it," George said. "I get arsey."

"Mum'll be upset if you keep swearing, so pack it in."

"She's not here to listen, so it doesn't matter."

George got up. His soft side had been poking him ever since Greg had mentioned Rick being poor. Mum didn't have much money either, although she was good at 'making it stretch'. Francine helped her out if she needed it, bread and teabags, milk and cornflakes, a few quid for the leccy and gas meters, which always ran out in the winter. Jeff was nice to them, too, sometimes slipping them fifty p so they could get sweets at Bum Head's. Some days, they were that cold they had to put coats and gloves on in the house and their breath puffed in the air. Then Richard would come in, all bolshy because it was nippy, moaning that his dinner hadn't been cooked. Once, Mum had boldly said if he didn't drink all his wages and put some into housekeeping she'd have had the gas to cook his dinner, and Richard inevitably lumped her one for being gobby.

The merry-go-round did George's head in, as did those notes Richard left on the mantelpiece. What did they say? And why did Richard behave like a normal person for two days afterwards? Barely anything made sense in George's life. The only thing that did was loving Mum and Greg.

"Where are you going?" Greg asked.

"To make it right with Rick."

Greg scrabbled to his feet. "Blimey."

George frowned. "What?"

"Have you turned over that new leaf Mum talked about?"

George chuffed out a laugh. "Nah, I wouldn't go that far."

He stormed towards Rick a few feet away. The kid sat with his weedy mate, Adam, a hand to his bleeding nose. George had expected Rick to go running to Miss after the punch, but it seemed he'd taken George's threat of beating him up after school seriously if he so much as squealed to anyone. Rick stared at him, obviously scared, and normally that pleased George, but it didn't now. He felt like an arsehole.

George stopped in front of them. "Your dad got the sack and your mum's ill?"

"Y-yeah," Rick said.

"You hungry? Is that why you nicked them sandwiches?"

Rick's cheeks turned red.

George looked at Adam. "Why didn't you share your lunch, you ponce?"

It was the obvious solution, wasn't it? George and Greg shared when Mum only had enough bread to make one sandwich. These two were mates, so Adam needed to step the fuck up.

Adam shrugged. "I didn't have nuffin' either."

"Fuck me," George muttered, angry that he'd called him a ponce. Like Greg had said, George pounced before thinking. "Stay there." He jerked his head at Greg. "Come on."

He stalked off towards the gap in the hedge, keeping an eye out for the dinner ladies, not that they'd be able to stop him. He was leaving school grounds whether they liked it or not.

"Where are we going?" Greg jogged beside him.

"Bum Head's."

"But we haven't got any money."

"So? Since when did that stop me?"

"You're going nicking, aren't you. Bleedin' hell…"

Out on the other side, George ran down the lane, Greg keeping up with him. They rounded the corner and walked up the street, George with his hands in his pockets. They risked seeing Mum, maybe even Richard or Francine, but in that moment, he didn't give a shiny shite.

"Stay out here," he said.

Greg tutted. "I'm not a bloody lookout."

"Didn't say you were, I just don't want you involved if I get caught."

George pushed into the shop and checked the round mirrors in each top corner. Loads of customers were reflected back at him, Bum Head too busy at the till to even think about watching him, his wife probably doing more baking out the back. George went down the first aisle, skirting Mrs Deal who needed a cane now, and stopped at the bottom. Stared at the freshly baked loaves, hoping the old lady didn't toddle down there and want to chat.

He'd never nicked anything from here before, it was too close to home, and Ron Cardigan, on one of the twins' spying-on-a-gangster missions, had said you didn't shit on your own doorstep—unless you knew you could get away with it. But today was different.

156

George would be doing a great big crap as his way of saying sorry to Rick, because he wouldn't actually say sorry. He couldn't unless it was to Mum or Greg.

He snatched a tiger loaf, stuffed it under his top, and walked out.

"Come on."

Greg laughed. "You look like you're up the duff."

"I had to put it somewhere, didn't I."

Back at the school hedge, they climbed through, George unsurprised to find Rick and Adam still there and not tattling to Miss. He stood in front of them again and took the loaf out.

"Here." He dropped it into Rick's lap and walked away, returning to their previous spot. He flopped down, hoping Rick got as much happiness out of that bread as he did. Would he feel safe now, too? Safe in thinking, because George had been kind, that there'd be no more broken noses?

"Soft arse," Greg said.

"Yeah, well…"

"He won't tell on you now."

"I know, but he wouldn't anyway. He was too scared to."

"Why did you do it?"

George thought of all the times they'd gone hungry. This week was all right, Mum had stashed a few quid

157

away out of her wages from her cleaning job, but next week they might be back in Rick's position.

"I can't believe you even had to ask that. You know why."

"Yeah, but not the other why."

George thumped the ground. "Fucking hell, you're doing my nut in. What other why?"

"I can't believe you even had to ask that."

George glared at his twin, who smiled, clearly enjoying getting on his nerves by throwing his words back at him.

"All right, I wanted to do good," George said.

"How come?"

"I don't like hearing about people being Hank Marvin, that's why. I don't like knowing people live like we have to."

"Yet you go round like Richard, punching people. Makes sense…"

George ignored the sarcasm. "I punched Rick because he stole." *This was the mixed-up shit George struggled with. He was as bad as Richard sometimes, but why did it feel so right to behave that way? Because he'd learnt it from Richard? Or was it because he was trying to teach the bullies that there was always someone out there bigger and stronger than them? That he wished someone bigger and stronger would deal with Richard? Sultan... "I don't know why I do shit, I just do." But what if he stepped over the line and ended up arrested, Greg going down with him by association?*

"I'll always be here to stop you going too far, you know that," Greg said.

George calmed. Greg understood, he always had, he'd just been pushing for George to open up, to give him an insight into his damaged mind. And it was *damaged, George knew that, he just didn't know how to control it.*

Already, they'd made a name for themselves. Richard wasn't so handy with his fists now they were older, wider, taller. Mum likened them to brick shithouses, and people gave them a wide berth when they swaggered down the street, looking older than they were. George had so many dreams, to run Cardigan once the leader was dead, to be someone who righted wrongs and gave residents peace of mind.

He wouldn't let up until he'd achieved that.

"We're going to be kings of the East End one day, bruv."

"So you keep saying."

"You need to start believing it, because when we're blokes, we're never going hungry, and neither is Mum. We'll have grey suits and red ties, a BMW, and

everyone will know it's us driving it. We'll be famous."

"Famous? You're having a laugh."

George wasn't joking. He could see it all. Fuck the dream cottage, they'd have a massive house in London, loads of money in a safe, and he'd hurt everyone who hurt others. But most of all, he'd hurt the people who'd hurt Mum, whoever they were. Richard did, that was a given, but some other sadness, and fear, lurked in her eyes whenever Ron was mentioned, or Sam, his sidekick, or Stanley, the bloke who propped up the bar in The Eagle. Mum had something in her past, George sensed it, and he'd find out what it was one day.

Until then, he'd keep planning.

He stared over at Rick and Adam. They'd scoffed the loaf between them, Rick's nose swollen, the blood crusting in the heat. Rick gave a pathetic wave, then lowered his hand as if he thought George would think he was a dickhead.

He didn't.

I want more of that. People thanking me for saving their arse.

He felt like a king already.

Chapter Thirteen

The baby cried. Again. Becky sighed, wanting to sob she was that tired. Not just from dealing with three-month-old Noah but her predicament. Noah's dad, nicknamed Lemon (he refused to answer to anything else), had left her three weeks ago, saying he couldn't cope, and he'd gone back to his mother's. She now had to try and manage by herself, not just with looking after the baby but the financial side of it as well. She'd never have picked a house to rent on her wage alone, and as she was only getting maternity pay at the minute, she was strapped for cash.

She got out of her cocoon and walked down the stairs, leaving Noah to cry it out in his cot at the side of her bed. She shivered from the chill of the house; she'd only been putting the heating on for short spurts to take the nip off, so she rushed getting his bottle sorted and made her way back down the hallway.

An envelope stood out in the darkness on her fuzzy doormat, and she was going to ignore it, but something told her to pick it up. She reached out to switch the light on, then put the bottle on the bottom stair. The envelope had landed facedown, so she grabbed it and turned it over. Read the message on the front.

Tears pricked her eyes, but there was also an element of fear in play. And shame that she'd had to steal from the lovely Yiannis in the first place. She'd never nicked anything other than the bread and nappies in her life, but it had been a needs-must situation. She'd been hungry, and Noah had needed the Pampers. Mum and Dad were tired of helping her out with small loans (she'd had to go begging to them on occasion even when Lemon had lived with her), and Mum's sister had dipped her hand in her pocket occasionally but had said the last time that her job as a scene manager in the police force didn't pay as much as some people thought.

You'd think Lemon would have been more careful, considering Aunt Sheila was a copper, but he'd never seemed bothered about that. Thought himself invincible. He hadn't paid her a penny since a week after he'd fucked off, yet he was always loaded, and now she knew it was because of all the *shit* he got up to. Was that why he'd left her for days at a time, never telling her where he'd stayed? Did the jobs he got involved with mean he had to kip somewhere else, keeping his head down afterwards so he didn't get caught? Or was he having an affair?

The Brothers knew she was a thief, but they'd given her money, offered help.

Could she go to them with her other problem?

Noah had cried himself into screaming, and someone from next door banged on the wall, probably Mr Urwin, who was grumpy, yet his wife was always pleasant.

She took the envelope and bottle, returning to her bedroom and closing the door. She switched the lamp on and cuddled Noah, feeding him with the end of the bottle held in place by her chin, and managed to open the envelope with him safe in the crook of her arm. The amount of notes in there had her stomach rolling over. She put the envelope beside her on the bed, shaking, wondering whether they were fivers, tenners, or twenties. Or even fifties. God, she'd be proper sorted if there was a grand in there. She could pay bills and have some to spare.

Noah fell asleep while drinking. He had a habit of only taking a couple of ounces at a time when he should be on five, and she cursed the stupid 'feed on demand' advice she'd been given. It made more work for her, Noah seemingly forever needing milk every two hours, but he only drank enough to stave off the hunger pangs. She placed him back in his cot and prodded his nappy through his sleepsuit to see if it needed changing. It wasn't squidgy, so she draped his blankets over him then counted the money.

Five hundred.

Could she be rude and ask them for the same again? Promise to pay it back out of the Universal Credit when it finally came through? She'd made her claim as soon as Lemon had gone, but it still hadn't been processed.

She put the money back in the envelope and popped it under her pillow. In bed, warming up beneath the covers, she worked out which bills she'd pay first. Thankfully, the housing benefit and council tax had been awarded and backdated, so she didn't owe the landlord, but there was the catalogue and a credit card overdue, plus her car insurance. The car had been on her list of stuff to sell if things got really bad, but maybe she wouldn't need to now. Then there was food for her and more milk for Noah. She'd better go and pay Yiannis as well, apologise for even stealing in the first place when he'd been so nice to her ever since she'd moved in. He must have seen her then told the twins what she'd done. Why hadn't he stopped her when she'd walked out?

The shame returned, and her face grew hot, prickling. She'd shit herself while stealing, praying she wouldn't get caught, promising herself it would only be this once because she'd sworn she'd get the courage up to ask Lemon's mum for some money in a couple of days. Not that Faith would hand it over without sniping and making nasty comments. The woman had always disliked Becky, wishing Lemon had shacked up with his childhood sweetheart instead.

Becky, pleased she didn't have to approach Faith anymore, pondered on whether she should tell The Brothers about Lemon so that way the cash they'd already given her would be payment for information. She wouldn't feel like she owed them, then.

The problem was, would she get in trouble for not telling them sooner? Lemon doing his dodgy dealings on Cardigan was something they should know about, but she'd only found out about it the week before he'd left her. That was the *real* reason why he'd scarpered. She'd brought up what she'd discovered one too many times, warning him if the twins found out, he'd be up shit creek, but he'd told her to shut her mouth, and if she ever told anyone, the gang he was with would come for her.

And Noah.

"What kind of father are you if you can let them hurt your son?"

He hadn't had an answer to that.

Becky nodded to herself. She'd go and tell the twins in a few days, when she'd thought it all through properly. Her priority was keeping Noah safe, and if it meant grassing up his father so the gang could be caught and dealt with, that was what she'd do.

So long as her name was kept out of it.

No one liked a snitch, especially not the Sparrow Road lot.

Chapter Fourteen

Cinnamon woke to the sight of George's face too close to hers. His breath fanned her chin, and she'd have bolted upright in shock if he didn't hold her down by the shoulder.

"Morning," he said and moved away to sit in a nearby chair.

Confused, she asked, "Why did you…stare at me like that?"

"I wanted to test a theory."

"What theory?"

"That even when someone's asleep they can sense they're being watched. You were snoring just a minute ago, yet the minute I went up close, you woke up."

"Right…" She wasn't sure if he was all there up top, but he'd paid for her surgery, so she'd keep her opinions to herself. "Have they told you when I can go home?"

"You're not going home, you're off to the safe house, remember, but they're letting you go tomorrow."

Unease slithered through her. She was safe here if any stitches split. And paracetamol wasn't going to help the pain, which was all she had in her handbag, unless they gave her a prescription for the stronger stuff. "Is that normal, to be let out so soon after being shot?"

He shrugged. "They reckon so, you've just got to take it easy. I've spoken to Anna again this morning on the phone, and she'll be your nursemaid."

"Right, okay."

She surprised herself by managing to get out of bed well enough, hardly any pain, although she suspected medicine from the nearby drip had solved that. Her legs were weak, and she sat on the edge of the bed for a moment to balance her equilibrium. She didn't need a wee, just wanted to move her body so it didn't seize up.

"I paid Karen and Teddy a visit last night," he said. "He *did* go into another house, but it's nothing suss. His brother lives there."

"Oh."

"I'm glad you reported it to me, though. If ever there's anything else like that and it seems off, do the same thing. We can never be too sure."

She took a few steps without keeling over, thank goodness. "Did you bring my leccy card back?"

"Yep." He fished it out of his wallet and gave her the receipt.

She stared at the amount he'd put on it, and tears stung. "Um, thank you. That will help a lot. I'll pay you back."

He shook his head. "We need to discuss you either working at Jackpot during the day in a higher position or doing something else to earn better money. What's your dream job?"

"Sourcing things for Vintage Finds. Travelling round London to look for bits and bobs to be sold there. Visiting car boot sales to pick up stuff people don't know are even worth anything."

"What qualifies you to do that?"

She'd had enough walking and returned to the bed, oddly out of breath. She sat and thought about the times she'd rummaged in charity shops for hours on end to discover a bargain for her or the kids. "Experience."

"Fair enough. We'll have a trial run when you're better. I'll give you a week, and the money, to root out gear for the shop. If it turns out we can price them to double your expenditure, we'll take you on. Better wages, no more casino, and more importantly, no more worrying and having to think about nicking chips."

Her face flushed. "I said I was sorry about that, and I meant it."

"I know, otherwise I wouldn't be handing you this opportunity. In the meantime, while you recuperate, we'll give you full wages, none of that sickness pay crap. Anyway, I've got shit to do, I just wanted to pop in and see how you were. Enjoy the rest and peace while you can. I imagine the kids will be all over you when you see them again."

"I expect so."

"I've sent someone over with a load of toys for them. Anna said they're getting bored. She gave me a list."

He walked out, leaving her with tears in her eyes and a 'thank you' on her tongue.

She'd come up trumps for once in her life, and the kids had, too. Now all she had to do was get out of here so she could see them. She missed them, and they'd be missing her, although they were used to being with Anna.

She got back under the covers and dreamed of a better life, one that was within her grasp.

George poked his head back round the door. "Oh, and another thing. I broke into your flat earlier and had a look at that mould. Disgusting. The council ought to be ashamed of themselves. Anyway, we're sorting you out a nice little house in a street behind The Angel, a couple of doors down from Vic's therapy office. It needs painting inside and a few things doing to it, but it's yours if you want it. Five hundred a month can't be sniffed at. Our men will move your things in about a week, okay?"

"I-I don't know what to say."

"Thank you?" He smiled. "And you're welcome."

He disappeared again, and she cried, the tears dripping into her hairline. She'd hoped for a new home, somewhere the children wouldn't have to breathe in the mould spores, and a job where she wasn't scrabbling for pennies.

Maybe she ought to thank Goldie for putting bullets in her. If she hadn't been shot, none of this would be happening.

Chapter Fifteen

Ichabod had spent the night in the front
bedroom of the house opposite Goldie's, his car
out of sight in the garage. It hadn't been difficult
to persuade the homeowner to let him in. He'd
mentioned Goldie's name and that he needed to
spy on him. It had been clear she disliked the
over-tanned leader with a passion. Her nose had

turned up as if Ichabod had passed wind, and she'd gestured him inside as soon as he'd mentioned the names George and Greg.

Marleigh Jasper, a forty-something posh woman whose husband, David, was away for work in some foreign country or other, had fed and watered him throughout the night while keeping him company at the same time. When he'd napped, she'd watched Goldie's through a slit in her curtains and vice versa. They'd talked about their lives. She was a kept woman, glad to be in that role, although she'd become somewhat wistful when he'd mentioned he worked in a casino.

"Oh, we have so much fun when we go to Vegas," she'd said. "All that excitement. The hope of winning is in the air, isn't it, as if it's something you can touch. Those places buzz with it."

Ichabod had to agree, although he'd tuned that buzz out now, only interested in watching for scammers, thieves, and anyone out to cause trouble. He didn't need T-T or the other security men to protect him, he could take care of himself well enough, so if a disagreement or fight broke out, he was the first one there to deal with it, ready to break a nose or two.

He'd come a long way in the last few months, all thanks to the twins. George mainly, who'd had faith in him from the start, choosing him to spy on Janet, and what a can of worms *that* had opened up. He still couldn't get over what she'd done, how she'd lived with voices in her head yet had seemed as if she had a handle on life.

It just went to show, first impressions could be deceptive.

He quickly glanced across at the woman of the house then returned his gaze to the home opposite, eyes trained on the front door. George had agreed to pay Marleigh a lot of money for her time and involvement, but she'd waved it off, saying she had enough of her own, and helping to catch Goldie doing something he shouldn't was payment enough for her. Ichabod needed to find out what she'd meant by that.

This morning, instead of perching on the bed behind him, she sat at the window in an elegant Edwardian-looking chair while sipping tea from a dainty china cup. Ichabod drank his brew without taking the binoculars away from his eyes. The sun shone, giving the view a deceptively summery appearance, but he'd bet it was brass monkey weather out there, the same as yesterday. The air had been a chilly prick lately.

"Why, exactly, are ye willin' tae go against yer leader?" he asked.

"It's obvious, isn't it? I mean, look at the state of him. His appearance is a crime against humanity." She laughed.

Ichabod smiled. "What, the tan and yellow hair?"

"He's dreadful. Joking aside, it isn't what he looks like, it's what I believe he does, or did, at that awful tanning place of his."

Ichabod was almost tempted to lower the binoculars to stare at her again but couldn't risk it. If Goldie got away unnoticed, the twins would go mental. "What goes on there?"

"I think he's part of The Network, the one that was on the news not so long ago."

Ichabod's eyebrows rose. "In what way?"

"He had a party in his house once, lots of girls turning up in a minibus, many men in cars, but it's the other thing that concerned me and David, which is why I made a phone call to the police. I spoke to a chap called Keith Sykes, a detective."

"When did ye make the call? Before or after it hit the news?"

"Oh, months before."

"And what concerned ye?"

"We'd been out for a meal. David had to stop at the traffic lights outside Golden Glow. We were talking nonsense about some deal with his job, and he suddenly stopped speaking and stared across at the tanning shop. I did, too, and there was this young woman at an upstairs window. She'd breathed on the glass and had written a word, one I didn't understand. I had a horrible feeling, as if something was terribly wrong, so I Googled it."

"What was it?"

"*Pomoc*. It means 'help' in Polish. The lights turned green, so I put my thumb up to her, thinking she'd understand that I'd get help, but she was yanked away by someone, then a blind went over the window. David had no choice but to drive on, people were pressing their horns, and he told me to phone the police. Sykes said he'd deal with it, and the next time we went past Golden Glow, shutters had been placed outside over the windows, the same style as on his house. Of course, I didn't think anything of it, I assumed the police had been round there and found nothing wrong, but when the news came on about all those poor refugees, I had *another* horrible feeling—that the Polish woman had been one of them. So I phoned Sykes again to see what the outcome had been about Goldie, only to be informed he'd died."

"Did ye speak tae anyone else?"

"Someone took my details, and an officer phoned me back, one who said he'd go and pay Goldie a visit, but I never heard anything about it, no follow-up call. I thought, seeing as Goldie was still swanning around, that it wasn't anything to do with him."

Ichabod had heard about the refugee case, of course he had, but he wasn't as close to the twins back then as he was now. He hadn't been involved with them helping the refugees to escape, but the word was out that not all Network members had been found and it was a worldwide operation. Could Goldie be one of them? Or had he hired a Polish escort and she'd written 'help' because the sex games had got a bit rough?

"Can ye take over the binoculars while I ring The Brothers?" he asked.

"How exciting!" Marleigh placed her cup on the sill and swapped places with him, lifting the bins to her eyes.

"I'll trust ye tae call me if ye see him comin' out, all right?"

"Will do!" she trilled.

He left the bedroom and walked into one at the back. For guests, he assumed, given that towels in the shape of animals sat on the bed as well as a basket of posh toiletries. He pushed the door to, leaving it open enough that he'd hear her shout if Goldie appeared, then rang the twins' work phone.

"What's happened?" George barked. "Something must have if you've phoned instead of messaged."

Ichabod related Marleigh's story. "So if ye can't get him for shootin' Cinnamon, you might be able tae get him for this."

"The Network? Jesus. I'll have to let Janine in on it. She's going to want to know why the officer didn't follow it up, the one after Sykes. He could be a part of it an' all. Did Marleigh give you their name?"

"No. Hang on." Ichabod went back to the front bedroom and asked her.

She remained facing forward, spying. "A DC Mallard. I remember it so well because David joked as to whether his first name was Drake."

Ichabod stared at her blankly.

"You know," she said, "they're both ducks?"

"Ah, I get ye." He walked back into the other bedroom to George laughing in his earhole. "I take it ye got that?"

"Yeah. I reckon I'd like this David. Right, leave it with me. No movement there yet, then?"

"No. The shutters are still closed, although he may well have them up for more than just security. Marleigh said they're never opened."

"It's got the air of that Network house about it, the shutters, except that one had boards of wood. Bastard."

"I'd best get back tae the window, and Marleigh's on about makin' bacon sandwiches for breakfast."

"That's got my stomach rumbling. Keep us in the loop."

"Always."

Ichabod relieved Marleigh of her duty, and she stood behind the folds of the curtain to talk to him.

"George is gettin' hold of the police," he said. "He'll get it sorted."

"Thank God for that. I've thought about that girl often. I'll just put the bacon in the Ninja and have a shower while it's cooking. Won't be long."

While he kept watch, Ichabod sat and pondered what she'd told him. If Goldie was in with The Network, had he let the Polish girl go because there was too much heat? Where was she? Alive? Dead? Was Cinnamon a link, which was why she'd been shot? No, he didn't think she'd be an eejit and be involved with an outfit like that, but then again, he hadn't thought Macey Moorhouse would either, yet she'd done the refugees' makeup every night.

Something sprang to mind. Now Ichabod came to think of it, Goldie had only been going out with bodyguards since the refugee situation had been discovered. Members of The Network had been picked off by an unknown assailant, one of them a lad who'd been a babysitter for the refugees and the twins' mole. Then there was that fella who ran a pub. He'd been shot outside his house. There were the men gunned down and dumped in the river, too—they'd helped two Ukrainian women escape, the sisters who now ran Vintage Finds. Was Goldie worried *he'd* get the same treatment, hence the bodyguards? If so, why had he changed tack and gone out alone to shoot Cinnamon—if that had even been him? If Ichabod was worried about some creepy sex-slave organisation gunning him down, he was fecked if he'd put himself at risk like that. He'd have fled the bloody country, so he would.

Still no movement from Goldie's. Had the dickhead gone out the back way? No, Marleigh had said there were only fields that way, butting onto a dual carriageway, this housing estate on the outskirts of Golden Eye. Unless Goldie enjoyed a morning jog and his bodyguards picked him up on the road, it was doubtful he'd left yet.

Marleigh returned with doorstep bacon sandwiches and more tea. This time, Ichabod's was in a mug. Relieved he didn't have to be careful with the china effort she'd given him before, he held the binoculars in one hand and half a sandwich in the other.

Marleigh sat on her fancy chair, still behind the curtain. "I'd like to say I could help you with what time he goes out, but it's never the same each day, nor does he return at certain times either."

"Probably so no one can keep track of his movements."

"What are the twins like?"

"Believe it or not, despite what ye might have heard, they're good men. They just want justice, tae do the right thing by their residents and employees. I won't hear a bad word said against them."

"I wouldn't dream of doing so, I was just curious."

They finished eating in silence.

Ichabod felt he should warn her about her involvement. He liked her and didn't want Marleigh finding herself in deep trouble. "Ye know if ye open ye mouth about this and the twins find out, they'll come for ye."

"I'm well aware. If I didn't want to help, I'd have shut the door in your face yesterday. I promise you, that Polish woman has given me many a sleepless night. I want to know what happened to her, whether she's all right."

"If The Brothers find her, I'll let ye know." He sat upright. "Movement."

A car drew up, sleek and black, the windows tinted.

"I'm going tae have tae leave me breakfast," he said. "Sorry."

Marleigh handed him his rucksack while he kept an eye on the two men getting out of the car and approaching the gate between the bushes outside Goldie's.

"Off you pop," she said. "Don't worry about closing the garage door behind you, it shuts by itself. The gates have a sensor and will open automatically. I'll give you a shout and bang on the floor when he's in the car."

He rushed from the room, letting the binoculars swing on the strap around his neck. He sprinted into the kitchen, accessed the garage via the door there, propping it open so he'd hear Marleigh. He pressed the button on the wall to open the up-and-over door that led outside. He wasn't bothered about the men seeing it rise from the road—Marleigh had hedges like Goldie's, and they were too high for them to see over. In the car, he slung his backpack on the passenger seat, leaving his door open, again so he'd hear her calling out to him.

Then started the engine and waited.

Another engine rumbled over his own, a meaty rev, then came the thud of Marleigh stamping above and her faint shout. He shut his door and eased onto the driveway, the electronic gates at the bottom swinging wide. He shot onto the street, sighting the car ahead as it turned out of the cul-de-sac.

Ichabod smiled.

Let's see what ye're up tae, fecker.

Chapter Sixteen

"I heard Rick's nose is fixed," Gail said and tucked a strand of hair behind her ear.

They'd been best friends with her for so long, living in the same street, that George couldn't remember a time they hadn't known her. Richard didn't like his missus hanging around with anyone, so Mum and Francine's chats over a cuppa were done on the quiet *while he was working or at the pub—or trying to get into Ron's good books, always banging on about being let back into his secret poker games. Mum and Francine whispered a lot, as if they had a million secrets between them, talking about 'him', whoever that was, like the man in question was someone to be feared. Maybe it was Richard, but George didn't think so. Why would Francine be afraid of him, too?*

Was it Ron? Or someone else?

A week into the summer holiday, they sat at the park having one of their picnics. Gail's brothers had gone to the cinema with Francine, else they'd be here, too. Gail hadn't wanted to go, preferring to spend her time with the twins.

They all chipped in with the food—well, George and Greg did when Mum had enough to spare. It was mainly Francine who provided things, and she always, always put in Penguins and Jaffa Cakes. George loved her, she was like an aunt, and if Mum wasn't around to go to, they went to her. Today, Mum had done peanut butter sandwiches and handed over bags of cheese and onion crisps. Gail had brought her usual and a bottle of lemonade plus three triangles of Victoria sponge wrapped in foil, leftovers from their Sunday tea last night. Leftovers? There were never any of those in the Wilkes' household because there wasn't much on their plates to begin with.

It was all a bit warm, the food, what with the sun blazing, but George didn't care. He lounged on the grass, eating, one elbow digging into the prickly grass to prop him up. His stomach full, he took a gander around. Movement across the park caught his attention, and he sat up at the sight of two men striding in and going towards the slide which had a wooden triangle construction underneath like a shed roof, benches either side. A doorway was at the back. The front, where the slide came down, was open, so you could see whoever sat inside. Beyond, the iron railing that enclosed the park, back gardens butted against it, six-foot planked fences preventing anyone nosing. Someone had used creosote on theirs earlier, the scent strong as it dried, still hanging in the baking air if a gentle breeze came along.

The men ducked through the doorway, and a kid two years above them at school, Ollie Pickles, stood, running a hand through his ginger hair. George had assumed Pickles had come here for a smoke — his mum would do her nut if she knew he liked the fags — but it seemed he was here for another reason; he didn't look afraid of the newcomers like normal people would, just a bit on edge.

Why had the men come to the park? They didn't usually conduct business in places like this. Or wasn't it anything to do with business? Pickles had bragged he worked for them. Had he fucked up somewhere along the line and the blokes had come to teach him a lesson? But in a park, *with all those little kids around?*

George didn't like the idea of that. What if they brought guns out and hurt someone?

He got up.

"Where are you going?" Gail asked, squeezing her piece of tin foil into a ball.

"Just got to do something a minute." George looked at his brother.

Greg seemed to know George had decided to listen in on the conversation at the slide. "I'll come. Stay there, Gail."

George ran to the right so Pickles and the men couldn't see them. Once he was level with the side of the triangle, he darted left and came to a stop next to it. He strained an ear.

"...so you want me to drop the note round then follow her after she comes out."

"Glad to see you haven't got cloth ears," Ron said.

Sam chuckled. He was a bit of a simpleton, some said.

192

"When she gets to where she's going," Ron went on, "some rope will be there, hanging on the railings. Watch what she does with it."

George glanced at Greg: What the fuck?

Greg frowned then shrugged.

"What if she doesn't come out?" Pickles asked.

"She will."

"What's it for, the rope?"

"You'll see. Here's two hundred nicker for now, and there'll be more after once you get rid of the body."

"The body?" Pickles' voice had risen.

"Yeah, the body," Ron snapped. "Don't look at me like that, my old son. You wanted to take a step up, and this is your initiation. Do the job right, putting her where no one will find her, and you'll be on your way to becoming a proper member of the firm."

"I didn't want to dump any bodies!" Pickles sounded panicked, and he must be shuffling his feet, given the scraping noise and the skitter of loose tarmac.

"What did you think you were going to be doing?"

"I dunno, just not running messages no more. Maybe collecting protection money."

Ron's laugh, dulled by the wooden overhang, had George's hackles rising. He couldn't stand the bloke, not when Mum got funny if someone mentioned his name, but in order to take over the estate when they *were older, he'd* pretend *he liked him, he'd do whatever it took, whatever he said when they finally got a job with him.*

"Collecting protection money?" Ron sniffed. "You're not beefy enough for that, son. One look at you, and people will piss themselves laughing."

George didn't agree. People knew the consequences of not paying up, so they'd hand the cash over to a stick-thin kid if they had to. Ron was fobbing Pickles off. He wanted him to do his dirty work for him, nothing more.

"Who is she?" Pickles asked.

"Just a woman who's become surplus to requirements. She's got a bit too big for her boots, and I don't like it."

George hated violence towards women, of course he did, his mum suffered most days, so whoever this woman was, he had to help her.

He glanced at Greg who nodded.

"Just do as you're told," Ron said, "and everything will be fine and dandy. If you don't…"

"I get it."

"Glad you do."

George nudged Greg. They moved away from the slide and sat a few metres away; running back to Gail wasn't an option, not when George had a strong sense that Ron and Sam were leaving the overhang.

They did, and Ron glanced over, giving the twins one of his scowls.

"They might not have cloth ears either, boss." Sam stopped walking and folded his arms. "They could have heard everything."

Ron shook his head. "It's just The Brothers. They come from dumb stock, nothing to worry about."

The mad part of George ignited. Was he on about Richard or Mum?

If it was Mum...

"Oi." George stood. "Who the fuck do you think you're talking about?"

Greg leapt up. "Leave it, bruv..."

"No, I won't leave it." He glared at Ron. "Were you talking about our mother?"

Ron seemed taken aback for a moment, angry, then he smiled. "A lad who loves his mother enough to risk upsetting a leader, eh? Have you got a death wish, son?"

"I'm not your son."

Ron's smile turned knowing, and he chuckled. "You need to toddle off back to that cesspit street you live in and mind your own business."

Sam placed a hand on Ron's shoulder. Was he like Greg, the voice of reason? "You said they'd go far in the firm when they're older, boss, be an asset. Best to keep them sweet."

The reminder apparently sank in, and Ron shook out his arms as though ridding himself of tension. George filed that information away. If he could get them permanent jobs with Ron, his takeover bid could begin, but he couldn't let it go, what Ron had said about dumb stock, no matter who the bloke was or what the consequences might be.

"So? Were you talking about our mum?"

Ron sighed. "The bloke you call Dad— No, the less said about that scenario the better."

Satisfied with that, George nodded.

Ron's teeth spread in a feral grin. "Your mum's not dumb, she's proved she's very clever. She does as she's told, that one."

Ron walked away, Sam lumbering after him, leaving George staring at their backs.

What had Mum been told to do?

Pickles had stayed under the slide awning all afternoon, alternating between sitting smoking, pacing, and kicking a football against the wood (he'd nabbed the ball from a hedge where some lad had lost it). Gail had taken the picnic mess home, plus she had to look after her brothers so Francine could go to bingo, George and Greg staying behind. At six, Pickles stubbed one of his endless fags out and left the slide, the twins following.

They tailed him towards Queen Avenue.

"He's going to cop on to us in a minute," Greg said.

"We'll hide behind a car or summat."

Pickles checked the street for anyone watching, dithering at the gate of number six. He seemed reluctant to carry out orders, which was no surprise, considering a dead body was involved. He went up to the house and posted a note through the letterbox. He knocked, rang the bell, and retreated, going to stand behind a tall van.

From their vantage point round the back of a car, George and Greg crouched and watched through the rear window. A woman opened the door, note in hand, glancing up and down the street. Her expression would stay with George forever. She was afraid, the kind of afraid Ron Cardigan inspired.

The door closed, and George prepared himself for a long wait. She might not go to where the note said, she could call the police instead, because a message from

Cardigan to a woman surplus to requirements didn't signal hearts and roses, did it.

Or was she so afraid of Ron she'd do whatever he wanted?

"She's coming out," Greg whispered.

Pickles jolted, waited for her to pass the van, heading towards George and Greg, then he went after her. They neared, so George gestured for Greg to move around to the far side of the car so when Pickles and the woman passed, they wouldn't be seen. George peered through the passenger-side window, spotting something about the woman that boiled his piss.

Ron had gone below the belt here.

The pair went around the corner.

"Let's go."

George stood and casually walked after them, Greg by his side. The woman kept glancing behind her, then going faster every time she spotted Pickles. He didn't always anticipate her checking if he was still there, so at times he hadn't dipped behind a vehicle or tree. George and Greg had, adept at this because of the days they'd spied on Ron or people George wanted to teach a lesson.

The journey ended beside the river, near the archway where George wanted to kill Richard one day. No drug pushers were in attendance, so Ron must *have told them to stay away. The woman went down the slope that led to the river path, wandering away from the arch and reading the note again, her head bent. Pickles stayed at the top of the slope and observed her from behind some scrubby bushes.*

George crept up to his back and slapped a hand over his mouth. "No making a racket. We're here to get you out of a pickle, Pickle."

Greg guffawed.

Pickle stiffened, fists clenching at his sides.

"We heard what Ron expects you to do. You know what that rope's for, don't you?"

Pickles nodded.

"I'm going to take my hand away so you can answer my next question, but if you shout for help, I'll shoot you in the back." George poked the tip of his finger in Pickles' side. "Are you willing to let a pregnant woman top herself?" He removed his hand from the lad's face.

"No, I-I didn't even want her d-doing it without *being p-pregnant, but Ron, he'll hurt me. K-kill me if I don't do what he w-wants."*

"Not if he doesn't know you haven't done it." George took his finger away and made movements as if he'd holstered a gun, then turned Pickles to face him. "You're coming with us."

199

George led the way down the slope and headed towards the woman who stared at the rope, a noose already waiting for her at the end of it. She glanced their way, then grabbed the rope as though desperate to do what Ron had instructed before they forced her into it.

"Don't," George said. "Let me see that note."

She held it out, her hand shaking, the paper flapping.

George read it.

GO TO THE ARCHWAY BEHIND THE WAREHOUSES. THERE'S A ROPE THERE. USE IT SO IT KILLS YOU AND THAT FUCKING THING YOU'VE GOT INSIDE YOU, LIKE YOU SHOULD HAVE DONE WHEN I SAID TO GET IT ABORTED. THERE ARE TOO MANY OF THE LITTLE BASTARDS ABOUT, AND I DON'T LIKE IT. I TOLD YOU WHAT TO DO, WHAT THE ORDER OF PLAY WAS WITH US, YET YOU THREATENED TO GO TO THE POLICE ABOUT MY LITTLE ACT OF COERCION.

TREACLES NEED TO KNOW THEIR PLACE, AND YOURS IS DANGLING FROM THE END OF A FUCKING ROPE. DO IT OR I'LL PAY YOU A VISIT, AND YOUR DEATH WON'T BE AS QUICK THEN. IT COULD HAVE BEEN SO EASY IF YOU'D JUST DONE AS YOU WERE TOLD.

George's blood ran cold at that last sentence. Ron had said Mum knew how to do as she was told. What had happened? Had she been pregnant before him and Greg and got rid of it? No, she'd never have gone anywhere near Ron in that way, and the man asked a lot of people to do as they were told, but it chilled George, nonetheless.

He eyed the woman. She reminded him of Mum a bit, maybe what she'd looked like when she'd been younger. "Have you got anywhere to go?"

"W-what?" She twisted a ring on her middle finger.

George reckoned she was in shock, so he elaborated. "Somewhere to live that's not in London?"

She nodded.

"Go there."

Her bottom lip quivered. "I haven't got the money for the train. I didn't bring my bag and haven't got that much in my purse anyway..."

George gritted his teeth. When he was rich, he'd carry cash around with him in the pocket of the nice grey suit he planned to buy. He'd put it in the glove box of their BMW, too, so there was always dosh on hand for people like her. He'd save them, get them away from any danger, feed their leccy meters, fill their bellies, have loads of employees and give them flats to

201

live in, like Sultan did. But he wasn't rich now, and he didn't have an envelope of cash to hand to her.

Shit.

"Here, take this." Pickles handed her the money Ron must have given him. "But you can't say I helped you. Ron wanted me to make sure you...you did...did that, then I'm meant to dump your body. You have to leave, never come back."

She held her swollen belly, stroking the top. "But he'll find me. He said he always finds people who run away."

"Change your name, then," Greg said. "You can't kill that baby. Why does he want it dead anyway?"

She bit her lip. "I can't tell you. I can't tell anyone."

Pickles stepped forward and put the money in her hand. "Fuck off. Go on, get out of here. Send someone to collect the stuff from your house another time or whatever. Tell them to say that cos you've gone missing, they're collecting your shit."

She stared at them, tears falling, then ran up the path. George watched her go, so fucking angry at Ron. Killing a baby, a child, was the lowest of the low. If he ever found out anyone else had murdered a nipper, or planned to, he'd be gunning for them, sod the fact he was only thirteen.

Pickles had ended up dead in a gutter a month later. The stupid twat had caved under pressure, admitting to Ron that the woman hadn't killed herself, she'd run before he'd had a chance to get down the slope. He'd met up with the twins shortly after Ron had beaten the shit out of him over it, promising he hadn't dropped their names in it.

It seemed Ron let people think a beating was the end of it, allowing them to go on their merry way, then he killed them later. George liked that idea and might adopt the same process when he ran the estate with Greg beside him. Then again, it depended on the circumstances and whether his mad side would allow him to play with people that way or he'd sort them as soon as they pissed him off.

Time would tell.

Chapter Seventeen

On the way to Golden Glow, Goldie cursed himself again for his mistake last night. Never had he done it before, and he'd wouldn't do it again because he was getting rid of his little secret for good. He'd bloody well fallen asleep in the loft room, hadn't he. Waking up earlier beside Zofia had sent his skin cold, sweat breaking out in his panic. Thank God she'd still been cuffed to the bed by her wrists, otherwise it could have ended badly. While a security code was needed in order to even leave the house, and the shutters blocked the view, she could still have run downstairs to use a phone and call the police. He didn't need the shit that would have brought to his door. He'd purchased her fair and square from the Italian Network boss, de Luca, and, like so many other men, kept this possession locked up in order to force her into *wanting* him to touch her instead of doing it through fear.

Sadly, the treatment hadn't worked with Zofia, but now he had his retirement plan in place, he didn't give a fuck about her. There were plenty more younger-than-him women he could pick up at his next destination, and as he'd live where no one knew him, he didn't care so much about the paedo tag. Providing whoever he chose was of legal age, he wouldn't give a fiddler's about the filthy looks or being called a pervert. With no leader mantle to maintain, no one to make him feel ashamed, he'd be free to do whatever he wanted.

She'd asked him to set her free again last night, and he'd given in and told her what her fate would be.

"*Because you've never followed the rules, fighting me all the way, when you leave this house, it'll be dead inside a rolled-up carpet, love.*"

She stiffened beside him. "What?"

"*You heard me. You're an ungrateful cow. I put you on that English learning course so we could chat, I've fed you, bought you clothes, treated you well, yet you reckon you'd run the first chance you get.*"

"*You only teach me English so I understand filthy words you say in the bed. You feed me rabbit food. The clothes…*" *She laughed. "Underwear. That is all I ever put on."*

"*See? Ungrateful. I'm not taking you with me when I leave. You're untrainable, you're a liability, and I've burnt your passport anyway, so there's no changing my mind.*"

She cried, her sobs getting on his nerves, and he grabbed her hair and wrenched her head back.

"*Shut the fuck up, you stupid tart.*"

"*Please, I do whatever you want.*"

"*Oh, so now you'll do it, will you? You've got the gist you won't be seeing Mummy or Daddy again, so* you're prepared to play ball? Too fucking late. When I picked you, I thought you were golden, inside and out, but no, you soon changed, didn't you. What was it, all a ploy? Did you tell me what I wanted to hear before I bought you just so you could leave the refugee house?"

"I had to survive. I wanted better life."

"That's what got you in this shit in the first place, wanting more than you had. You got greedy. What did you need to leave Poland for anyway?"

"To get job. Send money to parents."

"Ah, that old chestnut. Well, you fucked up, didn't you. Once you realised I wasn't going to whisk you away to my house so you could play at being a rich wife, you changed your tune. So yeah, a carpet's your future, not this gaff, and you'll be dumped somewhere no one can find you."

She cried again when he forced himself into her, and he got off on her fear and anguish. He'd enjoy killing her. It'd be like the old days when he'd been in his prime. He'd strangle her to death, the sly cunt, and stare into her eyes while he did it.

Angry that some of the men had women who'd turned out to be gems, he slammed into Zofia with more force than necessary to get his point across, that she was his property to do whatever he wanted with, then he slapped her about a bit until she screamed and *her lip bled. Hand over her mouth, he gave one last punishing push, then rolled over, leaving her cuffed to the other side of the bed.*

Bitch.

It still got to him now as he stared out of the car window at everyone going about their lives. They were lucky bastards. He had so much on his plate, running The Golden Eye Estate and all the other crap he dealt with, it was a wonder he hadn't cracked under the pressure. He imagined walking along a sandy beach, nothing but girls and spending money on his mind, and when he got his hands on the takings from that safe on heist night, he'd feel like a king.

He'd instructed the driver to go directly to Golden Glow. Goldie had decided on another tan, a deeper one; he wanted to look his best at the alibi party he was attending on Friday evening. He'd arranged one at the social club, booking strippers and caterers, planning a big bash that would stick in people's minds should they be approached by the pigs and questioned. He'd speak to everyone there, be present at all times unless he had to nip to the gents, and there was no way anyone could accuse him of being at the casino during the robbery. None of his men would blab, they wouldn't get their cut if they did, and if they opened their mouths after he'd handed it over, he'd shoot them in the fucking head.

Anger still swirling inside him at his lapse last night, plus having to deal with Zofia being such a drippy, snivelling cow, he forced good thoughts into his mind. Palm trees, sunshine, girls in bikinis, cocktails, a beachside property where he'd host gatherings and make new friends. He'd have money dripping from his fingertips. All he had to do after the robbery was stick around for six months until the chatter about it died down, then he'd put his house up for sale, live in a rented flat for a while until his place sold, and give up his leader status at one of the usual meetings.

He wasn't married to his estate, he didn't have an emotional attachment to it like some of the others did. All it had been for him was to make him a known face, plenty of money, and finance his dreams.

"We're here, boss."

Goldie must have zoned out. At the rear of Golden Glow, he left the car and went inside, shouting for Tanning Tart Babs. She'd been the one to look after Zofia when he'd first bought her, locking her in the room upstairs, and Babs kept a lot of his secrets, seeing as he held many a meeting here while she was present. Babs had proved her worth and loyalty, and if she wasn't so clingy, he'd consider taking her with him when he escaped London. She'd go with him, too. They'd been an item once, and she'd told him she loved him—still did, so she'd said the other day. But she wasn't the type he craved. There was no refinement about her at all, not like that Marleigh woman. Now *she* was exactly what he was after, and she had blonde hair so was as golden as him. But she was married to that hoity-toity prick, David, who turned his nose up whenever he saw Goldie. Marleigh was the same lately, yet a couple of years ago she'd been as friendly as anything when she'd put out her bins.

Babs appeared, drawing him out of his thoughts. "What can I do for you, oh Golden One?"

"The usual breakfast and a couple of coffees from the café, love."

She frowned, followed him into the break room, and closed the door. "Are you all right?"

211

"No, I fucked up with Zofia last night."

"Oops, did you bump her off? What did I tell you about strangling people during sex? You almost fucked it up with me once, if you remember. When will you learn?"

He went over to the kitchenette and leant on a cupboard. "It wasn't that. I fell asleep next to her."

"Jesus *Christ*, Goldie!"

He raised his hands. "I know, I know. She was cuffed, but if she hadn't been…"

"I thought she always had a chain on her ankle?"

He looked at her sheepishly. "I take it off sometimes. The clinking gets on my nerves when we're, you know…"

"Well, *don't* in future, all right?"

"There won't be a future."

Babs stuck her bottom lip out. "Aww, is she boring you?"

"No, I need her gone. I'm…" No, he couldn't tell her. Couldn't tell anyone where he planned to go. "It's just time she wasn't there, that's all." He thought about how it had been with Babs. She was good in the sack, so he could use her for sex until he left London. "Fancy taking her place?"

"Not anymore, Goldie. I've got myself a fella."

That gave him a kick in the teeth. "When?"

She blushed through her tan. "Been seeing him for a couple of months now."

"You never said."

"Didn't know I had to."

He didn't get it. Didn't get women. "But you told me you loved me last week."

"I do. Doesn't mean I can't be with someone else, though. Me and you, we're not compatible, love, you know that." She smiled to take the sting out of it.

"True. I only meant for us to have sex. I didn't mean a relationship."

"No to both. Do you need my help with Zofia?"

He knew when to quit while he was ahead. "Nah, I'll deal with it."

She sighed. "Okay, but you know where I am if you change your mind. I'm off down the café. Back in a bit."

She swanned out, and he sat at the table, taking his little notebook out and jotting a few things down regarding Zofia's disposal. He'd have to get someone to clean her insides out, he didn't want anyone finding her body and his DNA being discovered. Maybe his man, Bronson, would burn her *up there*, then chop her up and bury her. Burn her whole body, even.

He doodled, lost in thought for a while, then nodded, pleased with the idea of Zofia turning into a char-grilled slab of human steak. He slipped his notebook away just as Babs returned. His breakfast was on his special plate, and she popped his gold cutlery down inside a cloth napkin. She walked out and came back again with two to-go coffees and a cup and saucer.

"Enjoy," she said. "I'll be ready to give you a top-up tan when you've finished."

"Just a tan?" He winked.

"Goldie…"

She left him to it, and he cut into his sausage carefully this time. He had a Blake Mill shirt on today and really did want to get oil on it. The bloody thing had cost him over a hundred nicker.

The sound of Zofia crying came back to him, her tears thick and fast when he'd left her chained to the bed this morning. She had a bathroom, and the chain was long enough for her to walk around. Books lined the shelves to one side, plus there was a telly and plenty of water. She was an ungrateful piece of baggage, that one, and tonight, she'd regret every nasty word she'd ever said to him.

Chapter Eighteen

Karen and Teddy sat at the kitchen table, a plate of toast in the middle, a pot of jam and the butter dish beside it. It had been weird, waking up with him in the flat, the sound of the shower letting her know he'd made himself at home like she'd told him to. She'd waited for him to finish then got in, the scent of men's shower gel hanging in the steamy air.

She'd made a tea for herself and a coffee for Teddy, who'd been chatting on the phone to Oakley just now, telling him what had been going on. It had sounded like everything was okay from what she'd picked up. Oakley was a laid-back bloke and knew there were things they had to do that they didn't want to. Teddy wasn't exactly here on sufferance, but he'd stayed over in case the twins had stationed someone outside to spy on them.

In the shirt she'd put on the back of the bathroom door last night, and his trousers from his work suit, Teddy buttered a slice of toast. "We're going to have to shack up together until this is all over, you know that, don't you. We should have done it ages ago, but I didn't want to drop Oakley like that."

She sighed. Karen didn't like lying to him, keeping it from him that she was going to grass Goldie up to The Brothers, but her plan was to be a mole for the twins, earn extra money to put towards the operation, and Teddy would need to be kept out of the loop. "Yep, but we can get away with you staying with Oakley a couple of times a week, though, surely, because of the story we told George."

"I thought the same. Glad you agree. I don't want to be away from him every day."

She shrugged. "George should understand. He thinks Oakley's your brother from another mother. He's with his nearly all the time, so he'd get it. Mind you, they went their separate ways last night, which is unusual. I wonder where Greg was when he went off with T-T."

"Probably looking for Cinnamon's shooter."

Karen put jam on her toast. She wanted to test Teddy's loyalty so she knew whether to get him in the shit as well, even though she didn't want to. If he stood up for their boss, she'd know she couldn't trust him.

She took a deep breath. "Between you and me, I don't believe Goldie."

His frown pulled his eyebrows low. "What about?"

"That he wasn't anything to do with it."

Teddy's eyebrows went up momentarily. He seemed to be having an internal battle, maybe asking himself if *he* could trust *her*. But she'd touched on this subject when they'd talked about her phone call to Goldie last night, so what she'd said shouldn't come as a surprise.

"Go on," she said. "You can tell me anything. We've been thrown in this together, and if we can't talk to each other, it's a sad state of affairs."

"Okay…"

Her stomach rolled over. Was he going to tell her she'd fallen into the trap of confiding in him and he was now going to tell Goldie what she'd said?

He sipped coffee. "I don't believe him either."

She relaxed, letting out a breath of pure relief. The twins wouldn't have to hurt Teddy now; he was on *her* side, not Goldie's. She'd tell them lies so they didn't go after him, just like she'd lie about herself, too.

But what if he's pretending? What if he's making out he's on the same page as me but plans to grass me up? Shit.

"Thank God it's not just me," she said. "And just so you know, I'm being genuine here by trusting you with my thoughts. I'm worried you're going to go off and tell him what I said."

"Um, no. I told you about the farm, how I want to get away from him. That kind of information could get me killed if he found out, yet I told you.

He's not going to want to let me go. I've even considered changing my name so he can't find me. Oakley said he would, too."

She relaxed even more. He sounded sincere.

"It was him," he said. "Or he sent someone to shoot her. It's too coincidental that you told him about Cinnamon, then she ends up injured."

Karen bit her lip. "What if she works for him and we don't know it?"

Teddy paled. "Fuck. We haven't said anything iffy around her, have we?"

"No."

Teddy sighed. "Goldie would have said she was one of us, surely."

"Not if she's been sent to spy on us two. Him finding out she was going to nick that chip would have got right on his nellies. She could have compromised everything and he got arsey about it, shot her to teach her a lesson."

"I didn't think of that. Blimey. What the hell have we got ourselves into?"

She thought about mentioning the twins to see what he said, then talked herself out of it. It was one thing for them to share their feelings about Goldie, another for her to reveal she was hoping

221

to work for the opposition. Teddy might not go for that.

They ate in contemplation, Karen mulling both scenarios over and still coming up with one answer: Goldie *had* shot Cinnamon. But had she got away before he'd had a chance to kill her? Or had he only meant to give her a warning? Not knowing *where* she'd been shot prevented Karen from knowing the correct version of events. If it was near her head, then he'd definitely been going for the kill. Then there was a third scenario: Goldie hadn't shot her at all.

Karen thought about Cinnamon's life, or what they'd been told about it. She was single, no kids, loved to party, loved her brand-name clothes. What if she'd pissed the twins off regarding the chip and *they'd* done it? Jimmy Riddle hadn't given much information away, just that she'd been shot, and when she'd asked him why, he'd ignored the question. He'd mentioned Handsy, though…

What if they wanted to keep Handsy coming to the casino because *he'd* shot her? No, he'd been in the casino when Karen had arrived at work and had mentioned he'd been there since three. He could have got someone else to do it, though.

Maybe he'd taken offence because Cinnamon wasn't interested in his advances. God, he could come after Karen next because she'd taken his hand off her arse.

"I'll go and collect a few clothes from home in a minute," Teddy said.

She blinked out of her thoughts and nodded. Once he was gone, she could go and meet George and Greg, providing they had time to see her today. "I'm off to do a bit of shopping. Take the spare key. It's on the hook in the hallway."

"I'll be back before we go to work," Teddy added. "If anyone's watching, they'll see what we want them to see—a couple who live together going to their job."

She nodded again, finished the last of the toast, and drank her tea. Teddy left with a smile and a wave, and she went into the living room at the front to watch him walk up the road. No car followed him, so maybe they were being paranoid about being spied on, but it wasn't just the twins she was worried about, there was Goldie, too. If he'd gone after Cinnamon for whatever reason, who was to say he wouldn't go after *them* for some minor infraction?

No, we're too important to the heist.

She returned to the kitchen and picked her phone up. Held her breath. Released it through pinched lips and tapped out a message. Since she now didn't trust Goldie, she couldn't be sure he'd even pay her a cut of the heist cash. He could have lured them into being involved with the promise of riches but didn't intend to give them anything after all. She *had* to have that money, and if getting Robyn her operation meant grassing him up and going to Sienna instead, then that's what she'd do. Robyn's happiness was everything.

KAREN: IT'S KAREN FROM THE CASINO. I NEED TO SPEAK TO YOU BOTH. I HAVE INFORMATION YOU NEED TO KNOW BEFORE FRIDAY. PLEASE CAN WE MEET SOMEWHERE PRIVATE? I CAN'T BE SEEN TALKING TO YOU.

GG: GO ROUND THE BACK OF THE ANGEL. PRESS THE BUZZER. AMARYLLIS WILL LET YOU IN.

KAREN: OKAY, LEAVING MY FLAT NOW.

No response came, so she put her shoes and coat on, grabbed her bag, and walked out into the sunshine, the cold air sifting through her hair. There was no going back now, she'd taken the first step in a bloody dangerous game, but what choice did she have if she wanted to repay her sister for everything she'd done for her?

Chapter Nineteen

*T*hey sat in the living room watching telly, Mum out at her cleaning job, Richard upstairs getting ready for the pub. He drank so much it was a surprise his liver and kidneys hadn't packed up. If they did, it meant George wouldn't have the pleasure of killing him, so he sent up a prayer that their father cut back, having a sudden epiphany that he wasn't getting any *younger and he ought to start thinking about his health. Chance would be a fine thing, Richard enjoyed going to the pub and getting drunk too much, so as soon as George reached the proper end of his rope with the bloke, he'd do the deed.*

They were almost fifteen now but looked eighteen. George could take Richard, no problem, but his mother pleading with him to leave things alone had so far prevented him from laying the bastard out. Once Richard had gone to the pub, George could relax, but until then, he sat on pins and needles, Greg tapping his foot on the floor, showing he felt the same way.

Footsteps thudding had George glancing at the doorway. Although Richard didn't hit them as much since they'd grown as tall as him, he still regularly threw verbal abuse their way or clutched their T-shirt fronts in his fist to spit nasty words in their faces. The threats towards Mum always had them taking whatever he dished out in case Richard took it out on her, but, as George had done since he'd been little, he bit back at the prick more than he should. Goaded him. Wanting Richard to beat the crap out of him so badly that George could kill him and claim it as self-defence.

Richard appeared in the doorway, tucking his shirt in. "What are you fucking staring at?"

George shrugged. "Dunno. Shit doesn't have a label on it."

"Say that again."

"I said—"

"Don't," Greg butted in from beside George on the sofa. "Just don't."

George couldn't resist whispering something from their childhood. "Spiteful little cunt. Fucking little bastard."

Greg managed to keep his hilarity inside; he was still so wary around Richard that he wouldn't outright piss himself laughing in front of him, but George let his out.

Richard stepped closer, his face red, his fists clenched.

George laughed harder: Come on, Dick. Do your worst, I dare you.

"You'll be laughing on the other side of your face if you don't shut up," Richard said.

"Why's that, then? Are you going to pull my trousers down and slap the backs of my legs because I'm such a naughty boy? Or punch me in the stomach? Crack my rib again? Nah, I don't think you will, not now I'm big enough to do it back. And I wouldn't stop at a kick in the nuts either. I'd slice your fucking face up, then get Sultan to bury you."

"Sultan? How do you know him?"

"Wouldn't you like to know."

Richard inhaled deeply. "D'you know what? Since your mother had you two, my life's been hell, living with...with this crap, her, you, not allowed to do anything about it because of her mistake. One day, kid, you're going to come up against someone who doesn't stop when he's hitting you, then you'll realise what an easy ride you have with me. If you knew the truth..." He clamped his mouth shut.

"The truth about what? That you're a bullying tosser? I already know that."

Greg touched George's arm. "Jesus Christ, bruv, leave it, will you?"

Richard stared at George for a long time, his jaw flexing, his hands clenching and unclenching, eyes narrowed. Then he lunged forward and, still looking at George in a dare, gripped Greg by his top and hauled him upright. Greg put his hands on Richard's chest to push him off, but although the bloke was no Muhammed Ali, he was strong and didn't budge.

Anger birthing, George stood and reached between them to put his left hand around Richard's throat. "Let him go. If you ever touch my brother again, I'll fucking kill you."

Richard scoffed. "You? A fourteen-year-old kid? Don't make me laugh."

He released Greg, though, stepping back, George's hand going with him.

George marched him to the wall beside the door and pinned him there. "One day, when you least expect it, I'll come for you."

Despite looking as if he'd realised he'd better watch himself now, Richard said, "Take your hand off me, you little cunt."

George squeezed. "Can't you think up any new names? They're all getting a bit boring." He paused. "Oh, and punch our mum again, and I'll slit your bastard throat." He let go, took one pace back. "Go and do what you do best. Get so pissed up you can't see straight. Try and get in on one of Cardigan's poker games, like you always do. With any luck, you'll open your mouth the wrong way to him and he'll shoot you, doing us all a favour."

"What do you know about him?" Richard seemed panicked, his eyes darting from brother to brother.

"What everyone knows. That if you need someone sorting, you go to him."

"Is that a threat?" Richard rubbed his red neck. "Waste of time. He wouldn't help the likes of you two. Especially *not you two*."

231

"We'll see. He already thinks you're dumb."

Richard's eyes widened. "How do you know that?"

"Because he told us."

"You should stay away from him."

"Should we? But Sam said he wants us in his firm, so you'd really have to watch your step then."

Richard swallowed. "Does your mother know?"

"Not yet, no."

Richard closed his eyes, facing some kind of inner battle that piqued George's curiosity. What was going on in the head of the man who treated them as if they were shit on his shoe, a burden he didn't want to carry? Had never wanted to carry?

"Why don't you just go?" George asked. "Pack your bags and sod off? It's obvious you hate being here. Hate us."

Richard opened his eyes. "I can't."

"Why?"

"I just can't, now leave it at that." He walked out, slamming the front door behind him.

"You all right?" George asked Greg.

"Yeah."

"I meant what I said, you know. I'll fucking kill him if he hurts you again."

"I know you will."

"If anyone *hurts you, I'll maim them, murder them.*"

"I know. *Christ!*" *Greg sat on the edge of the sofa, hands between his knees. "You shouldn't keep pushing him."*

"I can't help it."

"But what if he loses his shit and takes it out on Mum, even though you said you'd slit his throat? What if she ends up dead because you couldn't keep your big mouth shut?"

George couldn't imagine a world without their mother in it. He didn't want to. Couldn't even begin to contemplate what the grief of losing her would be like. When she died, he'd lock all the memories inside his mind, because there was no way he'd cope otherwise. A life without her...no, he wouldn't entertain it. She'd live forever, she had to.

The front door opening then closing and her heels tapping on the hallway floor took George right back to the day he'd kicked Richard in the dick, and he laughed to himself, because since then, he'd thought of him as Dick, not Richard.

Mum poked her head around the living room doorjamb. "What have you said to him? I just saw him, and he's fuming."

"I only let him know how things stand," George said. "If he hits you again, I need to know. None of this hiding it business if he does it while we're not here."

"Why?"

Greg stood. "You don't want to know, Mum. As usual, George lost his shit." He took her bag of shopping and left the room.

George walked over and hugged his mother. "You're everything to us. If he puts a foot wrong…" He drew back to look at her.

"Don't say it," she said, tears pooling. "I didn't want it to be this way. I'm so sorry for everything, but I'm stuck and can't get out."

"We could just go. Take a bag and run." He'd give up his dream of running the estate if it meant she was happy elsewhere, or get her settled, then they'd come back when they were eighteen. He'd send her flowers and chocolates in the post every week so she knew they were thinking of her.

"We can't. It's not allowed."

"Not allowed?"

"Leave it, son. Please, just leave it."

She walked into the kitchen, and George followed. Greg had put the shopping away bar the Pot Noodles, tiger bread, and butter. Mum filled the kettle and switched it on, took hold of the loaf, and got on with cutting it into thick slices. Greg opened the new pack of Anchor and buttered them, George standing there staring at the two people he loved more than anybody else in the world.

Yeah, he'd kill anyone who hurt them.

Do time.

Stay in prison forever if it meant they were safe.

The front door bashing open had him turning to face the hallway. Richard kicked the door shut and stomped towards him. Had something happened on the way to the pub? Or had he had one of his usual moments where, after he'd seen Mum on her way here, he'd been thinking and had come back to teach her a lesson? For what, the shopping he hadn't given her permission to buy?

Richard brushed past George and stopped at the worktop by Mum and Greg. "I didn't like your tone just then, Dolly."

Mum gripped the bread knife.

Stab him. Stab the bastard in the throat. When the police come, I'll say it was me.

"What tone?" she said.

"The one where you told me if I wanted any dinner, it was those fucking shitty Pot Noodles or I had to get something from the chippy. You're my wife, and *you're supposed to look after me. You promised him you'd make this work, not create any waves."*

Him?

For a moment, George thought Mum was going to bite back at Richard, but she made eye contact with George and must have seen his face, how he was telling her that one wrong move, and Richard would be dead on this kitchen floor, his blood coating George's face.

"I'm sorry," she said. "I can make you something else if you want."

Richard looked at George over his shoulder, smiled, and gripped Mum's wrist as if to say: Well, it's not a punch, is it? You didn't say anything about me hurting her in other ways.

George took in a deep breath. Waited. Richard held Mum's hand up and used that position to shove her back into the cupboard under the sink, testing George, like he always did. The knife clattered from her hand to the floor, and George swiped it up, taking two steps up to Richard's back and putting the serrated blade to his throat.

"Didn't you hear what I said?" George whispered. "About slitting your throat? Take your hand off my mother."

Richard obeyed.

"I didn't like your tone just then," George went on. "My mum isn't your skivvy. If you don't like what she's provided for dinner, with money she earnt slogging her guts out cleaning for other people because you don't give her much housekeeping, then she's right, buy your fucking own. Now, either sit down with us and eat, or piss off up the chippy." He pressed the blade harder. "Or do you want to call my bluff and see if I'll speak to Ron?"

Mum gasped. "Don't. Don't ever go to that man."

"Sultan, then," George said.

"Listen to your mother," Richard snarled. "For once, she's talking sense. You'd do well to stay away from them."

It took George all of his strength not to saw into Richard's neck. "You never let up, do you. Always got to have a dig at her. This is your last chance. I might only be fourteen, but there are younger killers out there, and I will end you. Now fuck off to your cronies and leave us alone." He took the knife away. Stepped back.

Richard turned and stared at him. "You're not right in the head, kid. The apple doesn't fall far from the tree."

He strode out. George caught Mum's sigh of relief, so he didn't chase after the bastard because she'd had

237

about all she could take. But one day, Richard would never be able to speak to her like that again.

George stared at the table. Three bags of Revels sat in the centre.

She was learning. She did *matter. She* did *deserve nice things.*

"I've got something for you." He dug in his pocket and brought out a small blue velvet box he'd pinched at the market earlier.

Mum took it. Opened the lid and peered inside.

She lifted her head, tears in her eyes. "Where did you get this?"

"Doesn't matter."

"It does, George. If you stole it and someone saw you, I'll have the rozzers round here, and I can't let that happen because he'll *think I've —" She buttoned her lips.*

"Who's he?"

"No one."

"What will he think you've done?"

"Nothing." She took the necklace out of the box and held it up, the silver angel pendant swinging. "Is that how you see me? An angel? Because I assure you, I'm far from being one of those."

George didn't get how she couldn't see herself like they saw her. "Whatever you've done in the past, it doesn't matter. You're an angel now, our *angel, and we won't ever let you forget it."*

Chapter Twenty

In her office, the door closed, DI Janine Sheldon stared at DC Steve Mallard. The DCI had put him to work on The Network case when it had all flared up, and after George had warned her this morning that Mallard might be another copper in with the organisation, she'd recalled a chat she'd had on the phone with the DCI after she'd interviewed the two Ukrainian sisters who'd escaped.

"Have you had a chance to review Oleksiy's and Bohuslava's statements yet?" she asked.

"Err, no."

"Granted, I've not long finished speaking to them, but I thought someone would have passed on the information to you. I did flag it as priority and asked DC Mallard to let you know. Maybe he was too busy…"

"Ah, Mallard was sent out to investigate something so probably forgot…"

Now, she wondered what he'd been sent to investigate, and who'd sent him? The DCI? God, was her *boss* involved in The Network as well?

Mallard stood on the other side of her desk, clearly uncomfortable. He shifted from foot to foot and clasped his hands over his groin. Did he think she'd pulled him in here for a bollocking regarding the current case they worked on?

"You *can* sit, you know," she said, drawing her coffee towards her. She'd been in the middle of going through her emails and doing paperwork, something that swallowed up her time. This was a welcome interlude.

Mallard sat, propping his ankle on a knee. Going for casual? Trying to hide the fact he might be shitting himself?

"Everything okay?" he asked.

She smiled. "I don't know, that's why I've called you in."

He fiddled with his fingers. "Right."

"I actually need your help with something."

This brightened him considerably, and he puffed up with self-importance. She wasn't his biggest fan, he had a bit of an ego which clashed with hers from time to time, but she'd had no reason to suspect him of being a bent copper until now. Yes, *she* was one, so she couldn't be too hypocritical, but in order to keep herself safe and appear as a good officer in her colleagues' eyes, she'd throw any other bent ones under the bus if it meant she retained her current halo.

"What's that, then?" He rested an elbow on the wooden chair arm and held his cheek in his hand. "You know I'm always happy to help."

"As you're aware, the person who shot DI Sykes told his wife he was from The Network. We can safely assume Sykes was their 'man in the police' who gave them information as and when." She paused. "Or *one* of them anyway."

"There are more? Bloody hell!" Mallard appeared suitably shocked and disgusted.

He's good, I'll give him that. "I want to touch base on a call that was made to the station by a" — she consulted her notes for effect — "Marleigh Jasper regarding an incident she'd witnessed involving Benjamin Winston, otherwise known as Goldie. That call was passed on to you. I have a record that the call exists from our logs, obviously. Do you remember that?"

Mallard shrugged. "We get loads of calls. It was all a bit manic around that time, so no, I don't remember."

"Maybe that's why her report wasn't followed up."

"What do you mean?"

"Prior to us even knowing The Network existed, she gave information to Sykes that a woman had written the word 'help' in Polish on a window at Golden Glow, a tanning shop owned by Goldie. No visit to Golden Glow was logged by Sykes or any other officer. Once The Network hit the news, Mrs Jasper phoned in again, worried the woman was a refugee held against her will. That's the phone call *you* took. Do you remember it *now*?"

His cheeks gained a slight pink hue. "Can't say I do, no."

You're guilty as sin, you fucker, I can smell the fear on you. "There's no log of a visit to Golden Glow *then* either. Can you explain that?"

He let go of his cheek and sat straighter, dropping his hand to his lap. "If I can't remember even getting the call, how can I remember following it up? Come on, you know what it's like. We get so busy, so I probably forgot to deal with it."

"Forgetting or not, you should have put the actual call in your notebook. It should be in your end-of-shift report, but it isn't. I checked. Every incident *must* be logged, you know that, so why wasn't it?"

"I don't know. Like I said, we were busy back then. The DCI had me doing all sorts."

"That segues nicely to my next query, although, if you can't seem to remember anything, I doubt you'll remember this either, but our boss will..." She smiled again. "After I took statements from Oleksiy and Bohuslava, I had a conversation with the DCI. I asked him if he'd read the reports yet and mentioned that I'd flagged it and asked you to let him know they

245

were available to view. He said you'd been sent to investigate something and you possibly forgot. It seems you do a lot of that, forgetting."

"I'd have to go through my reports on that date to see where I went."

"But what if you 'forgot' to log that, too?" She drank some coffee. "Actually, you *did* forget. There's no mention of where you went. I checked the timeline. Sykes was still alive at this point. Is that where you went, to talk to him about Oleksiy's and Bohuslava's statements? Did you need to get everything in order because they'd given me several names of interest? Were you worried they might remember *more* names, like yours and Sykes', and drop you in the shit?"

His cheeks flared brighter. "But that would mean I was in with The Network, and I wasn't."

"Did you take Sykes' place as head bent copper after his death and that was why *you* chose to deal with Mrs Jasper when she phoned because you'd read the notes on the nature of her call and *knew* it was about a refugee in Golden Glow?"

"What are you on about? You've got no basis for these accusations."

She leant forward. "Listen to me, *mate*. Everything about this is fishy, and unless you can suddenly remember what you were doing and can *prove* to me where you went, I'm going with my gut. You're with The Network. You were on the team trying to bring them all in. You knew *exactly* what tactics we were employing and probably warned them so they could go into hiding, which is why the main players are nowhere to be seen. I suspect the big boss didn't give two fucks about the little men and women we did bring in, he was only interested in saving himself and any of his higher-level employees. What did he do, get hold of you once he knew Sykes was dead and offer you his position?"

"With all due respect, this is bullshit."

"Really? Then why do you look like you're itching to get a burner phone out and tell him about this conversation? Then again, would that be wise? He's picked off a few players as it is, and you might be next. He could think you're a liability because your DI has worked out what you've been up to. Said with *all due respect*."

"Look, I fucked up, I'll admit that. I should have followed up Mrs Jasper's call. But that's all I've done. Well, that and forgetting to log things. I'll try harder in future."

"Try harder to what, cover your tracks?"

"Seriously, you're barking up the wrong tree, and I don't appreciate being accused of something that's nothing to do with me. I'm sorry I didn't go to Golden Glow. I'll go now, see what Goldie has to say."

"What's the point? The woman will be long gone by now. And if you don't appreciate me asking you questions, we can always go and visit the DCI now so *he* can ask them. He can bring HR in, I don't mind."

He almost shot out of his chair but thought better of it. "What? No!"

"Why not? If you're innocent, there's nothing to worry about, is there?"

"I'd prefer to keep this between us. I wouldn't want you getting into trouble for falsely accusing me."

She laughed. "Are you for bloody real? Why would I get into trouble for not wanting a pervert refugee shagger on the team?"

"Now hold on a minute, I never shagged them, I just..." His mouth dropped open. "I mean, I... Shit."

She sat back and folded her arms. "So I *was* right, then."

"It wasn't like you think."

"So tell me what it *was* like."

"Sykes roped me into keeping my eyes and ears open. He slipped me a few quid every week."

"How much is a few quid?"

"Five hundred."

"And you didn't wonder how a DI could afford that?"

"Well, yeah, but…" He rubbed his hands down his face. "I didn't know *why* he wanted me to tell him if certain names cropped up in investigations or whatever, just that I had to tell him when they did."

She didn't believe him. This had 'cover story' written all over it.

He rushed on. "When I looked through Oleksiy's and Bohuslava's statements and saw a couple of names he'd mentioned, I told him. I thought he was working on a specific case relating to the names, which was unrelated to The Network, and he needed my help."

"And the five hundred pounds he paid you for it wasn't suspicious at all? Bollocks. If he was running a case, he'd have expected you to do it for *free*. As part of your *job*. Why did you ignore Mrs Jasper's call?"

"Because I was there when she phoned him about it months previously, and he moaned about her afterwards, saying he wasn't going to involve himself with the likes of Goldie because the bloke's a nutter. I didn't want to get involved either so…"

"So you left a Polish woman at the mercy of a 'nutter' based on Sykes's example? Right. Great work there." She let her sarcasm sink into him until he squirmed. "She could be anywhere by now. Buried like the other women. What the hell did you think when it came out that Sykes was in with The Network?"

"I shit myself."

"Why didn't you tell me, once he was dead, what he'd asked you to do?"

"Because I didn't want to get in trouble for helping him. You lot would have thought I was as bad as him."

"You could have redeemed yourself by following up Mrs Jasper's call, sending uniforms to Golden Glow so you didn't have to see Goldie. Or did you go to see him anyway, warning him to get the woman off the premises, and everything you've said to me is just lip service?"

He stared at the floor. "What are you going to do?"

"I don't know yet. You're on desk duty until I decide. For now, if anyone asks, we were talking about your career options. Now get out."

He left the room, and she watched him through the glass partition that separated her from the main area. He slumped on his chair, head in his hands.

Colin Broadly, her DS, got up and came in. He shut the door. "Everything all right?"

"It's fine. Thanks for asking, though. We were just discussing where he wants to go in the job, you know, take the exam for DI, move on to another division or whatever. Keep that under your hat, though, eh?"

"Will do."

He left, returning to his desk, and Janine got up to lean against her closed door. She took her burner out of her pocket and sent a message.

JANINE: MALLARD IS A PART OF IT. GET RID.

GG: WILL DO.

JANINE: SEND SOMEONE TO WATCH GOLDIE'S PLACE IN CASE THE WOMAN'S THERE AND HE TRIES TO GET RID OF HER.

GG: ON IT.

Having The Brothers at her beck and call was as handy as them having her on tap. Now she had to hope they saved the woman before Mallard got hold of Goldie and tipped him off about disposing of her. Sadly, it was out of Janine's control, she couldn't use her powers as an officer now she'd given the twins the green light to kill Mallard. And that poor refugee, assuming she was one, might well end up as collateral damage.

You win some, you lose some.

God, she was sounding more like George every day.

Chapter Twenty-One

"You win some, you lose some, and you've just lost." Adult George stared across the reception desk at the weasel-like man they'd been sent to kneecap for non-payment of protection money.

Power surged through him—he was on his way to being a king, and the heady rush he got from doing this sort of thing for Ron sent his blood hot. He'd already rooted around in the man's past to see if he deserved being hurt this way, to check if Ron was just being an arsehole by ordering the torture, and the news wasn't pretty. Mr Mike Everton gambled, left his wife and kids to go hungry, and spent all his free time up the boozer. It was Richard all over again.

"Please," Mike said, hands up. "Let me just ring my brother, see if he can help me. We're down on takings this week, otherwise I'd have it. People haven't been renewing their memberships after the six months are up."

"What about next week? And the week after that? Will you go to your brother then?" Greg asked. "What is he, loaded?"

"He…he owns a shop, one of them little supermarkets. He does all right."

George glanced around Pro-Fit Gym. Plenty of people worked out, so Mike had been telling porkies. No memberships or not, there was money coming in here. George suspected a lot of it was going out — at the betting shop and into the till at The Eagle.

"You do all right by the looks of things," he said. "You just haven't got business sense like your brother. Too busy dipping your fingers into the pot. Cardigan wants five hundred. Now."

"Okay, okay…" Everton sidestepped behind the reception desk, stretching his hand out towards the phone. "Just…just let me see if Diddy can help." He dialled a number and explained the situation to his brother. "Thank God. Okay, I'll send them round." He dropped the phone into the cradle. "He said to go to his shop. Everton's on Staten Road."

"Right." George knew Diddy. They collected from him, too. He held up a mallet. "We'll be back next week. Make sure you don't lose any bets by the time we're due. Fucking prick. And get help for your addiction. You've got kids, and they deserve a better father than you. Your wife needs looking after, not sending out to work all hours so she can feed your daughters. You're a bastard disgrace."

Angry at how so many men felt they could treat their families this way, everyone else suffering for it bar the blokes, George stomped out of the gym and got into their battered little van they used for jobs.

Greg got in beside him and stabbed the seat belt connector into the hole. "Another Richard."

"That's what I thought. Maybe we should kill Mike like we killed him."

Greg laughed. "Lure him down to the arch and do him some damage. I'm surprised you didn't kneecap him just then regardless of us getting the cash off his brother."

"I will next time he doesn't pay up. I won't give him a second chance again. No money at the time of the visit, no leeway. He knew we were coming. It's the same time every week."

George drove to Staten Road and pulled up in the shop's small car park. They got out, George leading the way, his trusty mallet swinging beside him. He entered the shop, and a few customers gave him wary glances. People around here knew they worked for Ron and shouldn't be messed with, especially when George held a weapon.

He approached the counter. A young blonde woman smiled at him, although it was slightly skewed, and she fiddled with her fingers.

"C-can I help you?" Her cheeks stained red in the middle.

"Where's Diddy?"

"Um, he's in the office. I'll…I'll go and get him for you."

"Nah, we'll go to him."

"But he's busy…"

George didn't give a fuck. He stalked towards a door marked PRIVATE and pushed it open, going into a corridor. Each door had a plaque: TOILET. KITCHEN.

STOREROOM. OFFICE. *He swaggered down to the office and didn't bother knocking, just walked in, much to the surprise of Diddy giving a girl lying on his desk a bit too much below-stairs attention. She shrieked, Diddy stepped back and tucked himself away, and the girl scrabbled off the desk to grab her knickers off the floor and push past George and Greg. She ran up the corridor and into the shop.*

"Screwing the staff?" *George asked.*

"That's none of your business." *Diddy sat behind the desk, rummaging through his hair with a shaking hand.*

"It is my business—our business, Ron's business—if you're fucking someone under sixteen. She looks pretty young to me."

"She was seventeen last week. Listen, I'm all paid up, you know that, so what do you want?"

"Your tone needs some work, mate." *George smiled, although his mind ticked over Diddy asking what they were there for. He should already know. Unless Mike had phoned a dud number, pretending he'd contacted him.* "And you know why we're here." *He waited for Greg to come in then closed the door.* "Your brother phoned you. We've come to collect."

"Which brother? And none of them have got hold of me."

"Mike."

"Err, nope. Not heard from him in a month."

George glanced at Greg: The fucking tosser pulled a fast one.

"So you don't have five hundred nicker handy to pay us, then?" George asked.

"I do as it happens, but I'm not handing it over for Mike. We're all sick of him, the whole family. If he can't control his gambling habit, then he's on his own."

"So you're refusing to pay, is that it?"

Diddy puffed his chest up. "I am. As far as I'm concerned, you can use that mallet on him. He's a loser. The only time I pay anything out on his behalf is for his wife and kids. My missus and his are friends, and I get to hear all sorts."

"Do you see yourself as a loser an' all?"

"Absolutely not."

"I mean, shagging young girls when you're married seems a pretty loser-ish thing to me."

"That's my prerogative and nothing to do with me paying protection money."

"One day, it won't just be your prerogative. When the estate changes hands, things will be different around here. If any residents are upset by another, there'll be ructions." George wouldn't be like Ron and turn a blind eye when it suited him. If ponces like Diddy and Mike were around when they took over, George would be dishing out a lot of lessons.

"Is Ron jacking it all in, then?"

"Not as far as I know, but he won't live forever." George turned to Greg: Back to the gym, then.

Greg nodded and eyed Diddy. "That girl had better be seventeen."

Diddy smirked. "She is."

Greg smiled, appearing pleasant, but he'd grown into his role as Ron's hardman and didn't sit back and let George deal with everything as much anymore. "We'll look into it, and if she's not... Well, you won't be walking on those legs of yours for a while."

They went up the corridor and into the shop. The girl—because as far as George was concerned, 'just seventeen' was still a girl—stacked bread at the end of an aisle opposite the till.

"How old are you?" he asked.

"Seventeen."

"She had a party last week," the blonde behind the counter said.

George leant closer to the girl. "You shouldn't be messing with arseholes like him. Find someone your own age. He's got a wife."

"I know, but..."

George waved off what she was about to say. "Don't tell me, you *love* him. Christ."

He left the shop, gunning the van engine while Greg got in. George didn't feel like talking, he had to process what he'd just seen and heard. Whenever he found out more and more men were like Richard, it took him back to his childhood, which fuelled the flames of his anger and brought the mad side of himself out.

At Pro-Fit, he grabbed his mallet, jumped out, and thundered inside. Mike, the dick, still manned reception, and glanced up at him, his mouth dropping open.

"Didn't he pay up?"

"What does it fucking look like?"

George rounded the desk and advanced on Mike who reversed against the wall. Greg, at George's back, nudged him away so he could stand beside Mike, lean across, and press the tosser's shoulders to the paintwork. George stood on his other side, drew the mallet back, then swung it at Mike's knee. The sickening crunch and Mike's scream of pain had Mad George grinning, and he went beyond the one kneecap Ron had instructed, whacking the other one — twice — then dropping the mallet.

Mike, a gibbering wreck, tears flowing, bottom lip wobbling, mumbled incoherently, his eyes scrunched shut.

"Let him go, bruv," George said. "Go and have a sit down."

Greg moved away to take a seat. Mike dropped to the floor, his lower legs bent at unnatural angles, hands in his hair, gripping, likely trying to direct the immense pain elsewhere.

George felt around in his pocket and brought out a knife. He crouched between Mike's legs and, at the moment Mike opened his eyes, sensing him close, his lips parting so he could plead for mercy, George slid the blade between them.

"Keep nice and still," he said. "We wouldn't want a wonky second smile, would we."

He pressed the blade right to the back, just before where Mike's teeth stopped, then did a flick upwards to the bottom of the earlobes, the slice harder to do as it went through the gum. Mike fainted mid-scream. George had to give the knife a bit of a tug to release it, then he carefully drew it out of the mouth and stared at the blood, the way it poured and poured, filling Mike's gob then spilling out, dribbling down his chin to stain his once-pristine white shirt.

"Fucking hell," Greg said. "Ron didn't ask for that."

"Nope, but we'll agree he doesn't pay for any extras."

"I worry about you, George."

"I know."

George picked up the mallet and stood. He wiped the blade on Mike's shirt and tucked the knife away. Movement to his right had him turning to face a woman customer in front of the reception desk, her blue-eyed gaze captivated by Mike.

"Cardigan's orders," George said. "How can we help you?"

"I-I just came for a session." She clutched the strap of her pink holdall.

"Are you a member?"

"No, I p-pay each time I c-come."

George snatched up a membership card from a pile on the desk and handed it to her, conscious of the blood from his hand smearing it. "You are now. Next time you're here, tell Mike we gave this to you and you're allowed access for life."

She took the card, shivered at the blood on it, and rushed through a doorway marked CHANGING ROOMS. George laughed, holding his stomach, his eyes watering.

"Fuck me, I love this job."

Chapter Twenty-Two

Karen sat in a room in the parlour at the back of The Angel and drank the tea Amaryllis had given her. Nervous, she tapped her foot on the floor. She usually had her emotions under control when it came to the twins. Whenever they'd spoken to her at Jackpot, she'd acted like any other employee, the same when George had come to her flat, although *that* time she'd crapped herself, thinking he'd rumbled them, but she thought she'd hidden it well. Now, she was frightened about the fabricated story she'd be telling them. It would show she'd asked to speak to them as soon as she'd known there would be a robbery, not that she'd known about it right from the start.

It was the only way to keep herself safe, to stop George and Greg from killing her for agreeing to be a part of the heist. The Brothers had explained the rules to everyone at work, that their loyalty was to them and any information they came across must be passed on straight away. If they didn't, it was an act of 'treason' as George had put it, and they'd find themselves with an extra smile and maybe have their kneecaps shattered — that was the best-case scenario. The worst? She didn't want to think about it.

The door opened, and she jumped, spilling some tea on her leggings. She rubbed it in rather than see who'd entered, mainly to get her act together and compose herself for what she was about to say.

At last, she glanced up. The twins seemed to suck all the space out of the room, and she swallowed hard, shaking so much she had to put the cup down on a little table beside her. Door closed, Greg taking a seat on the sofa opposite, George folded his arms and blocked the exit.

"What's all this about, then?" he asked.

She had to be careful here. If she said she'd got a phone call, they'd ask to look at her mobile. If her flat was being watched, they could catch her out—but it was the better option, and at least she'd know whether they were keeping tabs on her. Anyway, you could enter her block via the communal garden at the back, so unless they had someone stationed in the street behind, they'd never know who'd supposedly visited her.

"Someone came to my place earlier," she said.

George's forehead furrowed. "And?"

"He said he'd seen me at Jackpot and had a proposition for me."

His cheeks puffed out. "What proposition?"

"He said he knew I used to live on Golden Eye and that Goldie wants me to do a job for him on a Friday night, but he didn't say which Friday."

George stiffened and let his hands drop by his sides. He clenched them into fists. "What kind of job? And you let him into your *flat*?"

She hugged herself. "I didn't have much choice. He pushed me backwards and forced his way in."

"Fucking cunt. What does he want you to do?"

"Let some men in the back way at Jackpot so they can rob the place. Armed men. He mentioned shotguns."

"You fucking what?" George turned and thumped the door, the strike damaging a panel and creating a jagged hole.

Amaryllis' face appeared in the gap. "Everything all right, George?"

"Yeah. Can you ring the crew and get someone to come here and fix it?" He faced Karen again, hiding the hole. "Sorry. I got a bit arsey there. That Goldie bloke's doing my fucking nut in."

Greg grimaced. "Keep that temper in check." He pinched the bridge of his nose as if exasperated with his brother. "What about this... Maybe Cinnamon was supposed to do it and she refused, and that's why she was shot."

Karen didn't furnish them with the fact she'd wondered if Cinnamon worked for Goldie, too. "What? That poor cow..."

George took a few deep breaths. "What else did he say?"

"He's sending me a burner phone so they can tell me when to open the door. I lied and said we're not allowed phones on the casino floor, and he didn't give a shit, said I'd have to hide it in my bra and have it on vibrate. I told him I couldn't just leave my post, and he suggested I make out I need the loo. There was the promise of money, a share of the cash they plan to nick, and I told him even if I was desperate, I wouldn't do it. And I *am* desperate, I could do with the money, but—"

"—you came to us instead." George nodded, apparently pleased with that. "Why are you desperate? What do you need that kind of money for?"

She told them about Robyn and Cal. "I've been saving for ages, and so have they, but none of us can put much by each month. The NHS appointment will come up before we've even got half. She's in so much pain, she needs that op sooner rather than later, and I'd love for her to go private. She's done so much for me, especially when we were kids, and I owe her."

George and Greg looked at each other for a long time, as if speaking without words. What had she said for them to do that? Was it the part about owing Robyn? Had one of them taken care of the other as they'd been growing up like Robyn had with Karen?

George said, "What about getting a loan?"

"We don't have mortgages to use our homes as collateral, and we've all been refused unsecured loans, including medical ones."

George glanced at Greg who nodded.

"What if we can get the op done?" George asked.

Karen's stomach lurched with excitement. "What? I can't ask you to do that."

He chuckled darkly. "You're not asking, we're offering. And listen, love, you've just saved us losing about a million—or so Goldie thinks."

She lit up inside at the thought of them getting Robyn's op sorted, she wouldn't have to go begging cap in hand to Sienna now, then she frowned, realising what he'd just said. "What do you mean, or so Goldie thinks?"

George looked at Greg again.

Greg took the baton. "If we help your sister, we need your promise that what I tell you next is confidential."

She bobbed her head. She'd do anything to get Robyn on an operating table. Including lying to these two men who had turned into angels. "I promise, I'll keep it to myself."

"I won't repeat what'll happen to you if you break that promise." Greg sat forward. "As you know, we've told all of our employees the takings are kept in the casino all week until Saturday morning for a reason—to root out anyone who'd think of robbing us on a Friday night when the most cash is supposedly on the premises. Seems it worked. There's a fucking mole in the camp, because how else would Goldie know to rob us on a Friday?"

Christ, Goldie will go spare if he knows this. "Oh God, that's awful if someone's a snitch. Other than me and Teddy, is there anyone else at work who used to live on Golden Eye and could work for Goldie?"

Greg shook his head. "Not that we're aware of. How long have you known Teddy?"

She widened her eyes. "You can't think it's *him*. No! I've known him for years. There's no *way* he'd do anything like that. He's so honest it isn't funny, and I'm not just saying that because he's my boyfriend either. He won't even cheat at board games."

Teddy's dream of owning a farm sprang to mind, and she felt so bad for ruining that for him because now he wouldn't be getting any money, but…

"Was he at home when the bloke turned up?" George asked.

"No, he went to see Oakley this morning and won't be back until just before we go to work. The man came right after Teddy walked up the road. I haven't even told Teddy about it yet, I wanted to see you first."

"Good girl." George paced, a finger on his chin. "How do you feel about keeping this from him? And by that, I mean *never* telling him?"

"I don't know. You're not meant to keep secrets from each other when you're getting married…"

"But you'll have to. We've got a delicate situation going on with Goldie ourselves at the minute, and the least amount of people who know about this the better. He's going to go *missing*, do you understand?"

They're going to kill him. "Yes, I get it."

"We don't need every Tom, Dick, and Harry knowing what's really happened, so you *have* to keep your gob shut."

"I will, I swear."

"How do you think Teddy would react if the man approached him?"

"He'd tell him to fuck off like I did. He can't stand Goldie, and neither can I, which is why we left Golden Eye in the first place. The way he runs the estate is rotten."

"And how did it go for you, saying fuck off?"

She winced and forced tears. "The man pushed me against the wall and put a gun to my head. Said I have no choice but to do what Goldie wants otherwise he'll shoot me, Teddy, Oakley, Robyn, and Cal. He knows where they live and that Robyn goes to my old flat sometimes. They've been bloody *watching* me."

"Bastard," Greg muttered.

George took a big sniff of air, maybe so he didn't punch a second hole in the door. "What op does Robyn need?"

"Laparoscopic ovarian drilling."

"Fuck, sounds painful, drilling." George jerked his head at Greg. "Go and get hold of the clinic to arrange it, will you?"

Greg got up and left the room.

"You're *paying* for it?" Karen squeaked.

"Yeah. We'll sort some kind of repayment plan for the three of you later, minus a chunk for you coming to tell us what happened."

"I don't know what to say…"

"Cheers will do. Now then, what does the bloke look like?"

She imagined Bronson, the horrible pig who worked for Goldie. He'd touched her up once in one of the meetings at Golden Glow, before she'd moved to Cardigan. She'd told him to get his hands off her, and he'd kissed her, sticking his tongue in her mouth. She'd reported him to Goldie, but he'd just laughed. What did *she* care if Bronson got a Cheshire or worse?

"Tall, about six feet. Black hair. He has a fat bottom lip, and it was wet." She shuddered, no need to pretend there. The memory of his sloppy kiss barged into her head and brought it all back. The revulsion. The disgust. "Blue eyes, grey flecks. And he's wide, had a black suit on. When he left, he got into a dark car with tinted windows. I think it was an Audi."

"I know who that is. Bronson. Goldie's right-hand man and driver. One of his bodyguards."

"What should I do now, then? There's the burner he's sending, and what if he comes back when Teddy's there?"

"Sounds to me like he waited until Teddy had gone to pay you a visit, so he's not likely to want him knowing about this."

"He did say not to tell anyone, that they'd know if I did. Shit, what if he followed me here?" She paused. "No, I walked and didn't see that car."

"Good. Normally, we'd stick you in a safe house, but that would get Teddy asking questions, plus tip Bronson off that you've blabbed. Unfortunately, you're going to have to ride it out and play the game of doing what he wants, although one of our fellas will sit outside your flat and follow you to work and back. So long as you're useful to Goldie, Bronson won't do anything to you. Not before the robbery anyway. Afterwards, well, that's another thing altogether. Goldie probably plans to off you so you can't tell us anything when we interrogate the staff."

She shuddered at the idea of that, *and* the subterfuge she was indulging in. How cruel she was, to lie to them so she could get what she wanted. Did that mean she was like Dad? Did she have his awful trait of manipulation?

Greg came back in. "We get reduced rates at the clinic, so it'll cost two grand. Elsewhere, you'd be looking at a starting cost of nearly four, plus the aftercare on top, but I imagine you've researched that and already know. She needs a pre-op consultation first, which is three hundred. It's been booked for tonight."

Karen's heart leapt. "So soon?"

"It's a private clinic," Greg said. "They don't fuck about. If all goes well, she'll have the actual op tomorrow. I'll text you the address and time for this evening." He took his phone out and prodded the screen.

"I…" Karen's gratitude eclipsed the lies she'd told, and she cried, the tears hot and fast. "I… Thank you."

"Don't be daft," George said. "We should be thanking *you*."

That piled the guilt on even more.

Her phone blipped, and she ignored it, thinking it'd be Greg. Then it blipped again.

Shit, what if it's Goldie?

"Aren't you going to check that?" Greg asked. "I only sent one message."

Karen swallowed. She had Goldie's name down as Paula, but the content might not be anything like what a Paula would say. What if the twins came close and read it?

Shaking, she took her phone from her bag and stared at the screen.

ROBYN: I'LL BE AT YOUR OLD FLAT TONIGHT. HAD ANOTHER ROW WITH CAL. I SWEAR, MY HORMONES WILL END THIS MARRIAGE. I'M SO SCARED OF LOSING HIM.

She held the mobile up for them to read it. "Can I tell her?"

George nodded. "Fill your boots."

She wrote back: OPERATION'S SET. YOU NEED TO GO TO THIS CLINIC. I'LL SEND YOU THE DETAILS IN A SEC. THE BROTHERS ARE PAYING FOR IT. DON'T ASK... WILL EXPLAIN LATER.

That should stop Robyn from replying with anything about Goldie, shouldn't it?

ROBYN: WHAT? OMG! THANK YOU!

"She says thank you." Karen switched her phone off discreetly and dropped it in her bag. She couldn't take the risk that her sister wouldn't accidently drop her in it with another message.

"Right then," George said on a sigh. "We need to discuss how you're going to behave and what

277

the next steps are. You're going to open that door at Jackpot exactly when they tell you to, got it?"

George had called Moon and Tick-Tock for an immediate meeting. He drove towards The Dog and Flea on Moon's estate where they'd hash out the details of how to deal with heist night. Karen had said it would be on a Friday but not which one. George would bet it was *this* Friday. Today was Tuesday, and Bronson's visit had been timed so they got her on board, gave her a couple of days to get used to being involved—or to bolt so they could find someone else in time—then it was the robbery. Any more days than that and they risked her caving in and telling someone, which would fuck their plot up.

"I got Rowan to check the Jackpot personnel file about Teddy, by the way," Greg said.

"And?"

"It's down as him living in Moorgate Street at the start of his employment, then it changes to Diamond Road."

"Good, so they definitely weren't lying." Pleased he'd read the pair of them right, George said, "Are you going to tell me I'm going soft by offering that op to Karen's sister?"

"With everything totted up, the op and aftercare, we're talking four grand. It's a hefty whack compared to what we'd pay her for information, which would be about five hundred to a grand..."

"But if the heist had gone ahead and they'd managed to get their hands on our Friday-night dosh, they'd have got away with *more* than the clinic is charging us, so this way we haven't lost much. We have a shit ton of cash in the safe at the end of each night, just not the amount Goldie thinks. Take five hundred off for Karen coming to us, we split the three and a half grand between her, Robyn, and Cal, and give them a couple of years to pay it off, seeing as they're all struggling financially. Actually, because Karen's our resident and employee and she's stupidly forking out for that second flat, she can work off her repayments by being our ears, not just in Jackpot but elsewhere."

"Fine by me."

George swerved into the car park at the pub and went round the back. Tick-Tock's SUV was there, as was Moon's new sleek sports car he'd bought to impress his bird, Debbie. They'd be steaming when he told them what Goldie had planned. He'd have a hard job convincing them not to go out and blow his fucking head off.

Chapter Twenty-Three

Night had been a long time coming, the day dragging on, Goldie's thoughts centred on getting rid of Zofia tonight so she wasn't on his mind in the coming days when he had to concentrate on the heist. He'd phoned Bronson so he was on standby, ready to come to the house once Goldie gave him the go-ahead. Bronson only lived around the corner in the next cul-de-sac, so he was on hand at a moment's notice, albeit living in a smaller, cheaper pad, as it should be.

Before his right-hand man arrived, a murder had to take place, and Goldie stood in his living room, gearing himself up for it. He hadn't been up to see Zofia since he'd left her this morning. Couldn't face seeing her smirking mug or hear her berate him for breaking one of his own rules.

"You fell asleep," she'd say. "You are pathetic man. Weak."

Excuse me, but why *haven't I killed her before now?*

Disappointment in Zofia had been the driving factor in him keeping her alive. He'd wanted to break her into complying, to prove *he* was the one pulling the strings, not her, but she'd been with him long enough now to have succumbed even a smidgen to Stockholm Syndrome, yet she'd pushed against it all the way. She was stronger of mind than he'd given her credit for, and no amount of manipulation and cruelty on his part had broken her.

She deserves to die just for that.

He went up to the next level and spied through the shutter camera out the front. Last night and tonight, Marleigh's bedroom light hadn't been on, *at all*, and that was unusual. She'd had lights on elsewhere in the house, so she was home — ah, but when they were both away, she used a timer to give that impression. Had she joined David on one of his work trips? She'd mentioned many moons ago she sometimes did that. He hadn't seen her going out, though, but then again, that didn't mean anything. He hadn't exactly been spying out there twenty-four hours a day, had he, nor had he been listening for cars coming along, except when he expected Bronson or to see if the twins had sent someone to watch his house.

Shame she wasn't in, he could have done with one of her little strip tease displays to get his anger level up. Did she know he watched her? Or did she think she was safe because of the shutters? Was she teasing someone else? Having an affair with the bloke next door to Goldie? What was his name? Charles or something. Her doing a sexy dance would have served to fuel the fire because it'd show Goldie how useless Zofia really was. How *she* should be at the stage of willingly stripping for him instead of him forcing her to do it.

That did it. The one thought that always tormented him, over and over, lit the touchpaper, and he stormed to the third level, stopping at the bottom of the bed, staring at where Zofia stood, naked, in front of the bookcase. She'd never get to read any of those novels now, their stories forever withheld from her as she rotted in a cold, dark grave, maggots feasting on her.

Slag. Useless whore. A waste of good money.

She turned, glared at him, then gave her attention to the shelf as if he was of no importance, an annoying insect who refused to stop buzzing.

Of all the cheeky cows!

Anger flared, bright and piercing and all-consuming and so fucking *argh*. He lunged towards her, gripping the back of her hair and dragging her across to throw her on the bed. She bounced on the mattress, the chain tinkling, and for once the sound didn't grate on his nerves—he loved it tonight, how it rammed it home that she was stuck up here, unable to get away. Caged, like she deserved to be. She should be subservient, desperate to please him, but the obstinate bitch had shown she was feistier than anyone he knew.

She clawed at his neck, her nails raking his skin. The sharp streaks of pain angered him further, and he planted himself on top of her to stop the slag from moving.

"Keep still!" he shouted, spit flying. "Now!"

She must know this was the night she'd be put in that rolled-up carpet, that this was the end of the line and all her dreams of going home were gone. She ignored him, writhing and trying to fend him off. He pushed to a sitting position, batting her hands away, straddling her, a big fight on his hands as he tried to pin one arm by her side so he could kneel on it. The strength in that arm surprised him; she pulled it towards her when he yanked it towards him and, like a game of arm wrestling, they fought for superiority. At the same time, she slapped his head and face with her free hand, calling him names, and he lost it. Who the *hell* did she think she was? Two quick punches to her face had her resistance fading, and he took that moment to trap her hand down. Her other one now covered her face, blood seeping between the fingers. He snatched the wrist, wrenched her arm in place, and knelt on that one, too, putting his weight on it for maximum discomfort.

She stared up at him, both of them breathing heavily through their mouths, sand-grain speckles of blood misting the air with each of her exhalations, landing on her chin, miniature freckles. He'd broken her tooth, and the gap in her usually perfect smile churned his guts. Unattractive to him now, she continued to stare into his eyes, likely cursing him in her head, wishing she'd never left Poland and met the likes of him. For someone who was so clearly clever, she'd been thick as pig shit to believe the scouts when they'd offered her a way out of Poland.

She drummed her heels on the bed behind him, jostling him, annoying him, and opened her mouth to scream. He planted his fist in it, one of her teeth sinking into a knuckle. It didn't draw blood, but what if his skin was on her teeth?

"Shut your pissing ugly gob, woman."

She choked on blood, and he hit her several more times about the head. She quieted, stopped trying to get away, and went still, chest rising and falling slower than previously. It could be a trick, this display of being either tired of fighting or in pain from his blows, but he took the chance anyway and got off her, positioning her on one side of the bed and securing her wrists to the iron headboard.

He left her there to go into his bathroom on the lower level and get a bottle of bleach, a toothbrush, and a tool he used to get bits of food out from between his molars. Upstairs he went and squirted the bleach in her mouth, on her teeth, brushing them. She heaved and coughed from the fumes, the taste, and turned her head to spit the fluid out, gagging so much she was sick on the sheet. Unable to stand looking at her, seeing that vomit, he dug the tool beneath her fingernails, cleaning them of any skin that might be there where she'd scratched him. He went downstairs to put the bleach and toothbrush in his sink for sorting later, then rushed down the next flight to prepare the poker. Fuck asking Bronson to burn last night's DNA away, he'd do it himself.

In the living room, he plunged the poker from the ornamental cast-iron companion set into his wood-burning stove, then had an evil idea and added the shovel and tongs. He paced to give them time to heat up, thinking of the three journeys he'd have to make upstairs with each piece to mete out his torture. No, it wouldn't work, she'd have to come down here so the tools remained at their hottest.

Back on the third floor, he uncuffed her, leaving them dangling on her wrists, and manhandled her to the top of the stairs.

"What are you doing?" She sounded raspy, as if the bleach had got into her throat and made it sore, burning her. She dug her toes into the floor as if that would stop him from taking her down. As if she still had *power*.

"What I should have done after you stood at the window in Golden Glow, you stupid little cow. When you tried to get help."

He forced her down the two flights of stairs, struggling at times and almost going arse over tit because she went rigid and refused to go with him. He'd have pushed her down the steps but didn't want to risk her dying before she had the chance to suffer. And God, did he want her to suffer.

In the living room, he thrust her to the floor and kicked her in the gut so the pain took her mind off escaping. He pulled her by the ankles to his heavy armchair that had wooden legs and cuffed her to them. She could kick if she had a mind, but he stood to the side of her, in front of the fire, and she wouldn't be able to reach him. He took the tongs out of the flames and bent over, clamping a nipple with the fiery-hot end. She screamed, her teeth bared, then her scream went silent and her eyes closed. He let the tongs go so they fell wherever they would, the heat of the handle scoring a red line on her stomach, her nipple all but scorched off and hanging. She bucked and jolted, arms tugging at the cuffs, the chair shunting forward to cover her head. He needed that head visible, so he pushed the chair back, grabbed the shovel, and pressed the back of the scoop end onto her cheek and over an eye.

Her skin sizzled, and he stared in fascination at her body spasming. Either she was having a fit or it was a reaction to the heat. Whatever the reason, he didn't give a shit, he just needed her concentrating on *that* pain before he administered more.

He tossed the shovel onto the hearth, wrenched her legs apart, and knelt between them. "Now *this* is going to *fucking* hurt." Leaning across, he removed the poker and, bending his head to get a better look at where he had to aim, he thrust it forward, into her.

She made a noise he'd never heard before, not even when he'd tortured people in the past. The three points of pain, the newest one so much hotter as the poker had been in the flames for longer, and she was a jabbering mess. He wrenched the poker out, heated it for a few more seconds, then drove it into her again. Higher. Past a wall of resistance.

Blood gushed, her pelvis rising, her arse thudding back down. Once again, she spasmed, then stilled, but she breathed. She was holding on, as stubborn as ever, maybe telling herself she could get through this, escape, then she wouldn't end up in a carpet shroud. Her eyes closed, her face burnt on one side from the shovel, and she lay perfectly still.

The tongs had slipped off her stomach and onto the floor. He tossed them on the hearth, did the same with the poker, and watched a river of red seep from between her legs. Even if he were to keep her alive, she'd be ruined now. No children in her future, no playing happy families with him, which was how it was *supposed* to be. She only had herself to blame. *She'd* done this with her refusal to comply, not him.

Would the internal burning be enough to get rid of his DNA?

He left her there to collect some tea towels from the kitchen. He placed them under her arse to soak up the blood flow—he'd have to get someone in to clean the polished floorboards if the red stuff had seeped through and ruined them. No one would want to buy the gaff with a ruddy great bloodstain in full view, not to mention there'd be questions as to how it had got there.

Fuck's sake, Zofia really had messed things up.

He wanted her lucid when he killed her so was prepared to wait for a while, but not too long. The cover of darkness was important when he and Bronson got rid of her, and waiting until tomorrow night to dump her wasn't an option. He didn't fancy a dead woman in his house all that time, thanks very much.

She slept.

He made a ham and Branston pickle sandwich and a cup of tea, sitting at the kitchen island to contemplate his next moves. Tomorrow, Wednesday, he'd sleep a lot to catch up on what he'd be missing tonight. Thursday was him going over the plans with a fine-tooth comb, then Friday was D-Day.

An hour had passed. A groan came from the living room, so he nipped in there to see what her problem was. Ah, it was just the pain upon waking, and she sobbed quietly. The presence of more blood annoyed him. It had soaked through the tea towels and spread further on the floor. Jesus, he'd be better off having that section replaced now.

Enough was enough. He sat on her sore stomach, laughing at how his jeans would aggravate the burn, and wrapped his hands around her neck.

"You know, it could have been so different. You could have had everything you wanted if you'd just behaved yourself. Now look. You're about to die, and nobody you care about is going to know anything about it. Maybe they already think you're dead, what with having no contact for so long."

He squeezed, her good eye bulging, the other almost shut where it had fused together from the heat. Her tongue popped out, part of it fitting into the gap where her tooth had been, and with no energy to fight him, she let him kill her.

Let him.

It hadn't been as satisfying as he'd imagined. He'd wanted her to fight, not lie there like some limp bitch. It was a kick in the nuts that she gave in to him now, she allowed him to have his way. Welcomed it, almost. Too late. Way too fucking late to behave how he'd always wanted.

He stood, couldn't stand to look at her, and went off to collect the old rug he'd stored upright in the cupboard under the stairs. He hefted it into the living room and laid it out in a clean section, then messaged Bronson. They'd lift her onto it together; there was no sense in Goldie struggling to do it alone.

He returned to the cupboard and removed thick plastic sheeting, rolling it over the rug then using his penknife to cut it to size. The plastic immediately curled back into a tube, so he grabbed a few books off the shelf and piled them in each corner to keep it down. In the kitchen, he filled a bucket with hot soapy water and took that and the mop into the living room. He'd use it to clean the floor once she'd been moved.

His phone beeped.

BRONSON: OUTSIDE, BOSS.

GOLDIE: I NEED YOU IN HERE.

Let the disposal begin.

Chapter Twenty-Four

George and Greg sat at Francine's table in her kitchen. Every so often, they came here to see her. Each week, they dropped two hundred quid round to her. If they couldn't bring it in person, being too busy with Ron, George arranged for a messenger to deliver it. Francine was like a second mum, and they owed her for looking out for their mother all these years. They

earnt well over the odds, what with Ron's payments plus they moonlighted for other people who needed someone beaten up or whatever, so they had spare cash. More than Greg had ever thought they'd earn, but George wanted more—and he'd get it one day.

He opened a packet of custard creams Francine had placed on the table for him. She knew he liked them, and she'd also bought bourbons for Greg.

"There's something I wanted to ask." It had been bothering George since he'd been a kid. "Why, when Ron's name was mentioned, did you and Mum go all weird?"

"What do you mean?"

"You used to always whisper, looking worried."

"Oh, everyone's like that where Ron's concerned."

"So it's nothing specific?"

"No, of course not!"

"How's Gail?"

Francine jumped. "What's she got to do with anything?"

"Blimey, just asking. We haven't seen her for a while, that's all."

"She's fine."

Something told George there was more going on here.

And he planned to find out what it was.

Chapter Twenty-Five

The twins had been right. In Marleigh's front bedroom, Ichabod stared through his night-vision binoculars, his stomach going over. Goldie and a big black-haired fella carried a roll of carpet through the gates, paused to check the cul-de-sac, and put what was clearly a body in a rug into the back of the Audi that had turned up an hour ago.

Thankful Marleigh was in the bath, Ichabod grabbed his backpack and moved across the room to tap on the en suite door. "They're leavin', so I have tae go. I'll be back, though."

"Okay, don't forget the key I put on the windowsill. The alarm code is five-nine-six-one—I expect I'll be in bed when you get back."

"Cheers."

He returned to the window, snatched the keys up, and put them in his pocket, repeating the alarm code over and over. A quick glance through the binoculars to check the status—the men were getting into the car—and he left the room, made his way to the garage, and pressed the button to raise the door. He got in his vehicle and listened for the sound of them driving off, then he followed.

On the way into the countryside, he kept back enough that they'd think he was just another driver on his way home from a night out. As soon as the Audi's indicator lights blinked to go into Daffodil Woods, he went left into a turning several meters behind them. He parked on the verge and switched off his headlamps, the spears of brightness from theirs bobbing as they drove farther into the trees. They'd hadn't taken one of the many left or right forks, going straight.

Gloves on, he trekked over the field, keeping close to the hedges at the verge so he didn't stand out in the moonlight. Walking through the woods proved problematic—twigs snapped underfoot, and several times he disturbed wildlife, sending the creatures running to safety. Goldie and that bloke might take the noise as animals, not a person, but Ichabod remained vigilant as to where he put his feet the closer he got to them.

Now, having crept as quietly as he could to where the Audi was parked, the light of a big torch on the bonnet splashing on the two men, Ichabod stood behind a wide tree and observed. They already had the makings of an extremely shallow grave in the time it had taken him to get here, but it would need to be much deeper than that. That would take hours if they were going six feet down, so he prepared himself for a long wait.

"Fuck this," the unknown man said.

"Put your back into it, Bronson. I can't do it by myself, for fuck's sake! If it wasn't for you going against my idea of burning her, we wouldn't have to go so deep."

"The light would attract people's attention, I told you that."

"Jesus, we'd be unlucky to have anyone else around at this time of night."

"There was that car on the way here."

Goldie tsked. "We could at least burn the bit of her that will get me in trouble. Dig downwards rather than lengthways for a while so we have a pit deep enough to hide most of the flames. I only need her fanny burnt again."

"That means chopping her up."

"So? It's what you're paid for!"

Bronson huffed and left Goldie to dig while he poked in the boot and brought out an axe. Ichabod knew how this sort of shit went down, he'd been involved in it in the past, but viewing someone else doing it, and to an innocent woman at that, churned his stomach. Bronson whacked the axe into a nearby tree trunk, leaving it stuck there, then helped Goldie go deeper into the earth.

"Good job we've had a lot of rain, that's all I can say," Bronson grumbled.

The earth would be looser, true, but they could leave footprints for Janine to find. It'd help with her investigation once Ichabod let her know the body was here, but the twins didn't want evidence like that left behind. They planned to kill Goldie, and if the coppers had any inkling this had been him before Friday, he could be arrested, and if not, there would be questions as to him going 'missing'.

George had messaged him earlier with instructions on what to do, and Ichabod patted his pocket to make sure the items were still in a sandwich bag in his pocket. Marleigh had put gloves on to go and buy a new notebook, pen, and a box of bags with cash earlier so it couldn't be traced back to anything in her house. Not that he thought for one minute Janine would ever go to Marleigh's, but there was a chance she'd have to question Goldie's neighbours if some bright spark twigged the murder was his doing. It was best all round to cover Marleigh's back, so she'd burnt the rest of the bags and the notebook in her fireplace.

A sharp wind blew between the trees and whipped up forest debris, sending it spinning in a mini tornado then releasing its hold so it landed gently in the greenery.

Goldie stopped digging. "Someone just walked over my grave."

"It's called the wind getting under your coat," Bronson said. "I just had the same thing happen."

An hour passed, or what Ichabod had estimated was an hour, and Goldie declared the middle of the hole deep enough to put the pelvis in.

"If you look at the depth of the sides, once the first flare-up dies down, the flames won't be seen." Goldie speared the shovel into a shallow end farther along, circled his hips, and stretched out his back. "Hard work, that. Come on, we'll go and get her."

The pair returned to the Audi and hauled the carpet out. They placed it beside the hole, and Bronson unrolled it.

Christ alive, the state of her...

Goldie folded his arms to observe.

Bronson wrenched the axe out of the tree and walked back to the body. The poor cow was a mess. What appeared to be burns had ruined one side of her face, and an angry line across her stomach had scored pretty deep. It was the sight between her legs that almost had Ichabod retching. Blood coated the area, including her inner thighs, and whatever had been done to her private parts was brutal and unnecessary.

Bronson swung the axe behind him and brought it down. It embedded just below her belly button, and on the upswing, Ichabod judged that she'd been dead for a while as not much blood sprayed off the blade. It had already begun the coagulation process, so it was more like thick gloop than free-running claret. Bronson hacked on until he'd separated the bottom half from the top, then he got to work on the legs.

Ichabod turned away, partly because this was a scene out of a nightmare but also to check for anyone coming. With the torch being on—*feckin' stupid tae do that*—someone might come along to investigate, and he didn't want to be caught here.

"That axe is the business," Goldie said. "It's cut the fuckers clean off."

Ichabod gave the chop scene his full attention. Bronson had picked the pelvis up and placed it in the hole so the lower half faced upwards, her private parts on show. He tromped to the car, took a towel and a petrol can out of the boot, then doused the body part with it. He chucked the towel in, soaked that with petrol, then, taking a box of matches out of his jacket pocket, he struck several at once in a bunch and threw it into the hole. The resulting whoosh of flaming tongues writhed high then settled down, but they still peeped over the edge.

"Shit." Bronson put the can back. "Didn't consider the smoke either."

"No one will see it in the dark," Goldie said.

He got on with digging to one side of the deeper centre. Bronson chopped a leg into smaller chunks and threw the top parts, that had been closest to the woman's vagina, into the fire.

Burning DNA evidence...

Ichabod had to admit, they were covering their tracks well. Or Goldie's, as he was the one likely to have had sex with her. Bronson repeated his actions with the second leg, then hewed at the remaining torso until it was in smaller chunks. This took a while—the axe was bloody sharp, but hacking through a body wasn't as easy as it sounded. The plastic on top of the rug had split in several places from each downward stroke, the carpet beneath the same, and even if they took those with them, the police would work out what had occurred—there'd be marks in the ground. Ichabod had been told to give Janine a heads-up anyway so she could make suggestions during her initial sighting of the scene and get the investigation moving to a conclusion quicker.

Who knew how many hours had passed by the time enough holes had been dug to hide all the body slices. Only the head and neck remained, and Bronson cleaved her face in half down the middle, three chops, each side falling away so the dead eyes stared left and right.

"So she *did* have a brain, then," Goldie said, staring at it. "Shame she didn't use it to her advantage."

"I warned you she wasn't the right type." Bronson grabbed some of her hair and slung one half of her face into a hole. "But would you listen?"

Goldie shrugged. "We're all entitled to make mistakes. Granted, she was a big one, but the stubborn Miss Zofia Kowalczyk didn't get what she wanted in the end—a one-way ticket back to Poland. She begged me enough for it, but fuck that, she was my property, so why should I let her go?"

"You should have got rid of her yonks ago. Or better yet, you shouldn't have bought her in the first place." Bronson lobbed the other half of the face into the hole with its twin. "And there's no chance of you getting a replacement, not now The

307

Network's stopped bringing new ones in until the heat dies down."

"There's plenty more fish in the sea. Besides, I reckon I can be celibate for a few months."

"Don't make me laugh. You, not getting your end away on the regular? I'll warn the others we've got tantrums coming our way cos you'll have blue balls."

They laughed and covered up the remains, suffocating the fire and stamping the earth down. Bronson found a branch and windscreen-wipered it across the grave so it erased their boot prints. Goldie snatched up handfuls of greenery to make it look like it was a carpet of foliage like it had been before they'd started. Ichabod shook his head. If they'd have cut the top layer like turf, they could have laid it back down and patched it together, no one any the wiser.

Bronson put the shovels and axe onto the middle of the plastic sheeting, folded them up inside, and carried the rug parcel to the boot. He pulled out a roll of black bags, big enough to line a wheelie bin, and Goldie opened one up so the carpet could be dropped inside. With another bag on the other end, the torch lobbed in the boot, they were done.

In the darkness, Ichabod stared at the patch of ground where the carpet had been. The greenery had flattened, and he waited for either of them to notice so they could fluff it up again. They didn't, instead getting in the car. From what Ichabod could make out from the internal light being on, Goldie poured a hot drink from a Thermos.

They were having a feckin' *brew*?

Whatever their reasons for taking the risk of staying here, Ichabod took it as a win. He pulled the sandwich bag from his pocket and removed the pen and paper. Leaning the paper against a tree, he wrote a few words.

Paper back in the bag, the pen in his pocket, he waited for them to sod off.

A while later, Bronson reversed, and Ichabod stayed where he was for the count of five minutes. Sure they weren't coming back, he stepped out from behind the tree and approached the grave. Sourcing a sharp stick, he placed the bag on the burial site and speared the stick through the corner of the bag so it wouldn't blow away.

"God rest ye soul, ye poor feckin' cow," he muttered and ran back to his car. Inside, still

309

jittery from what he'd witnessed, he sent a message to the twins, then one to Janine.

ICHABOD: TOO MUCH TO TELL YOU IN A MESSAGE. CAN YOU TALK?

JANINE: WELL, YEAH, I'M IN BED!

He rang her.

"What have you got for me?" Janine asked.

He related everything he'd witnessed, including where each section of the body was and that they were in pieces. He mentioned where they'd chopped her up and that despite there being a plastic liner on the carpet, fibres and any of Goldie's hairs may have transferred to the body or onto the ground through the slits the axe had made.

"The twins don't want it pointin' back tae Goldie, so if any fibres that are found can meet a dead end for now…"

"I'll try. Can't promise anything, though. His DNA is already on the database from when he was arrested in the past, so a match might crop up. I can't hide that. When are they getting rid of him?"

"Likely Friday night."

"It'll take a while for forensics to sift through all that lot, so we should be safe. Then, if by any stroke of luck his DNA is on that rug, a hair, whatever, when we go to his place, he won't be there. It'll be put down to him disappearing after murdering her, so I should be able to tie this up in a neat bow."

"I tell ye, what I witnessed goin' on in them woods would give ye nightmares. She's been burnt. Was wrecked down below."

"Jesus. I'd better get on, make out I got yet another anonymous call. I take it you've used a throwaway phone to ring me?"

"I wasn't born yesterday, ye eejit."

Ichabod pressed the red button, switched the mobile off, and slipped it in his pocket. He'd dispose of the SIM on his way back to Goldie's street. His part in this was far from done, though. He drove back to Marleigh's, parked in the garage, and left his muddy shoes in the passenger footwell so he didn't traipse it into her house. He let himself in via the connecting kitchen door. The alarm didn't go off, and he was surprised she hadn't gone to bed like she'd said she would.

She sat at the window in her bedroom, staring at Goldie's place between a crack in the curtains.

"I thought ye'd be in bed," he said, taking his seat and lifting his night-visions from his backpack.

"I couldn't sleep and wanted to see when he came back."

"Not long ago, I'd wager."

"No. That man didn't stay with him."

The black bags containing the rug came to mind. "Did Goldie take anything inside with him?"

"No."

Bronson must be getting rid of it. "Right."

"Where did they go?" she asked.

He contemplated not telling her, making out they'd gone to a club. She hadn't been in the bath when Bronson had arrived, but she had when the body had been brought out. She could be left blissfully unaware, but she'd worried so much about the Polish woman, and he'd promised to let her know what had happened to her.

"They killed her." His delivery could have been better, but it was out now. "Took her to the woods in a rolled-up carpet. Buried her."

"What?" In the moonlight coming through the slit, tears shone on her cheeks. "Oh no. I thought... I wished..."

"I know. I've told the police, but it's a delicate situation, because apart from their dodgy copper, they'll never know who murdered her, do ye understand?"

"The twins are dealing with it."

"They are."

"Then I hope they don't go easy on him. He deserves everything coming to him."

Ichabod couldn't agree more, but for now, Goldie would continue to walk the earth until the heist attempt was thwarted. After that, all bets were off.

Chapter Twenty-Six

At four a.m., bright lights set up to illuminate the scene, Janine stood in Daffodil Woods with DS Colin Broadly on one side and Sheila Sutton, the scene manager, on the other. Jim Trafford, the pathologist, crouched in front of them by a hole containing two halves of a head that had carefully been unearthed over the course

315

of the past hour and a half. It would take some time to dig up the rest. All of the foliage and soil needed to be removed painstakingly slowly and placed in evidence boxes. It was Janine's 'guess' on where to start that had yielded the head, based on Ichabod's precise instructions.

Two other officers concentrated on a small patch to one side, which Ichabod had said contained the chopped-up arms. When he'd told her the Polish woman was dead, she'd wanted to cry. How cruel fate was to twice tempt Marleigh into phoning the police, only for the refugee to end up dead anyway because Sykes and Mallard had been too intent on ignoring her calls so perverts could get away scot-free. Going by when Marleigh had first spotted her in Golden Glow, the captive had been held by Goldie for ages. What had she endured during that time?

Had Mallard contacted Goldie to let him know he had to get rid of her as soon as possible because Janine was sniffing around? Or had Mallard told the truth regarding why he'd been involved with The Network—just to pass information to Sykes? Or, was he in this up to his armpits, but because Janine was onto him, he'd decided not to phone Goldie and the removal of the body was a coincidence?

Regardless, and to cover all angles, Mallard was being killed anyway. When, she didn't know, and it was best she wasn't aware of the time or day. That way her shock at the DCI telling them his body had been discovered—if it even was—would be a genuine response. The twins might do their usual and saw him up, put him in the Thames, but knowing George, he'd want The Network to know Mallard was dead and that someone knew who he'd worked for.

Janine stared at the sandwich bag with the piece of paper inside it that had been secured to the ground with a stick. An officer held it inside an evidence bag and perhaps studied the handwriting. The words, ZOFIA KOWALCZYK FROM POLAND, were wobbly from where Ichabod had written them against a tree, and it was obvious he'd penned it in the dark.

Already, two members of Janine's team had been called into the station to find out where Zofia had lived in Poland and whether she had any family who needed to be informed. She'd bet the story they had to tell was similar to the other rescued refugees—she'd been enticed here for a better life by Network scouts posing as people who wanted to help.

The officers working on the mound paused, one of them using a tool to move the last bits of earth away from a hand, the fingers curled almost into a fist, indicating she'd perhaps clenched them while being killed. Stripes, from handcuffs maybe, ringed the wrist.

Jim glanced over, pausing his visual examination of the pieces of head. "Going by that hand posturing and the marks around the neck, she was likely strangled. Sadly, the hyoid bone has been destroyed, and I can't tell just yet whether it's from the cut down the middle or throttling. I'll know more when I get her on the table. A sad state of affairs all round. She went through the mill prior to death. Something, I suspect metal, had been heated and placed on one side of her face. If you look closely, you can see the shape of it in the burn, rounded at the bottom on the cheek, straight on the top below the eyebrow—or what's left of the eyebrow. The lower hairs have been all but singed away."

Janine didn't want to take a 'closer look'. She wanted to find Zofia's family and let them know she'd been found. The sad part was, her body was evidence, and it wouldn't be released for a long time. If Goldie's DNA was discovered, and with him going 'missing', who knew how many weeks or months Zofia would be kept in storage. The Kowalczyks would have to wait to have her shipped over for burial, drawing out their torment for longer. Still, if it turned out the police had to search his house, him missing or not, if she'd been killed there, evidence would be found, pointing to him.

She viewed the rest of the scene. SOCOs searched the area, putting bits and bobs into evidence bags. There would be hundreds of them, all needing to be checked, stretching the time out even more. Markers had been placed where Ichabod had said the carpet was, and two women in white suits were busy searching for fibres, something, anything. A cut in a nearby tree had already been spotted, Sheila saying how pleased she was about that because it was obviously from an axe and it would give forensics a clearer guide as to the length and thickness of the blade, the make, and then Janine's team could try to find where it had been purchased and who by, a painstaking task. The tree trunk would be swabbed in case any DNA had been on it prior to the axe being whacked into the bark.

So much to do here and at the station, in the labs during the coming days. Janine and Colin were just getting in the way here if they stayed. They'd be better off back at the station. Colin wouldn't want to be here anyway, he was a few years from retirement and only wanted minimal effort on his part, something Janine didn't mind as it meant she could work for the twins freely without him looking over her shoulder or questioning her.

"Come on," she said. "The DCs might be close to finding the family. We'd best get back."

Colin sighed his relief, and Sheila nodded.

Janine bade them all goodbye and walked to the cordon to remove her protective clothing, Colin doing the same. They placed them in bags for the log officer to deal with and signed out.

In the car, she leant her head back and closed her eyes. Prayed any DNA wouldn't be matched until after Friday because she didn't want to be the one to apprehend Goldie, The Brothers should be doing it. And although she shouldn't, she hoped the pelvis had been burnt so badly there was no evidence left. Goldie didn't deserve the luxury of prison, and she wanted him dead for what he'd done.

Not exactly good police behaviour, but she wasn't good, not all the time.

Sometimes she was just as bad as the twins.

Chapter Twenty-Seven

*R*on stared at George from behind the desk in his office. *"When I send for you, you come. I don't care whether you have other jobs you're doing, I'm your priority."*

George stared back. *"If you paid us what we'd be missing if we didn't do other jobs, then maybe you could dish out orders, but you don't, so..."*

Ron studied him, bald head cocked. "You're a bit too gobby for my liking, son."

"Like I said before, I'm not your son. I don't dance to anyone's tune, not anymore. Those days are long gone with Richard being dead."

Ron nodded. Smiled. "A chip off the old block."

George's hackles rose. "Are you saying I'm like Richard?"

Ron laughed. "Fuck, no."

"Then what did you mean?"

"Forget I said anything."

George glanced at Sam. The bloke appeared confused by his boss' words, his forehead scrunched in concentration.

"No, explain what you meant," George said.

Greg cleared his throat, a warning for George to stop pushing, but George bowed to no man, even if his name was Ron Cardigan.

Ron tapped his fingertips on the desk. "You're like your mother, that's all I meant. Don't get your knickers in a twist. Now, back to the reason we're here. You're saying I'd have to pay you a retainer, is that it, then cash on top for each job you do?"

"That's about the sum of it, but I'd prefer to do other jobs for other people just the same. It's business, you know how it is. If we're not available to do something for you, then you'll have to use your other heavies."

"But no one scares people like you two, George. I'd be a fool to use someone else."

"Then you'll just have to wait until we can do your jobs, won't you."

Ron eyed him as if proud. "You turned out well. I should have known you would, really. Ever since you were little you've been a nutter. I could say you learnt from the master, seeing as you both followed me and Sam around, watching."

"Think whatever you like."

"Why did you follow us?"

George didn't know, he'd been drawn to Cardigan and wasn't sure why. He wasn't about to tell him that, nor that he'd been fascinated by leaders ever since Mum had explained what they were and what they did. "Dunno. I'm just a nosy little cunt."

Ron laughed. "That's my boy."

George inhaled. Maybe Ron kept referencing them as 'son' and the like because he only had a daughter and had always wanted a boy. In a way, it was nice to be thought of as a son—Richard had made it quite clear he wanted no part of them like that. They'd been an anvil round his neck, dragging him down.

"What do you know about Richard and our mum? How did they meet? Why did she marry him when he was such an arsehole?"

Ron's face blanked. "I know nothing. Why do you want to poke into the past? It's best left buried, believe me."

"I want to understand why she put up with him, why she said she couldn't leave him, it wasn't allowed. I thought you might know something about it."

"Why the fuck would I know?"

"Because you know the ins and outs of everything."

Ron picked up a cup and waved it at Sam. "Make us a brew."

Sam took the cup and went into the kettle in the corner.

"Listen," Ron said. "Your father was nice to her to begin with. It wasn't until she got married that Richard turned funny. What she chose to do after she got pregnant…" He paused. Seemed to compose himself. "The path she took was necessary for her. The life she lived was because of her own mistakes."

"What mistakes?"

"No idea."

George sensed he was lying.

Sam broke the tension by handing Ron a cup of tea. "It wasn't anything to do with Ron. If it was, I'd know."

Ron had a shifty look about him, as if he didn't tell Sam everything. George filed it away. Just one more black mark against the leader to add to all the others. George would kill him one day, but in the meantime, he'd play the game.

Chapter Twenty-Eight

In disguise, Greg beside George, they sat in their fake work van. This time, blond wigs and beards, George's long-haired, Greg's short. While they had a bit of time to scope out the street, George reckoned he could have nipped here as Ruffian and got the job done far quicker—Greg was being particular on this occasion, probably because their target was a copper. Or should George have come as Ruffian anyway, shown Greg what it was all about?

He thought about his need to hog that persona all to himself, how he wanted to be only him sometimes, which had stemmed right from when he'd been a child. Greg knew what George did as that side of his personality, going out alone to right some wrongs so he could get the urge to kill out of his system, but no, letting him properly in on it by being there when he was Ruffian probably wasn't going to happen in the future.

With Janet dead, there was no one to prove anything to, not even himself. He was at peace with his three selves and had even gone so far as to give in and look up the diagnosis Janet had shoved down this throat. He begrudgingly accepted that she might well be right about him having DID to some degree, although he didn't hear separate voices, only the usual inner monologue that most people had (and he'd been shocked that some people never even heard *that*).

Still, while he'd accepted he wasn't your average person, it didn't mean he'd get help, go on medication, or stop what his other personalities drove him to do. He enjoyed being

Mad and Ruffian, and he'd secretly acknowledged that with them taking over when he needed to do anything grisly, he could detach himself, blame *them* for the actions so his real self wasn't guilty. So he wasn't like Richard.

As far as he was aware, he didn't have the DID trait where an alter lived inside him that he was unaware of. He spent so much time with Greg that if George did something as an alter and didn't remember, his brother would say so. Greg had done that in the past when Mad had gone a bit too loopy, which was why George had sought out therapy in the first place.

Nah, he didn't want Greg to see him in action as Ruffian, to observe how he prowled instead of walked, how his whole demeanour changed, as if he really *was* someone else. Someone else, yet at the same time, Just George lingered within. As a twin, he'd always shared everything, but he needed the little patches of freedom as Ruffian. Greg had been a bit offended by that, he didn't truly understand, because he embraced their twin status, didn't mind being joined at the hip, but despite that, he'd given his blessing—so long as Ruffian didn't get caught and fuck everything up for them.

Enough of that bollocks. I am who I am. Deal with it.

He glanced at the clock on the dash. Five a.m. They were cutting it fine with all this sitting around lark. Some people got up early for work and might see them, but dressed as plumbers in overalls and gloves, they might not attract much attention beyond somebody thinking Mallard had called them out to an emergency leak or his boiler going on the blink. Getting him in the back of the van might prove problematic, but they'd done this numerous times in the past, so what was one more?

It wasn't like they could snatch a copper off the street in broad daylight, was it.

"Come on," he said, bored off his nuts. "Got your lock pick?"

"Of *course* I bloody have, bruv. Fuck's sake." Greg got out and, as it was still murky enough for him not to be seen clearly, he went to the front door and got on with letting himself in. He gave the 'okay' signal that the door had opened but made a cutting motion as if his fingers were scissors, indicating a safety chain was in place.

"Sod it." George left the van and went to the back, ferreting in the toolbox for bolt cutters. He found them and checked the street, then approached the front door. A quick snip, and he winced at the tinkle and slight knocking the two pieces made on the interior wall and the back of the door.

"Noisy fucker," Greg whispered.

"Piss off."

Greg entered the property. George put the cutters on the step and followed, closing the door to. Gun out, Greg did the usual sweep of the lower floor. George took the stairs slowly, one at a time, mindful this was a member of the Old Bill they were dealing with and the bloke might be more alert than the average person. At the top, he glanced through all of the open doorways but approached the closed one. He put his ear to it.

Silence. Perfect.

He waited for his brother to join him and, taking his own gun out, he turned the handle. Opened the door a little. Squinted through the small gap. The slice gave him the visual of a six-drawer pine chest to the left under a blind-covered window and the lower corner of a bed on the right, farther up the room. He pushed the door even more, stepping forward to peer around it.

Mallard wasn't in bed, but the covers were crumpled, so he'd either been in it or wasn't the type to make it once he got up.

George retreated and whispered, "Bed's empty."

"Look for an en suite door."

George poked his head around again. Ah, a door, partially open, the light on in there, and a foot and hairy calf where Mallard was on the loo. Christ, he must have been in there for a while as George hadn't heard any movement since they'd entered the house. Why hadn't Mallard picked up on the chain making a racket? Had he fallen asleep on the ruddy bog?

George walked towards the bathroom, sensing his twin at his back. He peeped through the gap. "Oh fuck."

"What?" Greg said.

George toed the door wide open.

Mallard sat on the closed toilet seat, a red hole between his eyebrows, a dribble of blood down one side of his nose which had continued its journey over his lips and down his chin, its terminus a furry man tit. George craned his neck to see better. The back of the plod's head didn't exist, unless you counted it splashed all over the wall, one half of the window, and the sink beside him. Pink-infused grey brain matter joined the claret festivities, and the blood had speckled in a fine mist as well as a concentrated splash, some of it dripping down the wall behind him.

It was dry.

"He's been dead for a while," George said.

"Well, that saves us the bother." Greg backed away. "Come on, we need to leave."

"Hang on." George stared at the glass shower screen. In blood: MINION-215. REST IN PAIN. "Look at that."

Greg came back. "That's what Janine said The Network employees are called. Minions."

"So he *did* work for them."

"We should get out," Greg said.

They left the property, the gory sight front and centre in George's mind, him wishing he'd been the one who'd created it. All that gearing himself up for nothing. Ruffian nudged him, asking to come out and play, but there wasn't time. George needed to sleep at some point. He collected the cutter from the step and tossed it in the back of the van.

Greg driving this time, George messaged Janine.

GG: NEED TO TALK. URGENT.

The phone rang.

"What's the matter?" she asked. "Bear in mind I'm dealing with Zofia's murder and can't talk for long. You caught me on the toilet."

"Oh, the parallels to what you just said…"

"What are you on about?"

"Caught on the toilet."

"Eh?"

"You'll see."

She tutted. "Being cryptic isn't helping."

"Probably not, but it's fun being a mysterious wanker. Where are you?"

"The station. I've been to the scene in the woods, though. It isn't pretty. He took a leaf out of your book, and this Bronson character chopped her into pieces. Jim says she's been strangled, burnt."

"Poor cow. Listen, we've been to Mallard's. Going through the backstreets now on our way home."

"Okay…"

"We didn't kill him."

She let out a screech, no doubt through clenched teeth. "Why the fuck not?"

"He was already dead."

"Oh." Heavy breathing. "Oh bugger."

"The Network got to him."

"How do you know, and how was he killed?"

"Isn't it better for you to discover that for yourself? Your reaction will be genuine, then."

"Are you saying I'm supposed to say I got *two* anon phone calls tonight? That's not going to look suspicious *at all* on top of all the other anonymous calls I get when it comes to you two."

He didn't appreciate her sarcasm but let it go. He was trying to do better with that. Less gung-ho and more measured thinking. Sort of. "How else do you want to play it? Leave him there until he doesn't turn up for work and you go round to see if he's okay? Or someone in his family finds him? Or he stinks to high heaven in a few days and a neighbour goes round there? Fair warning, it's not a nice sight, not something his sister or whoever needs to see."

"*Shh* a minute. I'm trying to think how to work it. Give me a second."

He listened to her footsteps tapping, then a "Why can't things ever be simple, for fuck's sake?"

He smiled. "Having a moment, Janine?"

"Yes, I'm having a bloody moment," she hissed. "Plus I'm hacked off. For them to have gone after him, he must have contacted them about me poking my nose in about the Zofia phone call from Marleigh. What if they come after *me* next?"

"If they thought you were a threat, they'd have bumped you off way before now, and the DCI. You two headed that case before it was passed to another team. You're still living and breathing, so I'd take it they're not bothered about you."

"*Then* maybe, but not now. Christ."

"Look, I'm just the messenger, so don't shoot me. It's your call as to how you deal with Mallard's body being discovered. I can always ring the station instead of you, if you like."

"Yes, do that. It'll be passed to me anyway as he was on my team."

"Enjoy," he said.

"Very funny."

"Do you want us to send one of our men to shadow you, keep you safe?"

"Oh, and Colin's not going to notice *that*, is he."

"You're an ungrateful cow."

"I'm angry and in the middle of a panic party, because, you know, I could have a hit out on me, so if you don't mind, I'm going to dance to the tune of self-pity in this loo for a while then get back to my job. And no, I don't want a sodding bodyguard." She sighed. "Thanks for the offer, though."

She hung up on him.

George laughed.

"Why do you like winding her up?" Greg said. "You can tell she's on the edge. She's got a lot on her plate, and she's right about the anon calls. It's getting old, and people are going to start wondering why *she* seems to get them and no one else. They probably have already."

"She'll cope."

George took a new burner from the glove box and Googled the direct number for Janine's station. He prepared himself to speak in his Ruffian voice, a Scottish accent.

A woman answered.

"One of your lot has been murdered at his home. Steve Mallard." He cut the call, removed the SIM, the battery, and lobbed them out of the window. "Drive round for a bit longer, in another direction so we don't get spotted when they check where that call was made."

"Like I didn't know to do that."

"Just making sure."

"I'm not stupid, bruv."

"I won't answer that."

"Knob off."

They laughed, George's a little manic.

Greg sniffed. Sobered. "I'm going to take your advice and get counselling."

George sat straighter. "Where did *that* come from?"

"Been thinking. We haven't dealt with Mum dying properly."

George had been thinking an' all. So many memories had been sprouting since he'd been having those sessions with Vic, where he was taken to a safe place in his mind and he saw her, always in the kitchen at their old family home. Memories he didn't want to recall but they came anyway. Maybe he needed to face them head-on instead of cutting them off when the going got too tough.

When the lump in his throat hurt too much.

"Grief counselling?" he asked.

"Yeah."

"Vic's excellent, just so you know."

"We wouldn't have employed him otherwise. Twat."

"Who, me or Vic?"

"You."

They laughed again, always the go-to for hiding their deeper emotions.

That or violence.

"He'll make us all better, like Mum used to when she kissed my bruises after Richard clouted me," George said.

"I hope so."

Me, too.

Chapter Twenty-Nine

Friday night had come. George and Greg had opted for different disguises so they didn't resemble twins. Greg looked disturbingly like Ruffian with his ginger wig and beard. He'd bought a black suit and dickie bow and sat at the one of the gaming tables. His appalling Irish accent was laughable, George had well taken the piss when he'd been practising, but Greg was supposed to be Ichabod's uncle, Rowan's father, here on a visit from Ireland. Rowan had been told to take the night off. Jimmy Riddle was their best bet as manager for tonight.

George had opted for a long brown wig he'd put in a low ponytail, his beard also dark, the East End version of Jason Momoa. He'd chosen to be one of the security team so it didn't appear suspicious when he cast his gaze around, scrutinising the customers. He acted new, letting T-T supposedly teach him the ropes in front of everyone watching. Specifically anyone in Goldie's team who'd been sent to spy. And they had to be here. If not, Goldie was a prick if he was leaving it up to chance. Or to the mole in the camp. Who that was, George had no clue. They'd viewed the security footage yesterday, a team of men going back months since the casino had opened, and no one stood out as off. With Cinnamon in the safe house now, if it was her, which he didn't think it was, they'd have sent someone else to take her place, probably posing as a player.

The casino crawled with men in the firm who fitted in as customers. George had ordered many of their male workforce to attend tonight, giving them instructions to observe but not why. While a warning as to what was going on would have been nice so they could be extra vigilant when the shooters entered the casino, if that was what Goldie had planned, he couldn't risk his men accidentally letting the cat out of the bag and Goldie finding out they were in the know. The men would just have to rely on their instincts if bullets went flying. He expected casualties, but that was par for the course, and he'd deal with the guilt of that, not to mention grieving widows, as and when.

Karen and Teddy appeared normal, although how Karen managed that, he didn't know, considering what she'd been through with having Bronson on her back and she had the job of opening the back door for the gunmen. Was she at risk? Would the gunmen shoot her as soon as she put the door on the latch? A burner sat in her bra; it had arrived on Wednesday via an Amazon driver; the man George had sent to watch her flat had clocked the van pulling up.

But was it a *real* Amazon driver? Could Bronson have been the deliveryman? The bloke who'd taken the package to the block of flats certainly matched his height and width, but unless he'd slapped a fake beard on and wrapped his head in a turban, it could have genuinely been an unsuspecting worker.

Jackpot Palace ran exactly as it always did, a good thing in George's eyes. If nothing seemed untoward, apart from his appearance as a new security guard and a few more customers than usual, then Goldie would still go ahead with the heist.

Ichabod was watching Goldie, his current position in a social club at a party Goldie had thrown. Ichabod had slipped inside in disguise without an invite, where he could keep tabs on how often Goldie used his phone—and when. If Ichabod reported Goldie sending a message or making a call at the time the burner vibrated in Karen's bra, well, it didn't take a rocket scientist, did it. Or maybe he would give someone at the party a nod for them to do the honours. Either way, it didn't matter. Goldie would be dying later tonight whether the heist took place or not, and any excuses he gave at the warehouse would be hot air. They'd be empty words, lies, to get himself out of trouble.

Moon had asked why they were even letting the heist go ahead when they had Goldie bang to rights for killing Zofia. He reckoned that was enough to haul his arse in. But George and Greg had agreed on this: they wanted to see how big Goldie's balls were and if he really did have the courage to play Russian roulette with his life.

George gritted his teeth and continued to observe.

In a pause between games, Greg nudged the player beside him. "If ye win any more, ye'll wipe the proprietors out, so ye will."

Handsy laughed. "I'm just a lucky man."

Greg leant closer. "Lucky, or did ye slip the wee fella there a fixed ball so it always lands on the red?"

Handsy widened his eyes. "I didn't even know such a ball existed. And I don't cheat!"

That's good, because if you did, you'd be dead. As for putting your hands on our girls, I might have to let George teach you a lesson for that. I see you're married. Bastard.

"So ye've got the luck o' the Irish about ye, then, eh? Have ye kissed the Blarney Stone for the craic?" *Over-the-top Irish? Fuck it, calm it down.*

"The what?"

"The Blarney Stone. If ye kiss it, ye get the gift." He gave Handsy a mysterious stare.

"The gift?"

"Of persuasiveness and eloquence, so they say. I can see wid me own eyes ye're eloquent, and ye're tryin' tae persuade me now that ye're not cheatin', so I reckon ye've puckered up tae that stone all right."

Handsy's frown scored deep. "I don't know *what* you're talking about."

"Ah, don't mind me, fella me lad, I had a few too many pints o' Guinness before comin' here, and this whisky's goin' down a treat." He glanced at the cold black tea in his glass and cursed himself. He was definitely going overboard with the Irishness. *Pack it in, you fucking dickhead.* "Why don't ye try that luck o' yours on the black this time?"

"I can't until I get the feeling."

"The feelin'?"

"Yes, of which one to pick."

"Are ye psychic or somethin'?"

"Err, no, it's just a feeling."

"Ah, the gambler's nudge."

"Um, yeah, if you say so."

The new game began, and Greg continued to be an irritating fly bumbling around Handsy to draw attention to himself so it was off George and all the other people they had in position, ready to go into battle against men with guns.

He looked forward to watching his brother kill Goldie, the gorier the better.

Teddy's nerves, stretched so taut he felt sick, wouldn't let up. As it was Friday, he waited for Karen to get the signal to open the back door, for her to tell him she needed the toilet. Goldie had sent the instructions to them again over WhatsApp earlier, an unnecessary reminder of the order of play, and once she'd unlocked the door and returned to her post, Teddy had to take his break and go and have a 'chat' with Casey in the money-counting room where the safes were.

Casey thought she was in with a chance. They'd shared a few secret conversations, ones he'd purposely engineered, and he'd told her wasn't ready to marry Karen, because if he was, he wouldn't fancy Casey. He hated lying to her, using her so she was the excuse for the cash room door being open when the gunmen came in, but if he didn't do it, Goldie would kill him.

He wished he'd never gone into this and consoled himself with the fact he didn't have much choice. He'd worked for Goldie in the dodgy side of his accounts business for about three years, moving money so it looked legitimate, arranging the laundering, the offshore accounts. He'd been eager to prove himself as a trustworthy employee, and that had been his downfall because it had led to this.

Oakley had got a case of cold feet this afternoon when Teddy had been at their place. "Don't do it," he'd said, as if it were that easy, and Teddy had explained, yet again, why he had to. Not just for the down payment on the farm, but because what Goldie wanted, Goldie got.

"It'll be okay, I promise," Teddy had said. "I just have to keep Casey chatting then go back to the blackjack table as soon as the men arrive."

"Have you met them? Do you know who they are?"

350

"I might have met them, but I won't know that. They'll be in gas masks."

"But what if they think you're just some random employee and shoot you? What if Goldie's ordered them to get rid of you and Karen because you might blab? Plus it means he won't have to pay you your cut if you're dead. How much are you getting? Is it even enough for a down payment?"

"I don't know."

Teddy felt stupid now, not knowing. He should have asked, but that would have been wrong as far as Goldie was concerned. You did what he told you as his employee and accepted his word as the truth. The bloke had always been fair in the past, but what Oakley had said had wormed its way into Teddy's brain and wouldn't go away.

What if Goldie's men *did* kill him and Karen?

The nerves got the better of him, and as the current game came to an end and all players left their seats, he turned to her.

"What's the matter?" she said.

"Something Oakley mentioned earlier," he whispered, eager to get his words out before new people arrived for a game. "That Goldie might

351

get the gunmen to kill us tonight. To stop us talking."

"What?" she squeaked. "Where did he get *that* idea from?"

"*Shh*, customers."

The strange, loud Irishman from another table lumbered over with Handsy, and they sat side by side, other gamblers filling the vacant seats. Teddy gave himself a talking-to. The heist might not even be tonight. It could be in the future and he was getting himself worked up for no reason.

He smiled at the men and one woman staring at him expectantly. "Karen will take your drink orders, then we can begin."

Karen's bulletproof vest constricted her breathing. George had left it in her locker in the staffroom, just in case anything went wrong later. She visited every customer, bending low to speak to each one. She had to do that so when she did it to Greg, Teddy wouldn't be suspicious. She used the electronic pad to send their orders through to the bar, then asked Handsy what he'd like.

"A brandy." He put his palm on her backside.

Tonight wasn't the night to give him one of her glares, so she smiled, sent his request through, and moved on to Greg.

"What would you like, sir?" She leant closer and whispered, "Worried Goldie will have given the order to kill me. Loose end."

Greg smiled. "A whisky. One o' the *special* ones. I want ye tae get it for me personally, and while ye're at it, ask that big bearded security eejit tae stop starin' at me. He's givin' me the willies."

She smiled back. "I'll do that right away, sir."

She glanced at Teddy to apologise for the change in her usual pattern, and he nodded, although he seemed worried, likely wondering what he'd do if her phone vibrated while she wasn't standing beside him, how she'd let him know if she was elsewhere.

He turned to the others. "Karen will be back shortly, but we'll start the game without her."

"Hear, hear," Greg said and slapped Handsy on the shoulder.

Karen had got the gist of what Greg had meant about the security eejit. She had to collect his tea then tell George her worries. Behind the bar, she poured his drink from the fake bottles in a crate beneath the counter, adding two balls of ice. She glanced at George who frowned. Pasting on a smile, she approached him and stood on tiptoes to speak in his ear, passing on Teddy's worries as if they were her own.

"You're probably right," he said. "You've got your vest on, yes?"

She nodded.

"Good. When you've opened the back door, go into one of the offices and lock yourself in. Stay there until I come for you."

She nodded and returned to the table, placing Greg's drink down. A waitress brought the others on a tray, then went off.

While Karen played her usual part, she thought about Robyn to take her mind off the heist possibly happening tonight. Her sister's operation had gone well, and she currently recovered at home. The clinic had given her some medication to help settle her hormones so she wasn't such a raging loon towards Cal. Both of them were so much happier now the prospect of a baby was in sight. They all just had to pray the op had been a success and had helped her chances of fertility.

Inevitably, the heist barged back into her head. If it wasn't tonight, all these nerves would have been for nothing. Anyway, why would Goldie have sent a message to reconfirm their orders? It *was* happening, she felt it in her bones, and now she'd been given permission to hide in an office, she felt better.

But what about Teddy?

She couldn't think about him now. She had herself to save so she could be an auntie to Robyn's baby. The best auntie, one who didn't lie anymore. Karen planned to turn over a new leaf when this was all over. But the biggest lie of all, the one she'd told The Brothers regarding Bronson coming to her flat…that would haunt her for the rest of her life.

Moon, disgruntled at having to sit in a booth, drinking cold black tea in this ridiculous getup, passing himself off as a rich sheik with his entourage, glanced at Alien and Brickhouse, also sheiks, his 'brothers'. They had guns hidden beneath their robes, robes that could be snatched off as soon as everything got going, the Velcro fastenings easily ripped apart.

Tick-Tock, Moon's supposed Arabian manfriend, in a black suit, dark wig, long beard, and Harry Potter glasses, didn't appear to enjoy having an itchy head and chin, and he kept scratching them.

"Anyone would think you had spiders in that Vandyke and syrup," Moon said quietly. "Pack it in."

"A sheik wouldn't know what a Vandyke and syrup was," Tick-Tock grumbled. "They'd say beard and wig. Get into character properly."

"Says the man who isn't wearing a fucking dress and worrying how he'll have a piss in the gents with all this fabric making matters difficult." Moon sipped his tea and winced.

They'd settled into a booth opposite the gaming area to observe. Jackpot Palace, separated into three sections, was a massive area to cover, so Moon had supplied extra men along with the twins' lot to watch from various places. As far as he could see, everything was hunky-dory, but the slots section at the other end might be a different matter. So much noise from the machines, so many people in there. He didn't envy the fellas who had to man it, sitting on stools trying to get three lemons in a row while also scoping the crowd.

"I'll be pissed off if it doesn't go down tonight," Tick-Tock said. "I've got myself all geared up for a gunfight."

"It'll be tonight," Moon assured him. "Goldie's been shouting far and wide the past couple of days that he's having that shindig at the social club, so he wants people to know where he is. Ichabod's already there. I bet Goldie's wondering why we aren't, why we didn't take him up on his invitation. The twins, too."

Tick-Tock's grimace split his cropped beard. "He'll think he was so clever to have asked us lot to go. We'd have seen for ourselves he wasn't anywhere near this place, which is what he'd have wanted. I wonder if any of the other leaders have gone."

"But he knows we don't like him, so why the fuck would *we* go? Prick."

"He had to try." Tick-Tock leant back. "We'd have done the same in his shoes."

"Hmm, except we wouldn't be after robbing other leaders in the first place. Who does he think he is? Fucking orange munter."

"*Shh*, that waitress is coming over again. Act all sheik-ish."

"Sheik-ish? What the chuff's that when it's at home?"

"I dunno. Mysterious. Foreign."

"Jesus Christ." Moon scowled at the young woman and adopted a 'sheik-ish' accent, whatever the hell that was. "We bought bottle. No need to come here. Go away."

She scuttled off, glancing at him over her shoulder.

"I said foreign, not rude," Tick-Tock said.

"Ah, fuck off and drink your tea like a good boy, there's a dear."

Jimmy Riddle needed to be cloned. Jackpot was too large for him to keep tabs on when a heist was imminent, and he found himself rushing from one end to the other before remembering he was supposed to act normal so no one cottoned on that anything was wrong. He could do with Rowan being here, but George had said *someone* with managerial status had to be ready to run the casino if Jimmy and Ichabod didn't make it.

What a prospect. Dying at work. Yes, he'd always known his various jobs for the twins could either see him in A&E or a coffin, but tonight… This was the biggest job he had ever taken on for them, one of the most dangerous, and his part in it was a tad daunting. He was responsible for spotting any spies, and that responsibility weighed heavy. What if one of them had a gun, and when he went up to question them, they whipped it out? He had a bulletproof vest on under his suit, all the men in the firm did, plus Karen, but there was always his head that could be blown off.

T-T approached him, as he usually would, to give a supposed security update. "George said you're better off in the gaming area because that's closer to the money room and any action will mainly be there. For all we know, though, they could just plan to rob the money and slip away quietly, not come into the casino and create a scene. He also said to stop darting round like a fart in a colander."

"Right." Jimmy straightened his tie and tugged down the fronts of his red tartan suit. "Right." Then he added, "Good luck."

T-T swallowed. Blinked. "Yeah, same to you, mate."

They'd become friends in the time they'd been working together. Jimmy didn't want to see anything happen to the younger man, but it was a given, if Goldie's men came into the casino itself and opened fire, that *someone* from the Cardigan lot could cop a bullet.

T-T walked off, and Jimmy followed at a slower pace to situate himself by the door that led to the offices, hands crossed over his groin, a stance he was known for here. He glanced over at George who stood by the front doors, probably so he could get a good glimpse of whoever entered, clocking potential spies.

Jimmy averted his gaze to look through the double doors and into the foyer. The greeters, two young women in black cocktail dresses and higher-than-high heels, chatted and laughed amongst themselves at the podium. What if Goldie also planned to send men in through the front and the women were gunned down?

Fuck's sake. This operation was full of holes and potential Cardigan deaths. Granted, the twins couldn't let everyone in on what was going on, but it bothered Jimmy that so many employees—those two laughing women, the croupiers, the waitresses, the bar staff—didn't know this night could be their last. No final phone calls to their families. No chance to say, "I love you, and thanks for loving me."

Knowing their potential fate when they didn't, it fucking hurt his soul.

Maybe The Brothers haven't let me in on the full order of play. I can't see them not trying to protect as many people as possible. There's no way they'll allow men to come in here, not with all these innocent customers.

He looked beyond the greeters through two more glass, bulletproof doors, at people going about their business in Entertainment Plaza. Jimmy would give anything to be in their shoes. Minding his own business, admiring the coloured water display from the fountain, maybe going for a bit of pasta in Bella Italia. Or even buzzing off to his favourite stomping ground, The Angel, where he was the twins' ears along with Sonny Bates when Sonny wasn't doing the same at The Eagle. But what if, for some of them out there, their meal would be the last one they'd ever eat? What if Goldie's men blasted their machine guns in other places to make a point and people ended up getting shot?

Jimmy had a horrible feeling he shouldn't have taken this manager's job two shifts a week, but saying that, he'd have been called in for this regardless of his employment status, so he'd have been facing death anyway.

Something didn't sit right, and he couldn't shake it off.

He mentally crossed himself.

May God have mercy on our souls.

T-T, as well as keeping an eye on his security staff, watched the punters. He'd be forever grateful to the twins for taking him on when he'd been involved with Sienna and her mad sister in a money-lending racket behind their backs. Still, he'd proved his worth, proved they could trust him, and now he had a posh-to-him flat with low rent and a job that paid bloody good wages. Tonight, he stood to get a bonus for his part in preventing the heist from going ahead, and while he was good at what he did, nerves still came for a visit.

They said even the most seasoned performer suffered from nerves. Well, he was on the biggest stage of his life so far, and all he could do was tread the boards and hope for the best.

Unfortunately, he had the nasty sense that something would go tits up.

He took a deep breath and prayed he was wrong.

Chapter Thirty

Goldie sat holding court, a bevy of women around him vying for his attention. They weren't Karen, and they weren't Marleigh, and it got on his wick. They were too eager to please him, simpering, none of them with an ounce of class in their marrow. They were like Tanning Tart Babs on speed, their commonness highlighted by their words and actions. In short, he wanted them to fuck off.

Instead of telling them that, he smiled. "Go and have a dance for me, ladies. Show me your strip tease moves, only, don't take your clothes off else you'll have a load of blokes come running."

They giggled and rushed away—*thank fuck for that*—and he nodded to a scrote who'd somehow got past the man on the door. Lemon, coming towards him. Highly rude to expect an audience without prior notice or permission, but this was a party, so Goldie supposed he could let him off. Although there was the gate-crashing he could bend the bloke's ear about…

"What do *you* want, and who the fuck do you think you are, just turning up without an invite?" Goldie shouted over the music. Any chance of a private conversation here was as remote as Zofia coming back to life, but he had a feeling he'd need to keep this chat on the quiet, so there'd be a lot of talking close to ears.

Lemon gestured to the booth seat for permission to sit, so he did have *some* manners and idea of protocol. Goldie nodded and switched his attention to the dancing women, giving them the thumbs-up and indicating they should keep entertaining him—ergo, keep out of his fucking mush.

Lemon sat, a whiff of strong aftershave coming off him, as if he'd bathed in the fucking stuff. Goldie liked a bit of Acqua Di Parma at four hundred nicker a bottle himself, but it seemed Lemon liked Joop.

The uninvited guest leant closer. "Word is, someone's selling cocaine on your patch without your permission."

Goldie kept an eye-roll at bay. Men like Lemon were always after a cheeky payout. They thought if they fed you bullshit, you'd swallow it like it was caviar and hand over a few quid. "How do you know they *haven't* got permission? I could have given it and they just haven't said so."

Lemon shrugged. "Don't say I didn't warn you."

Goldie got the right old huff. "I don't appreciate your tone, mate."

Lemon didn't seem to care whether Goldie did or didn't. That was the trouble with people from Cardigan, they acted entitled, like a lot of the younger generation today. Those twins were too soft to be running an estate, letting their residents gad about willy-nilly, actually letting them have a *say* in some things. Lemon should have been given a lesson in how to behave in the company of leaders before now, especially when Goldie was suffocating courtesy of Joop.

"I'm putting myself in the firing line for even telling you," Lemon said.

"Why? Afraid the twins might get upset you're helping another leader out?"

"Nope, I stay off their radar, I'd be a dick not to, considering what I get up to. It's the Sparrow Road lot I'm worried about."

Goldie raised his eyebrows. He'd heard about them via Bronson who kept his ear to the ground regarding the other estates. They thought of themselves as people to be reckoned with, although they went about their business quietly, and The Brothers didn't appear to be doing anything about them. Maybe they didn't know the Sparrows existed, which was lax on their part. Mind you, he'd cut them some slack. Cardigan was a bloody big estate compared to others, so they could be forgiven for not having their finger on all the pulses.

"Why's that, then?" Goldie asked.

"Because I'm one of them."

Goldie laughed. "Not exactly a trustworthy member, are you, if you've come to me with one of their secrets."

"Let's just say the bloke doing the main dealing isn't on my friends list. He pisses me off something chronic and causes problems within the gang. I want him out, so does the Sparrow boss, and we decided the only way to get rid of him permanently was by grassing him up to you."

"You do know you and your 'boss' are guilty by association, don't you. Just by knowing what this fella's getting up to, you're deep in the turd with me."

"We only found out today."

"Whatever you say, mate. So you want me to catch him and deal with your little problem for you, do you?"

"If you wouldn't mind."

"Come and see me tomorrow at Golden Glow. You can give me all the details then. The wheres, the whens."

Lemon smiled. "Cheers. Appreciate it."

Goldie watched him walk out, mainly to make sure he fucked off, *and* he was thankful the man's aftershave had gone with him. At least Lemon wasn't cheeky enough to stay and have a few free drinks and eat from the buffet. All this, shit like Lemon had just brought to him, only served to push Goldie farther towards his retirement dream. The constant ducking and diving, rooting out people doing what they shouldn't, had worn thin. He'd make a show by giving Lemon an audience tomorrow, and he'd send Bronson to catch the Sparrow cocaine dealer out, but Goldie's passion for getting pleasure out of such a thing was long gone. He just wanted the various orifices women provided and sand between his toes.

A few more months so suspicion didn't fall on him for the heist, and he'd be out of here.

He checked his watch. In twenty minutes, he'd be sending Karen her message to go and open the door. Then she'd tell Teddy she'd done it, and he'd go and chat up that Casey woman so the money-room door was open, all nice and ready for the gunmen to enter. In half an hour, his men would be inside Jackpot's money room.

Casey had better do as she was told and open that safe. He'd overridden his own rule of no one being killed on this job. If she didn't comply, her brains would be spattered all over the wall, his men now given permission to pull the trigger.

Ichabod had strained to hear the conversation over the music, but they'd spoken too low. Goldie looked at his watch. From his seat on a table next to the leader, Ichabod asked himself whether that young bloke had anything to do with the heist. Had he come for instructions? Had he been sent to round up the gunmen? Or was he now on his way to Jackpot?

Ichabod messaged the twins to let them know the score, plus he gave them a description of the visitor so they'd at least know who to watch out for. The man had a distinctive look: two-tone dark-green suit, his hair shaved at the sides and back, the top swept over, and he held a cap, a Peaky Blinder wannabe. He moved with stealth, too, as if used to creeping around in the shadows.

GG: UNDERSTOOD.

Ichabod drank some Coke then lowered his head, observing Goldie by slanting his eyes to the right so no one caught on to what he was doing. The leader had another couple of women either side of him, different to those he'd sent away to dance, and although he smiled and laughed, his eyes didn't portray a man pleased at having such company.

Two men in black clothing entered—more like barged in—drawing Ichabod's attention away from Goldie for a moment. They stuck out as people who weren't here to party, their combat trousers, boots, and turtle-neck jumpers not your usual shindig attire. Swaggering up to Goldie's table, they gripped a woman's arm each and hauled the birds out of the way, taking their places next to Goldie.

Stupid feckin' prick, allowin' them tae come here. They're givin' the game away.

Goldie deserved to get caught for that alone.

Goldie smiled, but he was far from amused. "What. The. Fuck. Are. You. Doing. Here?"

Phantom took a deep breath and leant in. "The van with the gunmen in it has been in an accident. They're currently being carted to hospital. The pigs are involved."

372

This was all Goldie needed. Eight men, gone, out of the equation. And pigs? *Fuck my life.* "And you couldn't have messaged me that? Look at you. Your clothes. It's obvious you're here for something other than a drink and a dance, and people are staring."

"I *did* message, tried to phone you an' all, but it says it's unread and the calls went to voicemail."

"That's because I've got my work phone off and you were meant to contact my fucking burner. Jesus wept."

"When did you tell us *that*?"

Fuck. Goldie couldn't remember even telling them. He'd had so much going on, and the Zofia issue must have prompted him to take his eye off the ball. Even dead she was bringing him problems. "Hang on."

He switched his phone on. Several messages popped up, and not just from Phantom. A couple of the gunmen from the van had let him know what had happened, and one of them had tried ringing.

"Bollocks," he muttered. "You should have got hold of Bronson."

"He's not answering either, so we thought, seeing as this is a massive spoke in the wheel, we should come here."

"It would have been better if you'd asked the bloke out there manning the door to come and get me. Now everyone's had an eyeful of me talking shop at a party, something I didn't want to happen."

"Are we still going ahead with the job?"

"Yes, get a few others in to take their places. Ferret and his lot will have to do; they can use their van, the Mercedes, just make sure they put fake plates on it. Torch the van later."

"Ferret?" Phantom shook his head. "Are you sure about that?"

"Are you questioning me?" Goldie waited for an answer. "Didn't think so. We only need them there to look scary. You two are the main players. Brief them on what's what. Now go. Fuck off."

Phantom and his brother, Checkpoint Charlie, stalked out.

Fucking imbeciles.

He read the messages.

BAZ: VAN CRASHED. COPPER'S BEEN ASKING US WHY WE'VE GOT GAS MASKS AND GUNS. WE'RE IN

THE SHIT, BOSS, BUT NO ONE WILL GRASS. THROWING
THIS SIM ONCE I HIT SEND.

KEV: RTA, BACK OF VAN TRASHED. GOING TO BE
ARRESTED FOR POSSESSION OF FIREARMS. DISPOSING
OF SIM NOW.

He deleted the messages and the record of the
calls. He'd keep his phone on, just in case one of
them had got away and sent more info, but he
switched off all the tones and left it on vibrate.
There would be a delay now while Ferret's mob
got ready, something Goldie didn't need.

Christ.

Ichabod sent the twins a heads-up. He'd heard
that conversation well enough as the song that
had been playing wasn't full of mad beats and
thumping drums.

ICHABOD: GUNMEN ARRIVING IN MERCEDES VAN.
RTA WITH ORIGINAL VAN. PLAYERS ON WAY TO
HOSPITAL. FERRET AND CO TO TAKE THEIR PLACE.
PHANTOM AND CHECKPOINT CHARLIE SOUND LIKE
THEY'RE THE ONES WHO'LL ENTER MONEY ROOM.

With the revealing information that Phantom
and Checkpoint were the main menaces, all the

others out of commission, a new lot being sent in, it meant tonight would go easier than they'd anticipated. Ferret wasn't well-known for being competent with a gun, he was more like Sonny Bates, a bit of a bumbler who was better at acting drunk, wheedling gossip out of people rather than being a big face. Why Goldie had chosen Ferret and his band of merry arseholes was anyone's guess. Had he panicked? Or weren't all of his men in the know about the robbery for a reason? Did he worry they couldn't be trusted, and he'd chosen Ferret because the bloke would piss his pants with fear if Goldie ever caught him spreading gossip?

GG: CHEERS. WONDER IF THE ACCIDENT WASN'T SUCH AN ACCIDENT AFTER ALL.

ICHABOD: SOMEONE ELSE TRYING TO DERAIL THEIR PLANS?

GG: MAYBE, WHICH MEANS WHOEVER DID THAT IS ON OUR SIDE OR WANTS THE HEIST FOR THEMSELVES.

ICHABOD: IF THAT'S THE CASE, GOLDIE SEEMS UNAWARE.

GG: KEEP ME POSTED.

Ichabod sipped some Coke and shifted his eyes towards Goldie. Mr Tanned Man now had another hanger-on, a blonde with long hair and even longer legs.

"Where are you from, gorgeous?" Goldie asked.

"Manchester."

"I thought I recognised that accent. Who are you here with?"

"Babs."

"Ah."

"She sent me over to make you feel better. She said you need some TLC."

"Maybe I do. Later. Now off you go, have some fun. If you dance nicely enough, I might take you to my gaff after the party."

She giggled and sauntered away, prancing about on the dance floor.

"Fucking Nora," Goldie muttered and glanced across at Ichabod. "Women, eh? I have to fight them off."

Glad of his disguise, Ichabod nodded and smiled.

"Who are you?" Goldie sound happy enough, but a touch of suspicion laced his tone.

Adopting a British accent, Ichabod said, "Ferret said I should come."

"And how do you know him?"

"He's my cousin."

"Figures. That family have multiplied like rabbits. Dirty load of bastards."

Goldie got up and skirted the dancing women, heading for the buffet and stopping to chat to as many people as he could along the way. He clearly wanted to be seen, remembered, but Ichabod had a feeling that when news of the robbery hit, the main thing people would recall was Phantom and Checkpoint bursting in. Not everyone in attendance tonight would be on Goldie's side, only here for the free booze and food. Someone would run to the twins and dob him in.

Shame it wouldn't make a difference.

Goldie would be dead by then.

Chapter Thirty-One

Karen's phone went off, the one Goldie had sent via Amazon. The buzz against her boobs sent her heart rate sky-high, and she almost lost her composure. She stopped herself just in time from darting her gaze about, and she successfully held in a whimper, but Teddy must have sensed what had happened because he stared at her. It felt like *everyone* stared at her.

"Go!" he whispered from the side of his mouth.

For the benefit of those at the table, she said, "Just nipping off for a break. I'll collect any more drink orders when I get back."

"Good," Greg said. "I need a Guinness." He winked at her then nudged Handsy. "She's a feckin' crackin' girl."

Handsy ogled her and licked his lips.

Greg nodded to himself as if confirming that Handsy needed sorting.

Shuddering, and not just from Handsy's obvious pervert-from-Hell leer, she checked where George was. He stiffened and gave a slight bob of the head, then spoke into the walkie-talkie on his lapel. Relieved he had her back and had likely warned everyone it was a go, she moved towards Jimmy, who glanced at her then looked away, but he'd realised what had happened, tilting his head to pick up whatever George said through his walkie-talkie.

At the door that led to the staff area, she whispered to Jimmy, "I won't be coming back out. George told me to lock myself in an office.

Will you watch Teddy, make sure he's okay? Tell him to go to the break room so he's safe?"

"Yep."

She pushed through into the corridor, going past the line of doors for the various rooms: the one for breaks, the money, the offices, the cleaning cupboard. At the end, the door that led to the staff car park. The dull steel seemed ominous, the voice of the frightened little girl inside her whispering, "If they're already on the other side, they're going to kill you." It only served to send her into panic mode. She wanted to run, to not unlock that door, to get someone else to do it.

She got to the end and stared at the three bolts, the heavy-duty chain, and the Yale. Reaching up, hand shaking, she drew the bolts across, imagining the gunmen hearing it on the other side and bracing themselves to fire.

Fuck, fuck, fuck.

She removed the chain.

Please don't let this be the end.

She turned the Yale handle down and popped on the snib.

Should I open the door to check if they're there?

No! She ran back down the corridor, barged into one of the offices, and slammed the door.

It didn't have a lock.

Panicking, she lunged back out and threw herself into the one beside it, relieved to see a key *and* a Yale. She secured herself inside and looked around for somewhere to hide in case the gunmen broke in. The desk had a solid back, so if she turned it around with the rear facing the door, she could stay under there until it was all over. No one would see her unless they came around the other side.

She got to work, rearranging the desk, and huddled beneath it.

The phone in her bra buzzed again. That wasn't supposed to happen. Goldie had said it would only buzz once. Had something gone wrong? Did she have another instruction?

She took it out and read the message.

TWENTY MINUTES UNTIL LIFT-OFF.

Confused, because Goldie had moved the goalposts by writing that, going against what he'd said about her genuine surprise showing when it became clear the casino had been robbed, she took a moment to process the change. *Was* it

Goldie, or had he handed the reins over to someone else?

At least I'm not going to die. If I've been given fair warning, he wants me to live.

Teddy waited, anxious for Karen to come back and give him the nod so she could take over the table and he could go and see Casey. The current game had ended, the customers leaving to play elsewhere, so he draped a red satin cloth over the table to show that his blackjack was closed for the moment. He placed the chips the customers had lost into the assigned briefcase that lived on the floor, attached it to his wrist with the lockable cuff, and headed towards Jimmy. This was usual practise, for Teddy to take the chips to the money room periodically throughout a shift—some people had a good sleight of hand, and chips went missing every now and then.

Because of the cameras, he had to appear normal, but he was finding it difficult.

He reached Jimmy. "Karen hasn't come back from her toilet break, so I've had to cover the table while I go on mine."

383

"Yeah, she said she had a dicky tummy, so she's taking a few minutes more."

"Right. She didn't tell me that."

"Probably didn't want to say so in front of the customers. Not what they want to hear on a night out, that a woman's got the shits."

"No. I'll just pop this to Casey, then."

"Get a move on, and once you've dropped the chips off, Karen wants you to go straight into the break room."

"Why?"

"Because she said so, and I agree. Don't argue, just do it."

Teddy frowned. Ichabod had never said anything like that to him, it was a given that Teddy would drop the briefcase off then go and have a cuppa. Had Casey made a complaint about him chatting to her? Had the camera in the money room picked him up while he talked to her, the door open, and the twins had been informed? Was he about to get a bollocking? The twins weren't here, but it didn't mean they wouldn't turn up at any minute.

He pushed the door open beside Jimmy and let it swing shut. Stared down at the end of the corridor. The steel door's chain hung where

384

Karen must have taken it off its keeper. He moved closer, squinting. The Yale snib was down. As far as he knew, this corridor didn't have cameras, but it should, considering the amount of times chips were brought here for Casey to hand them back to Brea in the buying booth for resale, plus Brea came along here to drop cash off.

Just because I can't see the cameras, doesn't mean they're not there.

And it hit him then, that if there were, Karen was right in the shit. She'd have been seen unlocking the door. Why hadn't they double-checked that with Ichabod before now instead of taking it for granted that they weren't being observed in the corridor?

Because Goldie knows the bloke who fitted all the cameras, and he said there aren't any.

But what if they'd been installed by someone else afterwards?

Or had Goldie lied, wanting Teddy and Karen to be the fall guys?

Panic laced his nerves, sending him jittery, and he had to force himself to walk along the corridor, act innocent, all the while waiting for the end door to burst open and men to come in. And what was it Jimmy had said? *Karen wants you to go straight into the break room.* She'd managed to let him know there had been a change of plan. Her pretending she had a stomach bug was her way of engineering things. How did she know to tell him that, though? She hadn't read the message that had come when her phone had buzzed.

She must have read it once she opened the back door. Stop overthinking things, just be glad she helped you.

He took a deep breath and stopped outside Casey's room. Knocked on the door. It had a peephole, and he imagined her getting up from behind her desk and looking at him through it. A clunk, and the door opened, Casey giving him a bright smile. Guilt had his shoulders slumping. He'd used her, put her in danger, and she might get killed.

He held the briefcase up. "One of my many visits to you this evening."

She waited for him to unlock the cuff then took the case, walking off to one of the two safes in the top-left corner—one for chips, one for money. He leant on the jamb, keeping the door popped open, and watched her, stopping himself from rearing his head back to check whether the men were creeping in quietly. Goldie had warned him to remain the same as usual, but fuck, it was hard when his whole body seemed on fire with nerves.

"Been busy?" he asked.

"God, yes." She knelt to put the chips in the stacker holders. "So many people in tonight. I saw them when I went to take some chips to Brea and make a money exchange. Has everyone had an influx of cash or what? As for the amount I've been counting, well... The takings are *well* up tonight."

That was good. More for them to share once this was all over.

Teddy had a twinge of remorse about that. Oakley was right, the twins had been good to Teddy and Karen, to all of the employees, and they didn't deserve to be robbed. Shit, Teddy wanted to go home, forget all about this, but he couldn't. He wanted the farm too much.

And to stay alive.

He was tempted to check with Casey whether the weekly takings *really* remained in the safe until Friday's had been put in, but that would look weird, especially once it was clear she was about to be robbed. She'd know he was involved, or at least suspect it. But his need to be sure he was getting a good whack from this wouldn't let up, and he had to suppress it by talking to her to take his mind off it.

"That's good, the takings being up. Means the casino's a success and we get to keep our jobs."

She locked the safe and stood. Brought the empty case over and handed it back. "True. And I bloody need mine. My mortgage has just gone up—by two hundred quid a month. Can you believe that? I mean, where the hell am I mean to get the money from? Work myself to death?"

Teddy attached the chain to the cuff. "Yeah, we had a letter the other day from the landlord. His has gone up, too, and guess who has to pay the extra in rent to cover it." He stabbed a thumb tip at his chest. "Muggins here."

"It's horrible. Can't Karen contribute?"

"She pays all the bills, like the leccy and whatnot."

"I don't know, something's got to give, surely. We can't all keep spending extra when our wages stay the same."

"Hopefully there will be light at the end of the tunnel. I can still afford to take you out for dinner, though." He smiled. He'd have to go through with it, too, when all this was over, because he had to work here until Goldie said it was okay to leave. "Only if you want, mind."

She bit her lip and sat behind her desk. "I don't think we should. I've been thinking about us. It's rotten on Karen. It's not her fault you fancy someone else, and going out with another woman's bloke isn't right. If you end things with her, fair enough, but in the meantime…"

"What, we can flirt?"

She blushed. "I don't mind that, as long as it doesn't get back to her."

The scuff of a footstep had him stepping back to check the corridor. Two men in gas masks came towards him, and although he'd been expecting the robbery, it still shit him up.

"Fuck," Teddy muttered, keeping one leg in the gap to ensure the door stayed open. He turned to face them and raised his hands. "Don't shoot!"

"Oh my God, what the fuck's going on?" Casey shrieked.

"Get under the desk," Teddy shouted, his legs going weak. "Now! Quick!"

The lead man pushed Teddy backwards and planted a hand on the door to stop it shutting. More men came in behind the initial two, eight of them, which wasn't what Goldie had said would happen yet. Only two were supposed to be here to force Casey to open the safe, then, and only if Casey was a pest, the others would appear so she was even more frightened, and they'd carry the money to the van.

What the *hell* was going on?

The second man gripped the front of Teddy's shirt and dragged him along the corridor a bit, slamming his back against the wall. He raised a handgun and pressed it to Teddy's temple. Oh God, Oakley's prediction was happening. Teddy's guts seemed to vacate his body, leaving only air, his limbs losing their strength.

The trigger cocked.

"Be a good boy and close your eyes."

The voice wasn't Phantom's or Checkpoint's.

Who the fuck *was* he?

The man dug the gun into him harder. "Thanks for doing your part, but it's over now. Night-night, mate."

Karen almost let her scream free at the sound of a gunshot. Footsteps thumped past the office, and she imagined men tromping down the corridor, heading for the casino. That wasn't supposed to happen, but perhaps someone being shot meant they had to run down to lean on the door so Jimmy couldn't come and see what was going on.

Would the gunshot have been heard in the casino? There was usually so much noise in there from talking, the low music, and people at the slots, their chatter and the machine noise drifting down to the gaming end. But Goldie's lot could have got lucky and Jimmy had walked away from the door to deal with something.

What if the gunmen had changed the plan behind Goldie's back and were about to burst in on all the players, innocent people?

What if Goldie had *told* them to, keeping certain parts of the plan away from her and Teddy?

And that shot…

"Oh God, please don't let it be Teddy," she whispered.

Then she hugged her knees and prayed it would all be over soon.

Casey had been through training with the twins for something like this, but acting it out with The Brothers as the gunmen and it actually happening were different things. Facing two men in gas masks, their machine guns aimed at her, ready to fire, was a whole new ballgame when those guns contained bullets.

She tried to remember what George had told her to do: "Whatever they ask for, do it. The money doesn't matter, your life does."

Man One shouted something at her, but it was indistinct because of the mask.

"I can't hear you," she said, voice wobbling. "The mask..."

"Open the fucking safes!"

She heard that all right and sidestepped over there, not wanting to turn her back on them. The gunshot had frightened her stupid, and she worried about Teddy because he wasn't by the doorway anymore. Was he dead?

Oh God.

She put the code into the keypad of the money safe and swung the door open. Man One came over while Man Two stayed in the doorway.

"Where's the fucking cash?" One asked. "Where's the rest of it?"

"That's all we have."

She didn't have to glance at the pile to know only a few stacks were there. Jimmy had come by earlier and, unusual protocol, had removed quite a few stacks saying George now didn't want the whole night's takings on the premises on any given evening so he was handing it over to their security man who'd deposit it elsewhere. He'd also cleared out all the chips and taken them to Brea, so the only ones in there were what Teddy had just brought. Now she wondered whether George and Greg had known these men were coming.

Why hadn't they warned her?

At the rapid waft of One's gun, she sidled along into the corner farthest from the safe, adjacent to the door. She squeezed between the wall and a filing cabinet, shuddering at their creepy gas masks, how shadows clouded their features.

Man One tromped forward and grabbed the piles from the safe. He stuffed them in a holdall Two held out, muttering something she didn't understand.

Two stared into the bag. "Is this a joke?" His voice, louder than One's, carried. He swung to face Casey and pointed his gun at her. "Open the other safe."

She dashed out of her spot and did as he'd asked, then retreated to the corner again.

"What's this?" Two shouted and grabbed the chip holder, dumping it and the chips in the bag.

"They're marked," she warned him in an attempt to get them to look at her in a good light for helping them—so they'd let her live. "We don't use the same ones every night, they're rotated, so if you take those and come back to cash them in, unless these chips match the ones being used that night, you can't get money for them."

"What?"

"It's policy. It's in the rules by the front door. Cash out the same night or wait until your chips are back in circulation."

"How are people supposed to fucking know when their type of chip is being used?" Two bellowed.

"It's just pot luck if you get it right. People drop in every night to check." She personally thought that was unfair, it was their money, but like George had said, if they didn't cash the chips in before they left, that was their problem.

"That's bullshit!"

"It isn't, I swear... Those chips you have are specific to tonight. If you try to cash them in before they next appear, they'll *know* they're from tonight."

"Get behind the desk."

She shot over there, one eye on their guns. She stood where he'd directed, her legs going weak.

"Sit. Swivel the chair round."

She did that.

Hands wrenched behind her, her wrists tied with something hard, then her ankles, she took the chance to look up at the hidden camera behind the grate of the air-conditioning duct. The cameras didn't pick up sound, so she mouthed, *Help me!*

"Don't turn around until we've gone," one of them said in her ear. "If you sit tight, you can live."

She closed her eyes and waited for them to leave. Counted to one hundred, then swung the chair around. She still expected them to be there, staring at her, but they'd gone. She glanced at her handbag, too far away and hanging on a coat tree beside the door. Her phone was inside it.

She wheeled the chair towards it using a back-and-forth motion to propel her. She bit her bag and jerked her head up, trying to get the strap off the hook. It kept promising to come free but flopped back down again, time after time. The bag itself was zipped shut, so she clenched the zip between her teeth and tried to draw it across.

The coat tree fell over.

Tears of frustration built, and she broke down in tears.

Why wasn't anyone coming to save her?

Hadn't the CCTV men spotted what was going on?

And where were Jimmy and T-T?

After shooting that prick just for being gay (he'd wanted to do that to Teddy for a long time), Ferret stood by the door that led to the casino, his shoulder against it to stop it from opening. Phantom and Checkpoint had come out of the money room with an all-but-empty-looking holdall and beckoned Ferret towards them. He gestured for the bloke closest to him to take his place and jogged up the corridor, skirting the body laid out on the carpet on the left-hand side. He stopped to stare at the briefcase, then turned to nod at one of his gang who trotted up to him.

"Get cutters out of the van. That case could have money in it."

Ferret turned to Phantom. "What's the score? Time's ticking, know what I mean?"

"We're going to have to go into the casino and get cash from the booths," Phantom said.

Ferret nodded. He could do with a bit more action, especially something as exciting as this, and the men he'd brought with him would be up for it, too. He spoke into the headset he had on beneath the mask which would filter his voice to his men's earbuds. He worked his own way, not Goldie's, who should have thought of the communication issue himself.

"Head for the booths. Sounds like we didn't get enough cash from the safe. The boss isn't going to like this."

Bronson stepped forward from his position at the steel door as overseer of what went on in the corridor. He hadn't been able to pick up the conversation because of his over-the-head gas mask, but it was obvious something was up.

"What's going on?" he asked Phantom.

"Fuck all money in the safe. I'd say there's only about ten thousand, and the bitch in there said the chips are marked, so we'll have trouble cashing them in on another day. We're going into the casino."

Bronson didn't like the sound of that. "Did Goldie tell you to do that?"

"No, but do you want to go to him basically empty-handed? There's got to be thousands out there. The place is packed, people spending money like water."

Bronson nodded. *They* could go out there, but *he* hadn't signed up for it, and he wasn't going to go against Goldie's orders. He knew George and Greg from watching them and attending the leader meetings. They were hard bastards and wouldn't think twice about shooting anyone who went through that door, providing they were in attendance tonight. As for the bloke called T-T, he was just as bad, according to Karen.

He made his decision. "You do that, and I'll wait at the back door to warn the van driver if the shit hits the fan. He might need to drive round the front to collect you in the car park."

Phantom handed him the holdall, then he and Checkpoint ran to the other end.

Bronson retreated to the steel door, staring at the body of the poor sod on the floor. There hadn't been any need to kill him, they could have just tied him up with that Casey bint in the money room.

Unless Goldie had given orders Bronson didn't know about.

He bristled at that. Why hadn't the boss included him in any changes?

With the urge to leave the building and fuck the lot of them, fuck *Goldie* for keeping him out of the loop, Bronson put half of his body between the open door and the frame and waited. If it sounded like World War Three had started, he was out of here.

Greg stared around the almost empty casino. As soon as Teddy had gone through that door with the briefcase, the customers and staff unaware of the heist had been ushered outside into the plaza and sent to the various restaurants with the lie that a famous actor was on his way who'd paid to have the casino to himself for an hour. The promise of their meals and drinks being paid for had the majority of them scurrying away, eager for a freebie, but some hung around outside, clearly waiting for the celebrity to arrive. George had locked the main front doors, then the internal ones on the other side of the greeter foyer, drawing the red velvet curtains across to prevent anyone out there seeing any carnage.

Teddy hadn't come back, so Greg could only assume he'd encountered whoever had come in, unless he'd gone straight to the break room after handing over the chips. Jimmy had moved away from his post at the door a while back. It had been a sodding pest that Teddy had even left his table, but Jimmy had felt if he refused to let him pass, the young fella would get suspicious. At the same time, it meant putting Teddy's life at risk along with Casey's, unnecessary in Greg's opinion, but it was done now, and if Teddy came a cropper, that was Jimmy's guilt to bear.

Shit, what if Teddy's in on it?

George had assured Greg that everything was above board with Teddy and Karen, but how many times in the past had his twin had a momentary lapse and took people at their word, things going to shit afterwards? All right, lately he'd stopped doing that, controlling the chunk of his heart that was too soft, but what if he'd fucked up again this time? What if he'd seen what he'd *wanted* to see, a couple about to get married and nothing more?

A quiet bleep on the walkie-talkies brought everyone's attention to them. Greg held up a hand to signal no one should answer and he'd deal with it. He sent two bleeps back, indicating it was safe for the head CCTV man upstairs to speak. Joseph had been told to only make contact if it looked like the casino would be ambushed — or once the gunmen had gone with their less-than-expected haul.

"Karen is in the main office. Casey is tied to a chair in hers. Teddy...Teddy's down; someone's just nicked his briefcase, but there's nothing in it, he gave the chips to Casey. One man at the steel door with a holdall. Ten men at the door that leads to the casino. Looks like they're going to come in."

Greg sent one bleep back.

Everyone looked at each other. Moon and his lot ripped off their sheik robes and tossed them aside, drawing their weapons. Tick-Tock pulled a gun from beneath his suit jacket and aimed it at the door. Greg followed suit, while George and the only men remaining from Cardigan and Moon's estate went behind the bar and collected the shotguns George had stashed in the bottom half of the spirits cabinet. T-T took his gun from his holster hidden beneath his suit jacket.

Then they all stood in a curved line three metres from the door.

And waited for the gunmen to burst in.

George and his supporters pulled their triggers as soon as the first gas-masked man entered. The bloke, momentarily stunned by the lack of customers in the casino and the fact he faced a firing squad, raised his weapon too late. He was gunned down and fell forward onto the floor. The one who came after wasn't so lax and, despite bullets going through his buddy and into him, he fired as he ran towards them, a yell of rage or pain muffled by his mask. They kept coming, one after the other, fucking lemmings with no sense of keeping themselves safe—like running up the corridor and leaving the scene. Their loyalty to Goldie and getting the job done no matter the consequences astounded George.

Or was that their stupidity?

With so many Cardigan and Moon men shooting, each of the men except for one littered the floor, either dead or injured. The final man, a big burly sort, stopped in the doorway, his gun aimed at them, a pause in gunfire from everyone else, as if they sensed this was a pivotal moment.

The fella slowly raised one hand to explain he didn't mean any harm. Then he took his mask off and threw it on the floor. Why? To reveal himself so they thought he was abandoning his allegiance to Goldie? He kept his gun up, though, and considering the amount of weapons trained on the last man standing, George would allow the threat to hover between them.

"*Phantom*?" George said.

"*George*?"

Stunned into silence for a moment, George stared at him, someone he and Greg had been to school with. He'd been a good mate back in the day, and George hadn't known he worked for Goldie. Last he'd heard, Phantom and Checkpoint had moved to Banbury with their parents just after George and Greg had started running errands for Ron Cardigan. Obviously, the siblings were back.

"Who sent you?" George asked.

"Am I going to stay alive if I tell you?"

George wished he could do that, but... "You may as well give me a name."

"Goldie."

"When did you get involved with him?"

"Does it matter?"

"Not really." George wrestled with his dilemma. Shoot an old friend or give him a second chance? "Well, this is a bit of a pisser, isn't it."

Phantom shrugged. "Life takes you down roads..."

"Yeah, for you, the wrong one."

Phantom dared to take his attention off George and glanced at the men on the floor. One of them groaned and held a hand out.

Phantom's eyes widened. "Charlie?"

Oh fuck.

How had Checkpoint got mixed up in this life? He'd been a computer nerd, so what the hell had happened for him to go in with Goldie? The fact two brothers stared at each other, one alive, one on the way to dying, stabbed a lance of pain into George's heart. It could so easily have been George and Greg in their places if things had gone wrong.

"Don't even think about it," Greg warned and shot Checkpoint in the head. "That's put him out of his misery. Now it's your turn." He swung his gun towards Phantom.

Phantom's finger tightened on the trigger, the gun aimed at Greg.

George sighed. Thought of all the times he and Phantom had fucked about as kids. Memories. Poignant, sweet. But they were in the past. Gone. They were different people now. Phantom was threatening Greg, and no one was allowed to do that.

George recalled the promise to his brother, to always keep him safe, to maim or murder anyone who posed a threat.

Then he pulled *his* trigger.

At the sound of the final gunshot, Bronson flicked the snib up and let the door lock behind him. He pelted to the van, jumped in the passenger seat, and whacked the dashboard. "Go, go, go!"

"But the others…" the driver said, switching on the engine.

Bronson recognised the voice of Waffles, the young bloke from Ferret's lot. *Eh? Why is* he *here?* "Dead, the fucking lot of them. Drive to the location." He settled the holdall on his lap.

Waffles drove out of the yard. "What location? Ferret told me jack shit."

Bronson took his gas mask off and threw it in the footwell. "Get yours off. If plod are around and they see you, you'll look suss."

One hand on the wheel, Waffles removed his mask, passing it to Bronson. "Tell me where to go."

"Goldie said to head for Baker's Crescent on Cardigan. Another van is there. The keys are on the front tyre."

"Right. Jesus, I can't believe they're all dead."

Bronson didn't give two fucks about that. He had more important things to think about. "What were you lot doing here anyway?"

"The original team were in an accident. Phantom got hold of Ferret for us to take over."

"An accident?" *Why the hell wasn't I told?*

"Yeah. The rozzers copped an eyeful of the masks and guns. The team have been taken to hospital for check-ups, all of them arrested on suspicion of intent to do armed robbery."

Shit. "Goldie's going to go nuts."

"Not our problem, though."

True. Bronson had stuck to his role—staying by the steel door to oversee the robbery then watch the money being loaded into the van so no one thought of taking a backhander. But would Goldie have expected him to deviate, to have entered the casino with the others?

Thank fuck I didn't...

Waffles drove on, and Bronson took his phone out to contact the boss.

ALL SYSTEMS DOWN BAR ME AND THE DRIVER. MINIMAL MONEY. PLAN WASN'T FOLLOWED. ON WAY TO VAN SWAP LOCATION. WILL AWAIT INSTRUCTIONS.

He rested his head back, waiting for a barrage of abuse to fly back at him in a message. He didn't care what Goldie said, this mission was a bust, and there was nothing anyone could do about it. Someone had grassed on them—they had to have done, because when that door to the casino had opened, the gunfire had been loud enough that more than one weapon had been fired.

People had been waiting.

Who was the snitch, though?

Teddy? Was *that* why he'd been taken out?

Angry at not being told these things beforehand, Bronson closed his eyes, thinking it was time he retired.

George trod on all the bodies on his way into the corridor. Still smarting from killing someone he'd considered a friend, he pressed the button on his walkie-talkie to contact the head CCTV operator. "No one's in the corridor apart from the stiff. When did they go?"

"Just now. Mercedes van, like you were told. I got hold of your man on the council CCTV to track it—outside cameras picked up the number plate.

The driver had a gas mask on, so no identification. The bloke manning the back door left with him, also in a gas mask. He took the holdall. From what I could make out in Casey's room, going by the wads of cash, she handed over ten grand and another ten in chips."

"Thanks." George stared down at Teddy. Why had he been killed? "When our man hit the deck in the corridor, what went on?"

"Teddy? Someone slammed him against the wall. Seemed like words were exchanged, then he was shot. Maybe he was the mole."

"Seems to point that way. He was surplus to requirements, no longer needed." *He knew too much?* "Right, I've got shit to do. I'm sure you'll see me doing it."

George took his skeleton keys out of his pocket and opened Casey's door. She lay on her side on the floor, attached to a chair, her face ruddy from crying. She stared at him, seeming confused, then he remembered he looked like Jason Momoa.

"It's George," he said on a sigh.

She blinked. "Why do you... The hair. The beard. What's that for?"

"Isn't it obvious? Someone just tried to rob us, but we stopped them." Well, except for the

409

money and chips they'd managed to get away with. A small price to pay, considering what they could have got if Jimmy hadn't taken the rest of the money away.

"And you didn't *tell* me?" Anger infused her voice. "You knew they'd come in here because of the safes, yet you didn't bother to let me know? I could have *died*."

He stuffed his guilt away inside a box labelled DO NOT OPEN. "But you didn't. You'll be heavily compensated." He hardened his emotions against how right she was to give him a bollocking and bent down to haul her and the chair upright.

"Money? You think *money* will help me forget this? What I've been through? I thought they were going to *shoot* me!"

"Thought and fact are two different things." He sounded such bastard. Hated himself for it. Keeping his soft side at bay, he untied the bonds around her wrists and ankles. With no response from her, he said, "Look, there are reasons most employees weren't in the know. It's over, so be grateful you're still breathing and tell yourself to live every day to the max from now on. Near-death experiences are a blessing because they change your perspective."

"A blessing? A fucking *blessing*?" She stood, rubbing her wrists. "I can't believe you're brushing this off."

He'd had enough of her gob, her words drawing guilt to the surface. "Listen to me, you. Working here, you knew the risks. Because of who me and my brother are, what we do. When we took you on, it was on the understanding that something like this might happen. You signed a waiver, you agreed to take the rough with the smooth. The rough was thinking you'd end up dead. The smooth is ten grand for being the one to cope with the gunmen ordering you about. Like it or lump it."

She swallowed and peered to the side of him, out into the corridor. "Oh my God, is that Teddy?"

George sneered. "You can thank him for your terror. He was a fucking mole."

"You killed him?"

"No, one of Goldie's lot did. Direct your anger at the dead man, not me. Now, believe it or not, bullet holes in the walls or not, we're reopening the casino, and I've got a few meal bills to pay, so you can either go back to work or get a taxi home. Your call. I've got too much shit to deal with."

411

She wiped her wet cheeks, more tears falling. "He used to come and talk to me a lot on his breaks." She tipped her head at Teddy. "Said he fancied me, that he shouldn't be marrying Karen."

Oh, fuck me... "He lied to you. Used you. He was the one who kept that door open for the gunmen. Wake up, love."

Should *he* wake up, too? Did Karen know about Teddy's involvement, if that was what had gone on?

Casey's shoulders slumped. Then they stiffened again, as if she'd suddenly remembered who she'd been speaking to with a tone sharp enough to wound. "I... Sorry. For being rude. I was in shock. I..."

"Forget it. It is what it is."

She nodded, her features turning calculating. "Ten grand, you said?"

"Yeah, ten grand, but that comes with a caveat."

"What is it?"

"Keep your mouth shut about this, or you *will* end up dead."

Chapter Thirty-Two

Someone tried to open the door. They knocked, three hard raps. Karen's stomach flipped. There had been so much commotion, all those gunshots, that she was convinced Goldie's men had won and had come to get her. To kill her.

"Karen? It's me. Do I have to use my key, or are you going to let me in?"

Relief at hearing George's voice had her scrambling out from under the desk, banging the top of her head on the edge. She staggered to the door, one of her legs asleep, and unlocked it. George stood there, his eyes dead, his mouth flat. Why did he look like that? Had something happened to Greg? Goldie would never see the light of day again if George's twin had been hurt. Or had they forced one of the gunmen to talk and her name had been dropped into the conversation? Shit, did he know she'd been in on it from the start?

"Come and sit down." George guided her to the desk and pushed her shoulders until she sat. He crouched. "Listen, what you're about to hear will rip you apart, but Jimmy said you passed a message on for Teddy to go into the break room, so hold on to that—you tried your best to save him without letting him know Bronson had contacted you to open that door. You did it in a way where you still followed our instructions to keep your involvement in this quiet."

You tried your best to save him? Alarm blazed through her. "What happened?"

"He didn't make it, love."

Tears burned. *Oh God, what about Oakley? How is he going to cope without Teddy?* "What... How?"

"He was shot."

So she'd been right. That first gunshot had killed her friend. She cried, for deceiving Teddy and not telling him she'd gone to The Brothers. For Oakley, who'd had a premonition, and now he'd mourn the man who'd ignored his warning. For initially needing the money for Robyn and Cal and having to tell the twins about the robbery, which had brought about Teddy's death.

For feeling so relieved *she* wasn't dead.

Guilt was a heavy burden that threatened to suffocate her.

"I'm sorry." George leant closer and put his arms around her.

She sobbed onto his shoulder, undeserving of his empathy—he should be killing her for what she'd done, for being deceptive when he and Greg had been so kind, arranging the operation and paying for it. She'd make it up to them, she had to. She would be the best ears they'd ever had, going above and beyond to overlay her treachery with good deeds. For the rest of her life, she'd try her best to right the wrongs. She'd say to Goldie it was better if they only communicated via the phone from now on so there was no chance of her being seen going to Golden Glow to visit him. If the twins didn't kill him as quickly as she thought they would, he could send her robbery cash via a courier, and she'd give it to Robyn for the baby she desperately hoped they'd have.

"What else happened?" She had to know, not that she'd be passing it on to Goldie, but so she knew how big her penance had to be.

George told her, and she closed her eyes, her tears soaking into his suit jacket.

"One man and the driver got away."

She pulled back, so tired now, the adrenaline that had kept her alert fading, replaced with lead in her limbs. "What about the police?"

"What about them?"

"Won't they be coming?"

"Err, no. All the customers and some employees have been stuffing their faces in the restaurants while all this was going on. No one but Goldie's two remaining men and our allies know what went down. The police have no reason to be here, because as far as they're concerned, no robbery took place."

She sniffed. "I have to tell Oakley."

George nodded. "I'll drop you round there. I want a word with him. Seems Goldie got to Teddy after all."

Her stomach lurched again. "What do you mean?"

"I think Teddy was killed because he was a mole."

He stared at her intently. Too intently. To see how she reacted? Too gauge whether she was in on it an' all?

"What? No! Teddy isn't like that."

"Wasn't. And I'll bet he was. He kept it from you."

"But he doesn't...didn't have it in him. He's too honest."

"Sometimes, people are good at hiding things. Like how he's been chatting Casey up all this time behind your back."

She'd known about that but feigned hurt. "W-*what*?"

"Sorry, love, but from what I can gather, he was a wolf in sheep's clothing, and unfortunately, you fell for it. You've got to admit, he was bloody charming."

She cried again, because while Teddy *had* known all along, he wasn't a bad person, and neither was she. They'd both gone into this for good reasons, and now…

Oh God, what if Oakley got distraught and blabbed? What if he told George about her role?

She'd have to face that if it came to it. She'd fulfilled her promise to Robyn, and if she had to die or get a Cheshire smile, then there was nothing she could do about it.

She nodded. "Shall we go now?"

"I've got some food bills to pay first. Oh, and in case the gossip's still burning by the time you come back to work, people were told a celebrity had hired the casino for an hour of gambling alone."

"Right."

"And if Handsy disappears at some point in the future, don't worry about it. When we viewed the CCTV this week to try to find the mole, we saw him touching you, Cinnamon, and various other girls more than had been reported. We don't like perverts."

So she had something else to thank the twins for.

Her guilt increased tenfold.

In Moorgate Street, Karen knocked on the door and dreaded what was to come. George waited in the car. On the way, she'd lied yet again and said Oakley was funny with strangers and she'd have to warn him one was coming first. George had seemed to understand, although he'd glanced across at her from the driver's seat, which had set her further on edge.

Oakley opened the door and smiled, then it faded as he looked over her shoulder at the BMW they'd got into in the plaza's main car park. "What's...what's *he* doing here?" he asked quietly.

"I've only got limited time before he gets out of the car," she whispered, "so listen to me. No matter what he tells you about Teddy, stick to the story that he's honest and would never be a mole, right?"

"Oh God, does George suspect him?"

"Yes, because...because of what went on. I've told him Teddy wouldn't ever do anything like that, and you can't tell him I was involved or we'll *both* end up dead. Me for playing a big part, you for knowing and not telling him."

"Where's Teddy now? Have they got him locked up somewhere?"

"George wants to tell you. Please, just stick with Goldie's rules. If he finds out you've tattled to a Brother… And act nervous. I told him you're weird with strangers."

"Okay, okay. Shut up now, he's getting out of the car."

Karen turned.

George walked towards them up the path. "All right if I come in?"

"Um, yeah," Oakley said. "Just…er, just… I don't know you so…"

"I get it. Regardless, I really do have to come in. You can have a wobble about me after I've gone."

They all settled in the living room, Karen's guilt rearing up again because she hadn't told Oakley about Teddy's death. It was cruel to let George do it, but he'd insisted, and she couldn't afford to piss him off.

George leant forward in an armchair and stared across at Teddy on the sofa. "There's no easy way to say this, and I'm a fan of not beating around the bush. I'm afraid your brother was shot tonight."

Karen cringed. He'd been so blunt. *Too* blunt.

Next to Oakley, she grabbed his hand and squeezed. "I'm so sorry…"

Oakley blinked as if what George had said remained unspoken. As if he hadn't heard a thing. "Um…" He swallowed. "Can you say that again? I didn't… I don't…"

George nodded. "The casino was robbed. One of the gunmen killed him."

"I-I don't understand." Oakley looked at Karen, tears pooling. "What gunman?"

George answered. "We believe Goldie, your old leader, gave one of his men permission to get rid of Teddy."

Oakley still stared at Karen. "Get rid of him? Why would he do that?"

The question was directed at Karen; Oakley clearly wondered if she'd known beforehand what was going down.

"It was such a shock," she said to let him know she'd been oblivious. "I was hiding in an office. Teddy had taken some chips to Casey… They came in and… I'm really sorry."

"You were in an office," Oakey said, his voice flat. "You weren't in the casino."

Shit, he'd known the order of play so was questioning why she hadn't followed the plan. Why *she* was safe and his boyfriend wasn't.

"She had a bad stomach," George supplied, giving Karen a warning look to let him handle this. "She was told to go and rest."

Oakley stared at his hand in Karen's. "Did he suffer?"

George shook his head. "It would have been quick."

Oakley switched his gaze to the floor. "Thank you for telling me. You can go now."

"I can't." George stood. "Do you know anything about the robbery and Teddy's possible part in it?"

Oakley's attention snapped up to George. "Are you *kidding* me? Teddy wouldn't get involved in anything like that. You suggesting it is well rude."

"How long have you known he was your brother?"

Oakley seemed confused for a moment, then their cover story must have kicked in, his features relaxing. "About three years."

"So you don't know him as well as you might had you grown up together."

"I knew him well enough. He was kind, decent, and just wanted to buy a farm and live in peace."

"So he could have needed money to do that. A payout from a robbery, perhaps."

Oakley's eyes narrowed. "You should leave. Talking about Teddy like that..." Tears fell as it finally sank in. Teddy wasn't coming home. "Oh God, Karen, what am I going to do without him?"

He rested his head on her shoulder, and she hugged him with her free arm while he clutched at the hand in his lap. That he hadn't dropped her in it in front of George was a testament to the kind of man he was. Good. As decent as he'd claimed Teddy had been.

Or it could be that if he opened his mouth, he knew George would kill him.

Chapter Thirty-Three

Goldie still seethed from receiving Bronson's first message. Goldie had sent instructions for him to follow the plan, as discussed, so what the fuck had gone wrong?

He paced his living room, having left the party in a snit, forgetting, until he'd come home, that he was supposed to stay there. Now he had suspicion to deal with—people would have seen him leave. News of the robbery would get out at some point, and the nosy fuckers would think he'd had something to do with it. He already anticipated being questioned at the next leader meeting.

While he waited for Bronson to turn up, he went through the points of the original message.

ALL SYSTEMS DOWN BAR ME AND THE DRIVER. Code for everyone else being dead. How had that happened? All of them had been tooled up to the eyeballs, so why hadn't they shot whoever had come to shoot *them*? Earlier, he'd given the order they could use the guns in self-defence.

MINIMAL MONEY. What? *What*? Where was the big haul? Had Teddy and Karen lied about the week's takings being in the safe on a Friday night? Or had they been fed a line?

PLAN WASN'T FOLLOWED. That fucking Ferret. He must have cocked things up. The original men in the van had been briefed to kingdom come. Hadn't Phantom explained correctly? Or had Ferret overridden him and taken matters into his own hands? If the dumb little weasel wasn't already dead, Goldie would kill the bastard himself.

On way to van swap location. Well, at least *someone* was doing something right. He just had to hope no one followed Bronson. If the twins had got wind of the robbery, they'd have had someone in place to tail him.

Why hadn't Bronson stopped whoever had changed the rules? He'd know not to deviate, and he should have insisted they all stuck to the original plan. So unless the rules not being followed was for a damn good reason, his right-hand man had some explaining to do.

Goldie's phone blipped.

Bronson: Outside, boss.

Goldie: Then fucking get your arse in here! And bring that munter of a driver with you.

Goldie went to the front door, peered through the spyhole and, satisfied all was well, let the men in. He stomped into the living room, standing on the rug he'd placed over Zofia's bloodstain that had been stubborn and wouldn't come out of the floorboards.

"Well?" he said.

Bronson and that Waffle twat stood just inside the doorway. What Bronson told Goldie had his blood pressure rising. *Phantom* had agreed to enter the casino in search of more money. What a dickhead.

"What gave him the right to do that? What did you say to him?"

"I asked if you'd given him permission to do it. He said no and asked if I wanted to come back to you basically empty-handed. I took it that he had prior knowledge that you'd instructed him to get the money no matter what."

Goldie thought about it from Bronson's perspective. He'd been told to stay at the exit door and stick to his job. Bronson would have wanted to follow his orders to the letter, but he'd know how pissed off Goldie would be at the lack of money, so yes, that explanation was satisfactory.

"How much did you get away with?"

"About ten grand. There are chips, but apparently they're useless until a certain time." Bronson clarified why.

"How come Karen and Teddy didn't tell me that?"

"Maybe they didn't know. It was the Casey woman who told Phantom and Checkpoint about it."

Goldie wasn't stupid, someone had tipped the twins off. Why else would Cardigan gunmen be waiting for *his* gunmen?

"Where's Karen and Teddy now?"

"Dunno about Karen, but Teddy's dead."

Goldie snapped his head up to stare at the ceiling. "Excuse me? Did I hear you right?"

"Ferret shot him."

Goldie lowered his head to stare at Bronson. "Pardon?"

Bronson shrugged. "I assumed you'd told him to. So he didn't blab."

"I gave no such order. Ferret did it off his own bat. Why?"

"To get a bigger cut? With you not having to pay Teddy, it'd mean we'd all get more money."

"Sneaky little shyster. And there's sod all I can do about it because *he's* dead an' all. Christ alive, this has turned into a fucking nightmare."

"What's the plan now?" Bronson asked.

Goldie stared at Waffle. "For a start, *he* can go."

Waffle seemed relieved and made to turn and walk out.

"Not that kind of go," Goldie said.

Waffle stopped. Stiffened. Realisation hit him, and he darted towards the hallway.

Goldie shot him in the back of the head and sighed. "I'm never going to sell this pissing house with all that blood in here. Help me put him in plastic. Jesus, this is the last thing I need, but he couldn't live. He's not trained right. Ferret's useless at getting his men in line. I couldn't risk him talking."

"No need to justify it to me, boss." Bronson stepped over Waffle. "I'll get the plastic."

George, Greg, Moon, and Tick-Tock sat at a table with the other leaders, minus Goldie, drinking a well-earned brandy after explaining what had happened. This hastily arranged meeting, allowed because of the gravity of the crime the orange bloke had committed, would only last as long as it took for their glasses to be empty.

An agreement had been made, and they'd reconvene at the warehouse in about an hour. Every leader would be there to witness Goldie's interrogation and execution, then his estate would be handed over to the next in line, Prince Judas as he liked to call himself. A bit of a poncy name if you asked George, but no one had, so he kept his opinion to himself for once.

Prince rose, necking back his drink. "See you in an hour. I'm going to love clocking Goldie's face when he realises he's been caught. Me taking over his estate has been a long time coming."

George nodded. He didn't think Prince ran his own estate very well, let alone another one. But he kept *that* to himself, too.

Marleigh slept in the king-sized bed behind Ichabod who watched Goldie's house through the night-vision binoculars. A message had finally come through after he'd got hold of the twins to let them know Goldie had arrived home. From the tone, Greg had replied.

GG: I'D HAVE THOUGHT HE'D HAVE STAYED AT THE SOCIAL CLUB UNTIL THE LAST KNOCKINGS.

ICHABOD: SOMETHING MUST HAVE MADE HIM LEAVE.

GG: PROBABLY THE FACT THAT ALL BUT TWO OF HIS MEN ARE DEAD AND THEY GOT AWAY WITH ONLY TEN GRAND AND THE SAME IN CHIPS. CONTINUE TO KEEP YOUR EYE OUT. WE'LL BE THERE AS SOON AS WE

CAN, THEN YOU CAN FOLLOW HIM AFTER WE'VE GONE.

Now, Ichabod could do nothing but wait. He'd enjoyed this job, mainly because of Marleigh's company. Weirdly, he'd miss having her there to chat to. David didn't know how lucky he was to have a woman like her. Or maybe he did, and he wished he didn't have to work away so much.

Or maybe he's living a dual life, and that's why she can't go away with him every time.

He canned that nasty little thought. There was no point in making up scenarios that probably didn't exist, just because he wished he had a wife like Marleigh.

He bit his lip, hard, to take his mind off her and focus back on the job.

The doorbell rang just as Goldie slapped the last piece of duct tape on the plastic body package in the hallway.

He glanced up at Bronson from his bent-over position. "Who the fuck can *that* be? Everyone else is dead."

"Dunno, boss. Let me check."

432

Bronson stepped over Waffle and moved to the front door. "Err, we've got unwelcome company."

Goldie stood upright and snatched his gun from his holster. "How unwelcome?"

"George and Greg unwelcome."

"Fuck. *Fuck*!" Goldie slapped his forehead with the heel of his hand a few times, hoping it'd dislodge a solution to this monumental problem. The twins were here, and that could only mean one thing: they knew he'd arranged the heist. Had Karen cracked under pressure? "Open the door."

"But the body…"

"What about the fucking body? It's not like they haven't seen one wrapped up like a pissing turkey before, is it? Jesus, use your loaf." He held the gun behind him and faced the door.

Bronson opened it. "Yeah?"

"We'd like a word with Goldie," George said.

Goldie moved to the side so he could see him. The pair of them filled the step, blocking all view of anyone who might be at their backs. Both had their hands clasped in front of them. Curious. Why no weapons? Why weren't they menacing

433

Bronson to let them in? Why did they look so…placid if they thought he'd robbed them?

"What can I do for you?" Goldie gestured to Waffle. "As you can see, we're in the middle of dispatching someone, so if you could make it quick…"

George peered inside. "Who's that?"

"Some prick called Waffle."

George seemed to relax. "What's he done?"

"None of your business."

George's nostrils flared. "The body will have to wait. A leader meeting's been called at our warehouse."

Goldie wished his stomach wouldn't play him up like that. It seemed to want to push his bowels out of his arsehole. "What for? And why didn't I get a text?"

"We sent one on the burner you use for leader discussions. Got no answer. It's important we have you there; it involves all of us."

"Hang on, let me check." Goldie went into the living room and snatched the burner up. Turned it on. "Fuck," he whispered and went back into the hallway. "I had the phone off. Only just seen this."

"You're not allowed to have the leader phone off," Greg said.

"I know, but I was at my party, wasn't I, and I fancied a night off from all the crap we deal with. Not a crime, is it?"

"Yet despite wanting a night off, you left to kill Waffle?" Greg said.

"Yeah, and let me tell you, it pissed me off, because I was having a good time."

George shrugged. "So, are you coming?"

"Why's there a meeting?"

"Some cunt's robbed our casino, so we need help to find out who did it."

Goldie laughed. "It's not other leaders' responsibility to do any detective work for you. Christ. Ask your pig to earn her money."

"Everyone else has agreed to help. Word is, there's someone going round trying to sabotage everyone's assets. Prince had a problem last week regarding his betting shop, and the next night, Rudy had his cocaine stolen from his lock-up. Now there's our casino. It's obvious someone's trying to fuck the lot of us over. There's a vendetta, which is why I said it involves all of us."

"Why am I only just hearing about this?"

"Maybe because you weren't listening at the last meeting." George shoved his hands in his pockets.

Goldie went on high alert in case he pulled out a gun. "I haven't had anything happen."

"Perhaps you're next. Maybe all that marijuana you grow at Golden Glow will get nicked. Look, the meeting's in twenty minutes. That should give us enough time to get to the East End if you put your foot down."

George and Greg walked off towards the open gate.

"Did you leave that open?" Goldie whispered to Bronson.

"Waffle was meant to shut it."

"Jesus! We'll have to leave him here. I need you to drive me to the warehouse."

"Isn't it a bit suss, the meeting being there?"

Goldie thought about that. "If no other leaders' cars are parked when we arrive, we drive past and come back here to sort Waffle."

"And that won't raise suspicion?"

Goldie gritted his teeth, his mind working overtime.

Ichabod followed the car to the East End, having left a note for Marleigh on her kitchen table to let her know his time there had come to an end. As she wouldn't let the twins pay her, maybe he could take some flowers and chocolates round as a thank you for all she'd done. Loaning your bedroom to some random bloke, whether he worked for the twins or not, should have fazed her, but she'd seemed to enjoy it.

She got lonely when David was away. If she was the cheating type, Ichabod would have solved that issue for her if she'd have him, but she was devoted to the bloke.

Shame.

Goldie's vehicle slowed, the men inside likely checking out the other leaders' cars along the kerb in a long line. Seemed Goldie must have approved being at the meeting, as Bronson parked behind a Ferrari Monza, and the brake lights went off.

Ichabod continued on, rounded the corner, and waited there for a couple of minutes. Then he emerged, driving to Jackpot to see what damage had been done to what he felt was his precious domain.

Chapter Thirty-Four

George had staged it to look like a normal leader meeting. The tool table had been pulled out, the tools put in the bathroom, and all the folded chairs sat around it, filled with the arses of the most influential men and one woman in London. At the end, the wooden torture chair, reserved for Goldie, who perched on it, likely thinking he was classed as super important because he was sitting at the head, the patriarch of the leaders. He had a cravat on, although it didn't successfully hide what he wouldn't want them to see: scratches peeked above it. Had Zofia fought back when he'd killed her? Would there be DNA under her fingernails? Hopefully. That would mean him going missing would save any fingers pointing at every other leader who was present here.

A takeaway from the Taj sat in the middle of the table, each foil tray open so people could help themselves, dishing it out onto paper plates, plastic forks at the ready. A pile of naan breads quickly disappeared with grabby hands drawing them closer to each person present, and paper cups, filled with brandy, meant Moon was happy. Normally, George would begrudge paying for Goldie to fill his stomach, feeding a man who'd intended to shaft them, but this little ruse would tickle his pickle, so the expense would be worth it.

Besides, all the other leaders had agreed that having a meal in their carefully constructed, calm atmosphere would lead Goldie into a false sense of security. George and Greg had purposely sat at the other end of the table so Goldie wouldn't get jittery in their presence, given the big fat secret he thought he kept. He was going to deny all knowledge of the heist, that was a given, and it would be interesting to see this little charade unfold.

"So," Prince said, dipping a piece of naan in his lamb bhuna. "Much as I'm enjoying having a meeting where so far we haven't hashed shit out, there's no getting away from it, we have things to discuss. All right for me to start?"

Everyone nodded or grunted. A few leaders, who usually remained quiet at the meetings, preferring to only speak when they had an issue, would do the same now, based on the agreed main players doing all the hard work in keeping the conversation flowing. Too many cooks might spoil the broth.

"My betting shop," Prince continued. "As you know, it's a big place, the betting area at one end, a restaurant and bar at the other. Unconventional, but you know me, I don't like being the same old, same old, I like to do things differently."

"Get on with it," Tick-Tock heckled.

The pair of them had never got on.

Prince gave him a filthy look. "So, some bastard decided it was a good idea to rob me. What with my shop getting hit, Rudy's lock-up being broken into, and now the twins' casino being raided, someone's in need of a lot of cash—or they're just being greedy. Why, we don't know, but I intend to find out once one of us gets our hands on them. What I propose is we up our security in all the venues that carry large amounts of cash or drugs. We work together to send messages if anyone's seen as being suspicious. That way, we have descriptions of who to look out for. What concerns me is, whoever is doing this—and I believe it's the same person—is specifically targeting leaders. Is it someone we all know?"

"It had better not be," Moon grumbled.

"Someone who's in the know about how we work, too," Rudy said.

"They've probably got people on their books," Mrs Whitehall added—she wouldn't let anyone use her first name; funny bird. "*Moles* who have infiltrated each of our large businesses."

Goldie didn't flinch. "Moles? Then that's easy to figure out. We all have a good think about who were the last people to join our ranks. Yeah, they all get vetted, but it's so easy not to dig deep and check properly."

Was that a poke at us? George held his temper in check. "But digging deep still might not reveal who they really are. There are ways and means of creating new identities and planting them online for us to find. This person is bloody clever."

Goldie couldn't help but preen, as George had hoped.

"Still," the orange bastard said, recovering quickly, "it won't do any harm for us to look into our latest employees. If we collect the names and do some cross-referencing, we'll probably find a link between them all."

"Like what?" Mrs Whitehall asked. She detested Goldie and never let a chance slip by without letting him know it. "A big shiny arrow in the air, pointing to their employer?" She laughed derisively, as she always did with him. "Come on, you don't think our man—or woman—has chosen people who have connections to each other, do you? No, they'll be unrelated, all chosen so they don't know who the other moles are. At least that's how I'd do it."

"Maybe it's you, then," Goldie sniped and stuffed half an onion bhaji in his mouth. He spoke while chewing: "Seeing as you were the one to suggest the method of mole selection… It's like a fart, isn't it. Whoever smelt it, dealt it."

Chuckles went round, the strained smiles and fake lilt to the laughter lost on Goldie.

"Are you accusing me, Benjamin Winston?"

"I don't go by that name, as you well know. It's Goldie, and if the cap fits."

Mrs Whitehall took the opportunity to bite back at him in her usual manner. "You really are a little scrote. A revolting human being. There's no way I'd hurt other leaders' businesses in that way. I'm far too busy coping with my own. I have no beef with anyone apart from you."

"Why single me out?"

"Because you make my skin crawl."

"Maybe they'll hit your sex shop next." Goldie sat back to wait for her reply, a blob of korma sauce on his shirt. "Think about all that cash. I mean, you run it like it's Ann Summers, but we all know what goes on upstairs. High-end girls."

"Girls you'll never get your mucky paws on because they don't go for fake-tanned, fake-blond men with a paunch and an ugly mug."

He opened his mouth to protest, but she waved away anything else he had to say and poked her fork into a chunk of chicken.

George fucking loved her. She was a diamond and had wound Goldie up, as promised, so hopefully he'd blurt something out in anger. Sadly, he didn't, scooping up some of his curry sauce on a broken-in-half poppadom.

"Fuck this arguing," Greg said. "We've spoken about moles, but what about the other employees on the mastermind's books? Ten men in black, wearing gas masks, came in from the yard and had no qualms about bursting into the casino where innocent people could have been."

"*Could* have been?" Goldie asked.

"We had prior knowledge of the heist so got everyone out."

"How did you get wind?" Goldie asked.

"A little bird told us." Greg smiled. "Shame he got killed — and not by any of us, I might add."

Goldie's cheeks took on a pink hue. He wafted his hand to fan himself. "Call this a fucking korma? It's ruddy spicy."

Nice save. "We lied to our casino workers. Told them the whole week's takings would be kept in the safe. The mole must have told their employer

445

the same thing. I mean, what *prick* would believe something like *that*? The amount of turnover the casino has, and we're talking a lot of fucking money here, so to leave that amount on the premises... The person who's doing this is a sandwich short to think we're that stupid, got to be."

"Maybe you two come across as thick and that snippet was believed," Goldie said.

George glared at him. "Are you having a pop at me and my brother, sunshine?"

"I was just saying—"

"Yeah, and *I'm* just saying, we know it was you."

Goldie's mouth sagged open. "You what?"

"Phantom told us before I blew his brains out."

"Phantom? Who's that?"

More chuckles went round, only this time, each leader didn't bother to disguise their contempt for Goldie. All of them whipped guns out and pointed them at him.

"Hang on just a minute," Goldie spluttered. "You'd believe some wally called Phantom over me? Who goes around with a name like that anyway? What, does he think he's Batman's cousin?"

"It's over," Tick-Tock said, "so shut your north and south."

Mrs Whitehall's eyes gleamed. "Goodnight, Mr Winston."

They pulled their triggers simultaneously, and Goldie's body danced in place, his arms flailing, torso jerking back and forth from the multiple bullets landing.

George squinted, got his aim right, and shot him between the eyes. "That's for Zofia, you nasty little bastard."

"Zofia?" Mrs Whitehall asked now the gunfire had stopped.

"He kept one of the refugees locked up at his place. Murdered her." George didn't bother to hide his disgust. "Now then, let's eat."

The leaders finished their food, drinking on into the early hours, chatting about anything and everything, Goldie staring at them blankly, his clothes riddled with holes, his korma tainted by the blood of a man who'd bitten off more than he could chew by playing roulette with the wrong people.

Tosser.

447

Chapter Thirty-Five

Cinnamon had moved into her new home three weeks ago, the smell of paint still fresh. Her children had a bedroom each now, and a conservatory sat at the back, all their toys up one end, her nice bamboo furniture at the other so she could keep any eye on them while they played. Two months had passed since her ordeal, and she worked days at the casino while she'd been recovering, but soon she'd be collecting things for Vintage Finds. She'd passed whatever test they'd set her, and they'd agreed she'd be an asset there.

News about the casino heist had just been revealed in a staff meeting, everyone sworn to secrecy. The reason the twins had decided to come clean after so long was Casey had been finding it difficult to hide her changed mood from her colleagues. Being tied up in her office had affected her badly, and she now saw Vic Collins regularly.

"It'll be all right, you know," Cinnamon said to her as they left the meeting in the gaming area and headed to the bar for a cuppa, the casino closed while the chat had taken place. "I get why you're angry, though."

"Vic's helping me to accept their reasons," Casey said, "but what I can't quite get past is how Teddy lied to me. I thought he meant what he said when he told me he fancied me, when it turns out, all along he'd used me so it wouldn't look strange, him keep talking to me at the office door. He didn't deserve to be shot, though. What if Goldie forced him to do it?"

"If that's what it takes to get you through it, thinking he was coerced, then that's a good thing, isn't it? It means you won't have hate festering."

"George told me to basically keep my chin high and suck it up, but Vic said it isn't as easy as that. I went through a traumatic experience, and not everyone deals with these things the same."

Cinnamon thought about hers. She'd rather have been tied up in an office than shot, but she didn't say anything. Diminishing Casey's experience by spouting that her own had been worse wouldn't help the poor cow.

They took coffees off a tray on the bar and moved to sit in one of the booths.

"Fancy coming to mine for dinner tonight?" Casey asked.

"I'd have to bring the kids..."

"I meant them as well."

Cinnamon had finally admitted to everyone that she had kids. There had been a few surprised glances but nothing major. Casey asking her over was new. They hadn't exactly been bosom buddies, and going out somewhere other than to work, the school, and to see Anna, who she missed like mad since she'd moved, had her a bit anxious. She had to remind herself that Goldie wasn't going to come back to finish the job. He was 'missing', and so was his right-hand man.

Anna had been given a payment for her part in looking after the kids at the safe house while Cinnamon had been in the clinic, plus being nurse to Cinnamon so well she was now going back to uni to study so she could become one.

Funny how life changed and sent you down different paths.

Cinnamon pulled herself out of her head, Casey staring at her for an answer. "Sorry, I was miles away. Shall I bring anything?"

"Just yourselves. The twins paid me for my ordeal, so I've got plenty."

Cinnamon had received some money, too, on account of her being a resident who'd been shot while minding her own business. She'd kitted the new place out with the majority of it and popped a couple of thousand in the bank. With her higher wages on top, she didn't struggle anymore, but that two grand wouldn't last forever, and she planned to use it for the leccy next winter.

"I'll miss this place," she said.

Casey's eyes popped wider. "Oh, are you leaving?"

"Yeah, the twins took me on as a finder at Vintage. You know, their shop."

"Nice!"

Despite everything, life was looking up, and she owed the twins everything. Now, she had a friendship on the horizon, and she'd jump into her new job with both feet. At last, there was no need to be ashamed of her situation anymore. She was getting somewhere—*and* she'd have her pick of all the designer gear before anyone else.

Chapter Thirty-Six

Karen had managed to stuff the guilt deep inside her, refusing to go and see Vic in case he told the twins what she said. There was client confidentiality, but when it came to The Brothers, she couldn't trust the old therapist to keep her secrets to himself. Nor could she trust any other therapist. The only person she could speak to about Teddy was Oakley, who'd stuck by her side, when really, he shouldn't. If he knew what she'd done, it would hurt him, but like Robyn had said, Karen had tried to keep Teddy safe, but he hadn't gone straight into the break room once the gunmen had entered. That had been his decision to ignore her warning, and he'd paid the price.

As had Oakley. He'd moved away, unable to stand living in the house he'd shared with Teddy, and he kept in contact with Karen on WhatsApp and the occasional phone call. Teddy's body had been placed inside Goldie's house along with someone called Waffle, and the police, having been tipped off, discovered them.

It was in all the papers that a manhunt was ongoing in search of Goldie. A dead woman's remains in the woods had yielded his DNA; although her fingernails had been scraped prior to her being buried, some had remained. He was wanted for her murder as well as Teddy's and Waffle's. Karen would have liked to see him in prison, but as George had told her, Goldie had gone missing, and that was all she and anyone else needed to know.

She stood at the blackjack table and glanced over at Ichabod who stood by the door that led to the staff corridor. A new door, the walls around it freshly plastered and painted to hide the bullet holes. On the night of the heist, a quick clean-up job had got rid of the blood, the carpet scrubbed, and holes written off as the celebrity snorting too much coke and attacking them with a hammer he'd brought with him. As no celebrity name had been mentioned, people were trying to guess who the fictitious star had been, social media awhirl with theories. The customers had come flooding back in, and it had been business as usual.

It was weird here without Teddy dealing the cards. In his place, a man called Daniel who was on loan from another leader's casino until a permanent replacement could be found. Karen got along well with him, and he'd even asked her out on a date.

It wouldn't do any harm to accept, would it?

She smiled. Apart from her guilt, life was perfect. Or it would be when Robyn announced she was finally pregnant. And if the op hadn't worked, there was always the surrogacy. As she'd proved, she'd do anything for her sister.

Including lying to two of the biggest gangsters around.

457

Chapter Thirty-Seven

George and Greg both sat with Vic, crying
after grief counselling. *Crying.* It was
unheard of, them blubbing like this, but Vic
seemed to be able to draw all the raw emotions
out of them when they shared these sessions.
Greg hadn't wanted to see Vic alone, he'd gone
back to being five years old and needing his

brother with him, probably thinking George would be the buffer against his emotions. That was all right, George didn't mind. He found this part of his therapy easier with his twin by his side.

George wiped the tears away and sniffed. "This is torture."

"But you'll get through it," Vic said, "and you'll feel all the better for it. Why are you crying with that particular memory when it was an occasion you'd dreamed of for so long?"

George imagined Richard, their fake father, dying under the archway by the river. "Because I saw us from the outside in, and we were just kids really. It got me choked up that we'd gone down a violent path so young. I wonder sometimes whether, if Richard hadn't been such a prick to us, we'd have turned out differently."

Vic leant back, elbows on the chair arms, and steepled his fingers. "But you didn't, and no amount of beating yourself up will change that. You have to face who you are *now*, who you were *then*, and deal with it. You mentioned you've been having a lot of memories resurfacing lately, George. How do you feel about not being able to stop them from emerging?"

"I was fucking annoyed at first, but I've learnt to 'embrace' them as you put it."

"To sit with them instead of turning your back," Vic said.

"Yeah. But it's weird, because I can see it all like it's on a telly, but it's in my head, and sometimes, like when I see Mum in the safe place, I can smell the dinner cooking and feel her hand on my arm."

Greg rubbed his eyes with the heels of his hands. "Next you'll be telling us you've got the gift of the second sight or whatever it's called."

"Bog off, bruv. I can't help the way my mind works."

Vic intervened, as he usually did when they picked at each other. "How do *you* remember it all, Greg?"

"They're like dreams. I close my eyes, and I'm in it, starring in them all over again."

"That's the same as *me*," George said, "so you can stop taking the piss."

"Yeah, but I don't smell or feel."

"How are you now?" Vic asked. "You both chose to remember the same moment, when you killed Richard."

George shrugged. "I'd do it all over again, given the chance. I've got fuck all remorse for that bastard."

Greg stood. "Same here."

"There's something you should read," George said to Vic.

Greg snapped his head round, picking up on what George referred to. "Are you off your rocker? That's private. It's all we have left of her."

George smiled. "If we show him, he'll understand us more. Understand why we find it so difficult to let Mum go. We've got unfinished business with her, we can't ask questions, tell her we still love her no matter what she did, what she was forced to do. If Vic knows the truth, he can help us get through it. We can't keep living like this, holding it all in."

Greg grunted. "So you brought it with you without asking me first?"

"Yeah. Because if I'd asked, you'd have said no."

"But you think I won't in front of Vic. That's manipulative, bruv."

"I didn't mean it to be."

Greg sighed. "All right, show him, but next time, fucking run it by me, got it?"

George nodded and took their mother's letter out of his pocket. She'd left it in the care of a man called Alfie Cuthbert, and it had sat in his safe for years until he'd found it one day and brought it to their attention.

He handed it to Vic, who bent his head to read.

To my lovely boys,

If you're reading this, it means Mr Cuthbert has delivered it, or if not him, someone else he trusts. This is hard for me to write, as even though I'll be gone by the time you see what I have to say and the outcome won't affect me, I'm still worried you'll hate me and you'll feel pain. Not for what I did, you'll understand that, but for allowing you to live with Richard.

Maybe you already hate me for that. As we age, we think about things, don't we, and ask ourselves questions. Two of yours are likely: Why did she stay with him? Why did she let us suffer?

The answer is simple. If I hadn't, Ronald Cardigan would have killed me. You'll learn to know how he works, how his word is law.

When you told me your plans to work for him, after you'd dealt with Richard, my blood ran cold. When Cardigan agreed and used you for jobs, it ran even colder. I wondered if he thought it would further help

keep me in line—more than the threat of murder!
Richard used the riddles as a way of keeping me in line,
too. He'd threatened to tell 'her', and also 'him'.

If an estate leader gives you an instruction, you
follow it, and that extended to Richard—or at least I
told him it did. He would never tell 'her' or 'him' that
he knew, but that threat still frightened me because if
he <u>did</u> tell them, Cardigan would know I'd spilt the
secret and I'd be dead.

Richard found out what I'd done when you were
born, and he used it against me, acting the way he did
to force me to stay. I'd stay anyway, I'd already been
warned by Cardigan. Whatever Richard put me
through, I endured it because I didn't want to die and
leave you with that horrible man.

This is the difficult part. I had an affair three years
after I married Richard. The man in question would
say he'd never have cheated on his wife, and the way
he outwardly adored her, no one would believe me if I
said he had. She was his one and only, so everyone
thought, except he had me tucked away over a period
of six months. We used to meet behind The Eagle and,
well, things happened out there.

I had the affair because Richard soon showed what
he really thought of me once I had a wedding ring on
my finger. The punches, the beatings, you remember

them well. I wanted love, or a semblance of it anyway, and for those six months, I convinced myself I had it. I pretended the man cared, that he'd take me away from it all, and when I told him I was pregnant, he showed his true colours.

Showed me that all those times he'd said he loved me, he'd lied.

Richard wasn't your father. I hadn't been with him in the whole time I'd been seeing the other man, so I played one of the biggest deceptions a woman can and had sex with him once I knew I was pregnant. Please understand my fear, my desperation. But he knew, once he saw you both, that you didn't belong to him, and he beat me into a confession.

Once I say the other man's name, many things will fall into place. Why Richard behaved as he did. He wanted to get even, to get close to the man and bring him down, hence him always going to The Eagle.

And now, I'm going to finish here and cry, and hope I haven't ruined your memories of me, and pray that whatever time I have left with you is good and happy.

I'm sorry, sons, and I love you more than anything, never forget that.

Your father is Ronald Cardigan. 'Her' is your elder half-sister, Leona. If you ever do manage to take the

estate, it belongs to you without question—it's your
birthright.

All my blessings,
Mum

"Ah," Vic said. "Yes, this will help. Thank you for trusting me with this."

Greg's face turned red. "I've had enough. I'm knackered."

"Same time next week?" Vic asked.

"Unless something comes up, yeah," George said.

Outside, they walked to the BMW.

"That session hurt," George said.

"I know."

"I can't believe we went through that shit. We were just boys."

"Yep." Greg got in the driver's side.

George climbed in and stuck his seat belt on. He nudged his brother. "You all right?"

Greg nodded. "Yeah. You?"

"Not really."

"Me neither. Fuck it."

They sat in silence for a while, George hoping the memories didn't turn into nightmares like they'd been for him as a child.

He sighed. Greg sighed.

"Fuck work for the rest of the day," Greg said, starting the engine. "Shall we go to The Angel for a knees-up?"

"As long as we can have lunch. And a pudding."

"I'd have thought you'd need a Pot Noodle after what we've just done."

George smiled. "Nah, I want a nice bloody steak. That way I can pretend I'm eating Richard."

"Now that's a step too far." Greg drove away.

George's recent memories about the past had brought a lot to light. Ron keep calling them 'son'; the way he'd worded things to do with their mother; him seeming proud of how they'd turned out, despite hiding the fact they were his kids.

And the woman at the slope, the one they'd saved…

"We've got another sibling out there," he said. "You realise that, don't you."

"We've probably got several."

"But there's one I know for sure is related to us."

Greg drove a little faster. "Do I want to hear this? Is it someone we know? And how did you find out?"

"Memories. That woman Pickles was supposed to dump."

Greg grunted. "Fuck, I'd forgotten about her."

"I wonder where she went."

"Do we *really* want to go poking into it? We don't want people to know Cardigan was our dad, and she might want the same for her kid."

George shrugged. "Just thought I'd put it out there."

"Well, we're better off letting sleeping dogs lie. We have enough shit to contend with regarding the estate, let alone adding more to the pile."

"Um, I've got a confession."

"Aww, what *now*?"

"I killed Bronson."

"I know."

"How?"

"Because he happened to disappear. How did you do it?"

George sniffed. "Chopped his knackers off and choked him with them."

They laughed all the way to The Angel.

468

Chapter Thirty-Eight

Becky still hadn't heard from Lemon. Noah needed some new sleepsuits, and it was about time his father stumped up for something other than the beer he swilled down the Lamb and Flag with the Swallow lot. Faith had sent her away with a flea in her ear when Becky had gone round to speak to him earlier, saying mean things and implying Becky was a bad mother if she couldn't cope on her maternity pay.

There was nothing for it now but to go to The Brothers. She couldn't involve Aunt Sheila, because Lemon would sling so many alibis at the investigating officers that he wouldn't get put in the nick, then he'd likely do Becky some damage. The twins, on the other hand, wouldn't let him get away with anything, and maybe they'd kill him.

She needed the cash her little snippet of information would provide. She'd held off since they'd given her that five hundred quid, talking herself out of grassing Lemon and the Swallow lot up, but after what Faith had said, well, he could take everything the twins dished out to him.

Becky wasn't jealous because of Faith's words, which had been Faith's intention. No, she was *angry*. She'd been manipulated, Lemon convincing her she was the light of his life at one point, then as soon as she'd got pregnant, he'd been gaslighting her, making out she'd said or done stuff when she hadn't. She'd got so confused, eventually believing she *had* done what he'd said, but she'd woken up now, and she had someone else to stand up for—her son.

"You're a scutty cow, so Lemon told me," Faith had said. "Barely doing any housework once Noah came along. Lazy bitch."

"I'd just had a *baby*! I was tired, and your precious son did sod all to help me, not to mention staying away for nights on end. All he was bothered about was gadding around with his mates."

"I wonder why? I mean, you must have asked yourself whether you were enough to keep him entertained, which you weren't, otherwise he wouldn't have left you."

"So you got your own way in the end, then. Me out of his life."

Faith had smirked. "I always do."

She'd folded her arms and leant on the doorjamb. She hadn't even asked Becky in, and it had been raining buckets. Noah was all right underneath the rain cover on his pram, but Becky had got soaked.

Spite rearing up inside her, Becky had snapped, "You'd better watch your back, woman."

Faith had laughed. "Are you threatening me? Get away with you. Why don't you piss off back to your nasty little hovel and starve to death, do us all a favour."

"Who'd look after Noah, then? You?"

"He isn't even Lemon's. Looks nothing like him."

Becky had stormed off, heading for The Angel, where she could get a message to the twins via Lisa who managed the pub. Or she could go up and see Debbie in the flat.

Yes, she'd do that.

Lemon didn't know who he was messing with. She'd bring him down, and the Sparrow Road pricks, and Faith, too.

The lot of them were nothing more than shit on her shoe.

To be continued in *Revived,*
The Cardigan Estate 21